WRATH & REDEMPTION

WILD SPACE SAGA BOOK 2

WRATH & REDEMPTION

BRANDON HILL & TERENCE PEGASUS

4 Horsemen
Publications, Inc.

DEDICATION

As always, special thanks to the entire staff of 4 Horsemen Publications.

Also, a big thanks to Bayou Pen 2 Paper for all your insight!

And a big thanks to our DeviantArt and IRL followers. You're what keeps us going! Keep following the Northwest Passage with us!

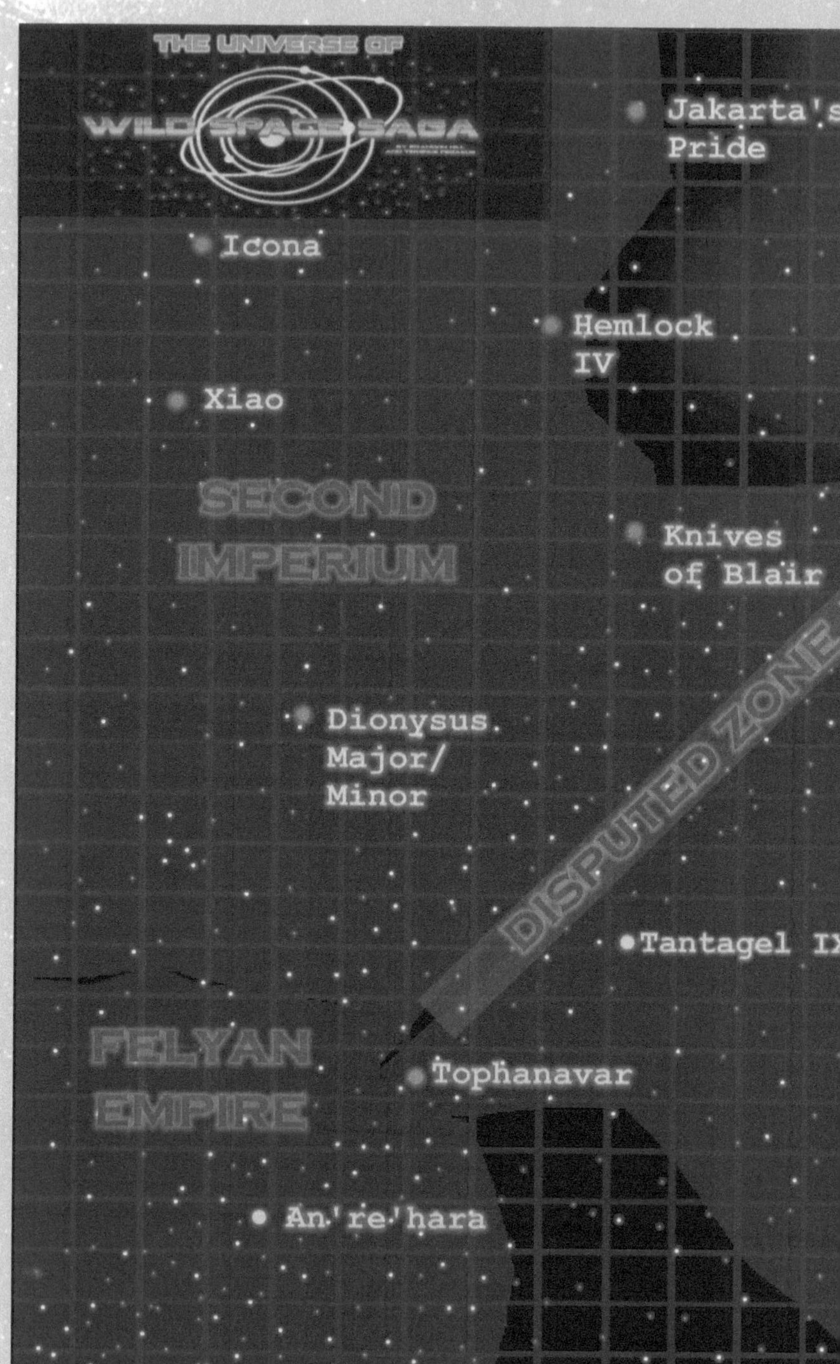

THE UNIVERSE OF
WILD SPACE SAGA
Jakarta's Pride
Icona
Hemlock IV
Xiao
SECOND IMPERIUM
Knives of Blair
DISPUTED ZONE
Dionysus Major/ Minor
Tantagel IX
FELYAN EMPIRE
Tophanavar
An're'hara

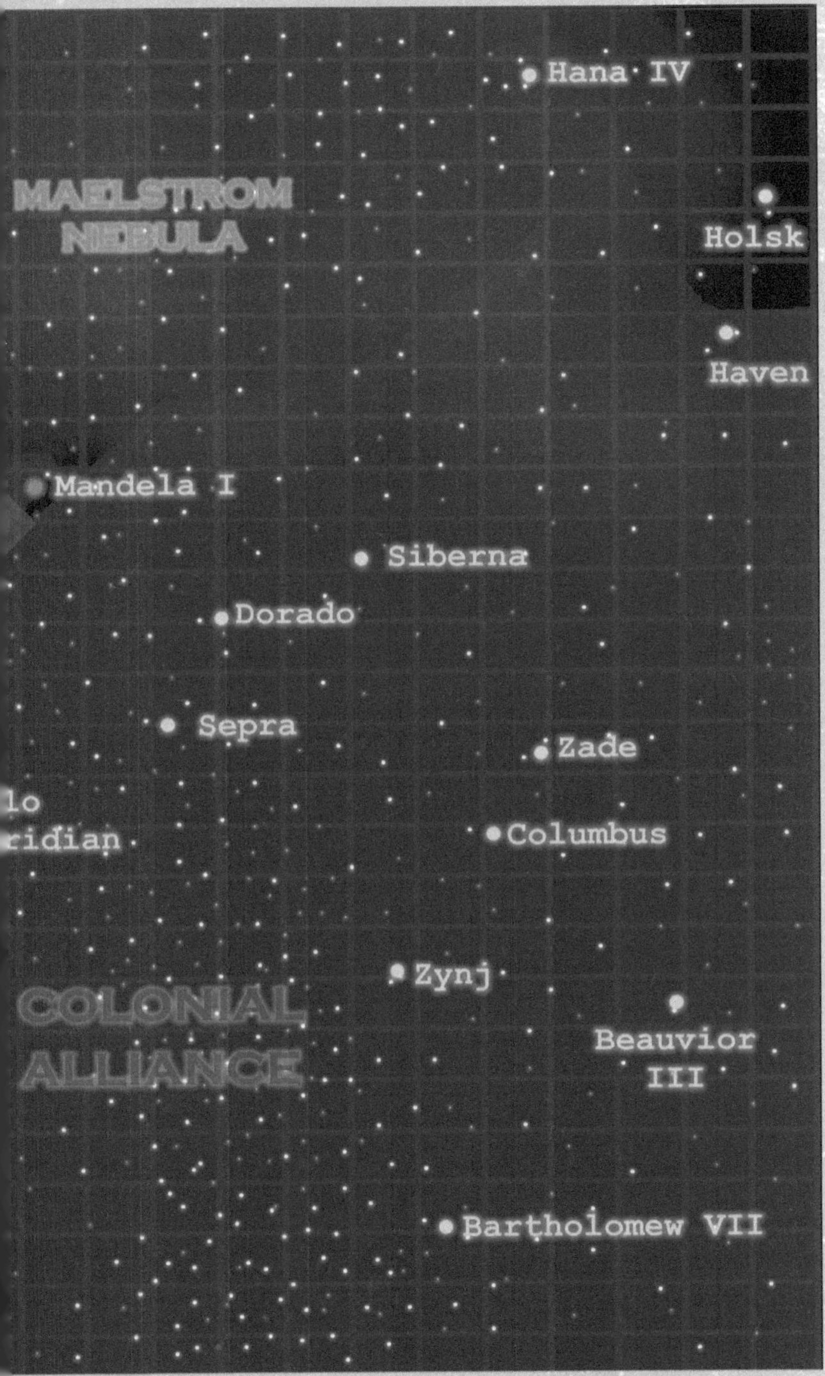

MAELSTROM
NEBULA

Hana IV

Holsk

Haven

Mandela I

Siberna

Dorado

Sepra

Zade

lo
ridian

Columbus

Zynj

COLONIAL
ALLIANCE

Beauvior
III

Bartholomew VII

TABLE OF CONTENTS

The images were at first shaky and blurred. With far too much going on outside, the cacophony of orders shouted over comms in Jakartan battle language were periodically drowned out by MAG fire in closed quarters. Surrounding the trooper from whose POV the helmet camera was broadcasting were the black and blue helmets of the battalion in subdued light. The location and time stamp remained redacted, but the surrounding steel walls were reminiscent of a military battleship or the service corridors aboard some orbital station.

"Enemy sighted! Weapons free!" were the words that Four understood as the image switched to another soldier, near the front lines, amidst the deafening staccato of gunfire.

The enemy—or rather *enemies*—flashed into view in the midst of the firefight: a knot of serpentine nightmares made from shadow and slime, snapping their toothy maws as they moved like a wave against the soldiers' well-coordinated, but seemingly futile efforts to extinguish, as if they were indeed being overcome by an actual ocean wave. Flashes of gunfire gave the entire scene an unrealistic, freeze-frame quality, as if generated by strobe lights in a dance party. But the occasional soldier that was caught by the undulating wave and wrapped in an inky black embrace of death quickly removed any semblance of entertainment from the venue.

The video ended with a nightmare: a loud explosion that sent multiple soldiers flying as shards of metal fired outwards from the left of the screen. A thunderous roar temporarily glitched the audio as the soldier's POV shifted and everything began to spin. It took Four a moment to figure out what had happened, but a view from the outside of what appeared to be a space station caused realization to dawn coldly upon him. Whatever had caused the explosion had sent shrapnel through the outer bulkhead, which appeared to be sealed by the flash of an emergency force field. The surrounding bodies of the other unfortunately spaced soldiers hurling into the void confirmed the explosive decompression that had preceded it.

The camera feed shifted once again, bringing the cacophony of gunfire and comm chatter to the forefront—and a full view of what had caused the explosion. At first, there was nothing but a toothy maw of black flesh, pelted with seemingly ineffectual MAG rounds, until the mouth closed, revealing a much larger version of the serpent creatures, easily the size of a car, reaching and snapping through the hole it made, even while the smaller members of its cohort continued their attempts at overwhelming the soldiers. The last thing in the recording was the soldier's groan of dismay as the massive serpent thing opened its maw yet again, this time spilling a new army of smaller serpents into the confined space ... then made her its next meal.

"Shit..." Four whispered, placing the tablet gently upon the table. He rubbed the bridge of his nose as he eyed Rico sitting in the chair across from him. He took a puff from his cigar as if what he'd just witnessed had been little more than a movie vid.

"Where did you get this?" Four asked.

Rico shook his head, barking out a quick laugh. "Oh, no, no, no," he said, waggling his finger. "I know you Agent types. I tell you anything, and people start disappearing." He shrugged. "Not like you could make those folks disappear, anyway."

Four frowned. "Have some respect for the dead." He removed his glasses and gazed upon Rico with his unnaturally green eyes. "Besides, I told you I'm getting out."

"Sure you are," Rico drawled. Then, smile fading, he leaned forward and pointed directly at Four. "Either way, you're not out *yet*. And I know precisely what ISID is capable of. You don't want to know how many lives just getting those few seconds of footage cost. And don't ask me to risk any more. I have my own family to think about."

A vague smile curled at the edge of Four's mouth as he placed the glasses back on his face. "I'm sure that she is perfectly capable of looking after herself."

"Who said I'm talking about Lex?" Rico said. "She's always been able to handle herself. And I'm damn sure you don't mean her, anyway."

"Indeed," was Four's enigmatic reply. "Fine, then. No further questions on your means of procurement.

But I would ask if you know any more about what happened here."

Rico shrugged. "Details are scarce, but there are a few rumors. We know the official line among the brass is the high casualty rate among tanks is the ongoing siege of Tantagel being more of an uphill battle than expected. But the big rumor is that the real meat grinder for ground tanks is them fighting something at the far borders, near the edge of known space. Comms are sketchy at the best that far out, but ... well, that's the rumor."

Less than satisfied with this paucity of information, Four nevertheless accepted what he could get. With a gentle sigh, he tapped the tablet and transferred the file to his private storage firm on the StellarNet, before wiping all memory of the transfer.

"Thank you for bringing me this," he said. "And I appreciate the risk you took in getting it here. Once I can get together enough evidence, I plan to expose this Imperial shadow war. The people of the Imperium need to know where the *real* fight lies."

"Good luck with that," Rico said, dipping his head before taking another puff from his cigar. "God knows you'll need it."

Sarah looked at the sky above her, except it wasn't sky. It was a mass of concrete that formed the base of the level above. Huge light panels sat dark, simulating night. She shifted uncomfortably as her back popped and clicked as it set itself back into place.

The fall had ended in a dumpster where Sarah now lay. It stank, and she hated it. Sarah rubbed her swollen belly as muffled pops sent ripples across it. Her body's inscrutable processes were quickly breaking down the body of her assailant. Ordinarily, she wouldn't have consumed a body in such large pieces, but there hadn't been much time. In truth, she hadn't meant to kill him. Things had simply progressed faster than expected, and she had elected to eat and run. In her hurry, though, Sarah had forgotten just how high up in the building the bar had been. She'd scrambled through a bathroom window, only realizing her error as gravity took hold and she plummeted toward the ground.

So here she lay among a different kind of trash she was used to being around. Another muted thump and her hip set itself. She lay her head back and contemplated her 'life' and the series of events that had led her to this point.

Life, when it came to Sarah, was a contentious issue for some. This was mainly because she wasn't strictly a lifeform in the traditional sense. Unlike her younger sister Alexa, she was a construct—not quite an android but not what one would consider organic either. If anyone had bothered to ask, she would have described herself as a synth or synthetic lifeform. In truth, her body bore no specific gender; she had simply chosen her name and form. In fact, when she had first become self-aware, she had been little more than a blob of black, shapeless goo.

Ultimately, she came to base her appearance on a lab technician who had been kind to her in her earliest days. In fact, she was probably the only person she had ever been sad to see die in the Second Imperium's first attacks on the world of Tantagel IX where the lab was based.

After escaping the lab prior to the attack, Sarah had turned to surviving on whatever she could get her hands on. Slowly, a primal urge led her to start hunting live prey: first vermin and stray dogs; then like an addict, it began to escalate, her desire for blood becoming like an itch in her mind, leading her to the consumption of homeless and vagrant humans. By the time she had managed to escape Tantagel and drifted throughout the outer colonies, she'd started feeding on local criminals and misfits, ultimately finding herself facing an eternity in a hole somewhere in the depths of the Alliance penal facilities. No one knew what to do with her. As a synthetic lifeform, she technically wasn't bound by the laws of the state; furthermore, she was also not protected by the inalienable rights of the Alliance.

Fortunately for Sarah, this is where Alexa had stepped in, demanding that they turn her over to her under the condition that the Royal House of the Pirate Clans kept her under their strict observation.

Thus far, the results of that act of kindness had been varied.

Now here she was, lying amongst rotting trash, working for her queen sister. It was no big surprise when she thought about it; it was rare for a job to go to plan, and this had been no exception.

She heard the cars arrive, blue lights reflecting off the brick wall above her. Another pop and her spine finished reknitting itself. Cradling her still-bloated abdomen, Sarah rolled onto her side and clambered to her feet … and found herself staring down the barrel of a pistol.

Slowly, she raised her hands, steadying herself on the slippery mess under her feet.

The officers were two Felyan hybrids: one male, with his weapon trained on her, the other female. Both were staring at her, slack-jawed.

Slowly, the female scanned the wall above her.

"Did you just fall from up there?" She finally asked, gesturing toward the shattered window where her gaze rested.

Sarah shrugged her shoulders. "I misjudged the drop; sue me."

Both blues looked at each other and then back at Sarah.

"Seems a bit irresponsible," she said.

"Especially while pregnant," the male growled, clearly not buying her explanation.

"Yeah…" Sarah drawled, "about that…"

Suddenly her stomach growled, and she unleashed a monstrous belch that sent the two blues staggering back with expressions, both aghast and disgusted. She sighed with relief and was still grinning as they cuffed her and placed her in the police cruiser. All the while inwardly laughing as their colleagues complained about the stench.

"So, are we done? Or do you want to play 'Ring Around the Rosie' a fifth time?"

Sarah rested her head against the cell's concrete wall. Thus far, she'd accepted two things that seemed to be ever more certain about her life. The first was that even her best efforts to do good would eventually land her in a jail cell; the second was that Alexa would always have to bail her out, even if it wasn't her fault.

It was her fault this time, though. And after all that had gone down, she was on the edge of deciding to declare this reaming the two cops were giving her certainty #3.

"If I were lying, don't you think I would've come up with a better story?" she said, looking neither of them in the eye. A vague impression then dawned upon her, which she decided to test. "Or maybe you're just hoping I'll slip up so that I can cover up for shortcomings on your part?"

"What are you trying to say?" the male asked testily.

Well, she'd definitely hit a nerve.

He was a hybrid like his companion, both of them human and Felyan crossbreeds, but his shorter ears could still flatten like any Felyan's. And he'd growled just as deeply when she pissed him off, Sarah noted with amusement. The way he so blatantly lost his decorum, he must have been a real handful for the chief.

"Just tell us again." The female laid a hand gently on her partner's chest. Her tone was far less abrasive. Sarah watched as her tail looped upon his. Hybrids were prosaically common on Tophanavar, but she did overhear that these two were a married couple. That was a bit more unusual for blues in their line of work. But it did make their "good cop/bad cop" routine almost adorable. Still, Sarah didn't answer immediately.

Instead, she watched the commercial playing on the tank across from the guards' desks on the other side of the force field: an animated depiction of a Gestalt battle, the two titanic, humanoid machines duking it out over Tophanavar's airless, cratered surface, coupled with animated text that advertised the GI charity expo that was scheduled to begin tomorrow. She'd bought tickets—not that she thought she'd need to, with Alexa arriving as a combatant. She just didn't want to be a charity case. Besides, her sister usually gave her free tickets to any matches she was in, but now she was fairly certain that she wouldn't be quite so charitable.

"Touchy now, isn't he?" Sarah remarked at last. She gestured vaguely to the bad cop but kept her eyes trained on the holos in the background. "Of course, I expect nothing else from blues missing the forest for the trees. You answer a call for a silly bar fight and then find little old me, not your real target."

"And just what do you mean by that?" Good Cop's voice was becoming strained, Sarah noted with mirth. *Naughty, naughty. Good cops keep their cool.*

"Describing it all again..." Sarah said, heaving a protracted sigh. "I was just doing a favor for my sister." She attempted the impossible task of making herself comfortable on the cushioned slab that even calling a bed would be considered excessively generous. "No good deed goes unpunished, I guess."

"What favor?" Bad Cop said.

"Your real target, as I said."

"What real target?" Bad Cop looked like he wanted to bash his way through the force field and try to pummel the answer out of her. She really hoped he would try.

The roughing up might certainly be kinky from a certain perspective, but to be honest, the really painful stuff was her sister's thing.

"Someone you need to worry about a hell of a lot more than me," Sarah said.

"You're not going to tell us, are you?" Good Cop's ears sagged with the dry look she cast her way.

"I'm not at liberty," Sarah answered with a shrug. "My sister will have to tell you about it. Clan business."

Like Alexa would tell you anyway, Sarah thought. Though these blues were amusing, she could not help but feel a sense of frustration at this unnecessary detour. And the fact that they seemed to show no real recognition of what she was talking about was convincing enough of their ignorance of the real situation. But that didn't stop her prey from being one of the biggest dangers in the colonies. The Doctor was wanted on five Alliance systems; there were orders to shoot her on sight in the Imperium, and the Pirate Clans had bounties on her head that could buy a planet. And so, she was more than happy to do the Clans and her sister a favor by ferreting the bitch out. The disappearances in Risstown, with victims turning up either dead or violently ill, weren't exactly the Doctor's M.O., but things went a lot deeper than this. Still, her going deep undercover to try to find out who had been behind it had proved to not be one of her best ideas.

"We'll certainly be looking into that," Good Cop said, her tone more contrite.

She must've looked up my rap sheet, Sarah thought. They would certainly have had records on past arrests and bails paid and by whom. It must have been pretty

—— XX ——

humbling to learn that their suspect was related to the Pirate Queen.

Bad Cop cut into the conversation with a hiss of such annoyance, it reminded Sarah of a death adder.

"Enough with the games!" he snapped. "Just get back to telling us what happened at the bar."

"Right, right." Sarah rolled her eyes. "The pimp tapped me on the shoulder—"

"And that's where you slammed his head into your wine glass?" Good Cop asked.

"No, he'd first been trying to sweet-talk me into going into business for him," Sarah explained. "I didn't realize they were so touchy about freelance call girls in Risstown."

"They are when you horn in on their territory," Bad Cop replied.

"Well, I'll brush up on my underworld etiquette next time," Sarah sneered back. "Besides, I'm not that kind of lady."

"So after that, you slammed his head into the wine glass?" Bad Cop said, gesturing to move the conversation along.

"Yes."

"Then you grabbed him and dragged him into the restroom... and you proceeded to," Good Cop continued, opening a note holo, "beat the shit out of him, and then tossed him out the window... and you expect us to believe that he survived a three-story drop into an empty dumpster?"

Sarah shrugged. "Why not? I did, didn't I?"

It was the third time she recited it, but it did not stop her from wanting to physically facepalm at her own explanation so hard that it would cause a singularity. Still, it was better than having to explain the actual truth: how she gave into her baser instincts and just so soon after having spotted the elusive Doctor. Or at least that was what she looked like. Sarah had taken plenty of pictures and videos, which the blues had confiscated along with the rest of her evidence. The only evidence they didn't have was the body of the pimp, which the impact with the wine glass had unfortunately killed. Thankfully, her digestive system was an efficient way of getting rid of evidence, though she found the bones distasteful and hard to keep down. Once that unpleasantness was finished, she'd made her escape through the window. There was enough blood on her to suggest some roughhousing and that the pimp had run off instead of having been made into her next meal. Without a doubt, these blues had expected more to this story, and Bad Cop most certainly wanted to nail her for murder. *Good luck with that.*

She only wished that they had known more about her actual target. Alas, no one on this asteroid had much of a clue as to the nature of the devil that walked among them or the worst one that was soon to come.

"So, are you satisfied?" Sarah said. "If you don't mind, I've grown rather enamored with staring at this wall for the past eight hours." She paused, then grinned slowly. "She posted bail, didn't she?"

Good Cop made a sigh that carried with it a tone of utter defeat.

"Yes. We received her money transfer. It'll be fully valid once she arrives at the spaceport tomorrow."

"Good." Maybe now they would leave her alone. "Now, if you don't have any more questions, kindly sod off."

Sarah watched as the blues exchanged dissatisfied looks, then ambled away. Good Cop, however, took several seconds longer than her colleague to leave, dropping her mask of false compassion and fixing her with a gaze whose suspicion spoke volumes more than any words. At last, however, even she left.

Sarah, a bit unnerved at Good Cop's actions but nonetheless satisfied that neither was the wiser, closed her eyes. She wished she could somehow will Alexa here a day sooner, but at the end of the proverbial day, it was best that she arrive when she would. Yes, she would be pissed about the situation, and understandably so, but her work would not be in vain. Her sister would at least be happy about what she was able to find. And the best part was that she wouldn't be alone.

Alas, if only her reputation for getting things done came with an assurance that she could do it neatly...

Alexa probably wished that, too.

PLANET SIBERNA
MILLION MAN STADIUM

The damage icon flashed in Xerx's field of vision immediately after *Tiberius'* sledgehammer blow.

Well, that's a new stabilizer, he thought with chagrin, shaking off the stinging system feedback. Even here, safe in *Imani*'s insulating nanofluid-filled cockpit, the impact had nearly rung his bell. He could practically hear the announcer's electrified chatter to the crowds, thinking that Artemis' beast of a Gestalt had done some serious damage. The truth was that *Imani* was holding together surprisingly well, in spite of *Tiberius'* superior strength. But even though victory could still go either way at this point, Xerx wasn't one to get ahead of himself. Neither he nor Artemis had put in enough damage to tip the scales significantly in either direction—unusual for an opponent who was known for her brutality.

And then he saw it.

On the analysis screen, a mote of red was growing deep inside of his opponent's heavily armored chassis.

Xerx grinned. He must have squeezed in a lucky shot in his last series of blows, causing a core-damaging breach in the casing somewhere. If the increasing heat readings were true, it was only about a minute more before *Tiberius* would go into emergency shutdown. He mulled this over in his head. He could continue the fight, which seemed to be well in his favor, or just toy with Artemis at this point and wait for the proverbial clock to wind down, allowing him to outright win against her for the first time.

But on top of his optimism, Xerx could not shake a niggling bit of suspicion. As fond as Artemis was of sticking sharp objects in vital places to finish the match as quickly as possible, it was puzzling that she had not been fighting in any way similar to her style. What was she playing at? Not that he wasn't thankful for the reprieve, but to drag out this fight for so long, the little pink-haired witch had to be up to something. She'd only been resorting to physical blows after exhausting her scant long-range ordinance with useless missile strikes that *Imani*'s low sensor profile could easily evade. Not like her at all.

In the end, he decided that toying with her would just be goofing off. Wasn't that old Earth saying, "Go hard or go home?"

Tiberius pressed into the gap between them, and Xerx pressed on the control rig. *Imani* made a sweeping block of the next incoming right hook before landing a smart kick to his opponent's midsection. If he hadn't been submerged in the breathable, oxygen-rich nanofluid, he believed that he would be sweating. But the way things looked, Artemis was having a tougher time of it. That was encouraging. With *Tiberius* "bleeding out," as it were, her controls had to be downright sluggish. He watched the titan stagger back, then fall into the fake nanofab building husks of the stadium's battleground simulation, demolishing them further from their war-torn disarray and buying him some time. Still, Xerx could not help but take note of the hulking Gestalt's sword scabbards. They were there, as well as its smaller blades, still sheathing their unused blades. Were her controls merely stuck? That was certainly a possibility.

Xerx shook his head. Matches weren't won by second-guessing oneself after all. And so he closed the gap, pushing *Imani* into a flat-out run, deciding to finish it, while *Tiberius*, who was down but certainly not out, struggled to lift himself from his prostrate position in the rubble. The Gestalt made a wild swing at *Imani*'s head sensors, which Xerx caught mid-blow, then used the momentum of his charge to push him deeper into *Tiberius*' small impact crater.

"Broke your robot?" Xerx teased over the comm as he brought *Imani* down to a straddling position about *Tiberius*' waist. He spun up *Imani*'s vibroknife option. The slot in her arm opened and ejected the weapon into her gray-black steel palm. Artemis, taciturn as ever, gave no reply as his trustworthy Gestalt raised her arm into the air, his targeting sensors registering their prize.

"Well, then, winner's bonus, here I come!"

Neela's voice broke into the coaching comm line, frantic. "*Kidege*! Look out! She's—"

Xerx's heart nearly burst out of his chest as his cockpit gave a shuddering heave that reminded him of that crash landing that he and Neela made in the *Reckless'* hangar mere days ago. The lights in the cockpit suddenly turned red, coinciding with a shrill whistle. He could feel the pressure of the nanofluid changing as his vision focused beyond the surrounding holoscreens, to the sight of webs of bright light that surrounded a massive slim object that tapered into sharpened edges.

A blade.

"Shit..." Xerx whispered, almost certain that he'd added urine to the slowly draining nanofluid. His vision focused back on the holograms in his field of view. Each was now banded with a red banner with flashing white writing.

"EXECUTIVE SHUT DOWN. COCKPIT BREACH DETECTED. TIBERIUS CORE DEPLETED. MATCH = DRAW."

"Draw?" Xerx's voice nearly cracked amidst the sounds of *Imani's* power systems cycling down. Unable to use the primary controls for anything now that the judges had forced their override, Xerx slammed his fist on the purge button, inhaling deeply. He then exhaled once the internal ballast drained the remaining nanofluid that had not yet seeped out of the damaged cockpit, forcing the remainder of it from his lungs. For a moment after, he gagged on the trace amounts left in his sinuses and windpipe, which created a sensation that was not unlike accidentally snorting water in a swimming pool. Once his fit had passed, he pulled the two levers that loosened the hatch. Beyond, he could hear the sounds of a clearly hostile audience, along with the announcer, beside himself as he attempted to placate them. The ladder extended as the emergency hatch cracked open, allowing the muffled jeering to become thunderous as Xerx climbed up into the perpetually hot Siberna sun ... and found himself face-to-face with Artemis, who was sitting on her haunches atop *Imani*'s spinal segment beside the intersection where her shoulder plates began. The woman's intense green eyes stared at him, unnervingly reminiscent of Nemesis, though hers had been yellow. The memory of that recent protracted battle aboard the *Reckless* sent an unwelcome shudder down his spine.

"You damaged my power core," Artemis said.

"You were on the ground and unarmed..." Xerx said, though he felt his confidence wavering with even these words, "weren't you?"

Artemis smiled, brought her closed fist into Xerx's view, then opened it to reveal a transmitter diode. It opened up a holo of the match's local broadcast, which featured an aerial shot of *Imani* and *Tiberius*. *Imani*, as she was doing now, was holding her vibroknife aloft, while *Tiberius'* fist was buried partway in the glacis plate that protected the cockpit pod inside *Imani*'s chest. From behind that closed fist, Xerx spied a hidden blade projecting at an angle and sinking into the jagged fissure.

"You aimed for my cockpit?" Xerx said, incredulous.

"I wouldn't have ripped it out," Artemis replied, sounding almost innocent.

No, she probably wouldn't have, Xerx mused. Only one pilot ever did that intentionally, and it was bad enough that ripping out an opponent's cockpit was considered by the GI Leagues to be a "dick move" at the best of times and desperation at the worst. He assumed that this had fallen far into the latter category. He sighed. Not ripping it out really was something of a courtesy, considering how expensive that kind of damage was to fix.

"Looks like we'll be sharing the prize money," Xerx said flatly.

"Mmhm," Artemis nodded, otherwise silent and looking like she had never been happier. It was the most disarming look she had amidst all her facial piercings.

"I guess I should at least be happy that we're getting something out of it," Xerx said to his wife as he stepped out of the shower and wrapped a towel about his waist. He'd tried to maintain a positive attitude about today's match, but he could not shake his lingering pang of annoyance. "After all, half is better than nothing."

"Now try telling that to our crew," Neela said. She was sitting on the bed as he passed her by on the way to the dresser.

"Geez, twist the knife, why don't you?" Xerx replied. "Besides, it's not like I threw the game. And yes, I know you tried to warn me."

"I never said you did," Neela replied. "And yes, I did."

"Then why make fun of me about it?"

For a moment, his wife seemed taken aback, but then her expression turned contritely pensive.

"I ... think that perhaps I was a bit more sanguine than I intended," Neela admitted after a tiny fluster. "But winning less off of this fight shouldn't really be a problem for us, should it?"

"Well, the trip to Tophanavar is all expenses paid, round trip," he said, fishing out fresh underwear, then a shirt, and pants from the dresser. "And I'm sure we can pull some job for Alexa if she's not too busy afterward. But that's a big 'if.'"

"How so?"

"Tyger's going to be there."

Neela shook her head with a rueful grin. "He's going to try to hide from her again, isn't he?"

"And he'll fail, as usual."

"Then we won't see either of them for at least a day or two."

"And when we finally see him again, he'll be walking bowlegged." Xerx suppressed a chuckle as he raided the closet for a fresh set of clothes. "I'll look for Alexa after all that, I guess."

"So it'll be an extended stay?"

"Probably so. We don't have any matches scheduled for a few weeks after that, so we can take our time getting back home. Besides, it all depends on what we find there."

"Well, I think finding a job on Tophanavar will certainly be a nice change of scenery," Neela said. "And the trip alone will get your mind off of that match."

"I still think the pink-haired witch got off on her little sneak attack," Xerx said, his prior frustration returning.

"It wouldn't surprise me if she did," Neela said. "You know her nature. She just got back to Siberna yesterday, and she loves messing with you. Besides, how many matches have you lost to her in the past?"

"More than I want to count," Xerx said, almost growling. "*Imani* doesn't do sneaky-stab-stab all that well."

"Ironic for a Gestalt armed with a knife." Neela's comment sounded less like a barb and more musing aloud this time and therefore peeved Xerx significantly less. "Well, considering the fact that *Tiberius* is clearly good at 'sneaky-stab-stab,' I should think that ending a match on a draw is an improvement on your track record with her."

"Can't argue with that," Xerx replied. "Still, I can't help wondering if she just threw the match."

"And risk a fine?" Neela raised an incredulous eyebrow. "Or worse still, a ban? Do you honestly think she'd do that?"

"When it comes to spending time with Maria?" Xerx countered. He then paused and chuckled in spite of himself. "I'm surprised she didn't make *Tiberius* turn tail and scale the arena wall just to head for the spaceport!"

"Wouldn't that be something now?" Neela said, then grinned, looking as if she'd been amused by a mental image that her husband's words had drummed up. "Well, those two do make quite the motley couple. Then again, you know more about Artemis than I do."

"Not much more, actually." Xerx scratched at the narrow strip of hair that grew down from his lower lip. "Speaking of the *Shadow Star* crew, I haven't seen Paige for the past few days, not since the finals started."

"She's a captain like you are," Neela said, "and with more responsibilities to boot."

"Or she might be sick."

"Even if that were the case, I'm sure the crew would have informed you. She just has clients is my guess. Mercs don't have the luxury of the GI."

"True," Xerx said, his thoughts drifting off again to today's battle. "As for *Slayde* not being part of the G1, I think that's a good thing. I've seen it in action. Even if you retrofitted that thing to make it league legal, it'd still kick everyone's ass and make change. And all things considered, I guess the match could've ended a lot worse."

"And some prize money is better than none," Neela said, seemingly pleased with husband's more positive turn.

"Even though the crew will probably piss it away on shopping and booze when we get to Tophanavar," Xerx added, that pesky realism once again intruding into his optimism. "Amenities will be on our dime."

At his wife's silence, he flashed her a shrewd grin.

"I see you didn't deny it," he said.

"I know them just as well as you do," Neela said, then sighed. "I just wish we were going there only for the charity match."

"Now don't start that again." Xerx at last shuffled off the towel and fitted himself into his underwear. "My mind is made up, *Kipenzi*."

"I know." Neela raised her hands in surrender. They'd argued about it once before, to no avail, and they were both aware that nothing would change his mind on this mission. After years of searching, his cousin Isibar had at long last found out the next destination of Dr. Hayashibara, the psychopathic scientist formerly in the Imperium's employ who had tortured him and whose ambitions had resulted in the kidnapping and subsequent murder of several Felyan hybrid children. This would be the best chance to at long last settle his family's vendetta with her. There was no way to talk him out of it. "God knows I know, my love. But I do worry."

Xerx, the hardness of his resolve softening minutely at the sound of his wife's words, flashed her a loving smile.

"I'd wonder who you are if you didn't."

"You can ask for your little cousin's help, you know?" Neela said. "I think I recall Cala mentioning that he lived on Tophanavar with Rinkya."

"Oh, right." Xerx chuckled as he leaned against the dresser. "Last I saw of those two, Rati was still scaring that girl with bugs. Makes me feel old now." He then shook his head. "But no, I don't want him dragged into this mess. Not unless he doesn't have a choice. Besides, he's not a pirate blood."

"Both he and Rinkya are cops, though," Neela said.

Xerx raised an eyebrow. That was certainly news to him, though with a family of fifteen-plus children, he had long since given up on keeping track of what each had been doing with their respective lives. Still, he could not deny the advantage that their position might give him.

"Well, that does change things a bit. But pirates and cops haven't exactly mixed well in the past."

"I suggest you think about it at least," Neela said as she stood and headed for the shower. "After all, it is a long way to Tophanavar."

Xerx paused in dressing, taking notice that his wife had already begun to disrobe, removing her shirt and leaving it on the carpeted floor in a very deliberate way. She passed him with a flirtatious smile, which he returned with a broad, almost salacious grin.

"You know, the team is almost done storing up *Imani* in the hangar," Xerx said, speaking coyly. "I'm sure I can trust them to finish up the job without me while I … maybe wash your back?"

Neela had disappeared around the doorway by the time Xerx had finished his question, leaving a conspicuous trail of clothing behind her, save her bra and panties.

"Well, my love, you might want to call them instead of staring at my clothes," Neela said, her hand extending from the doorway, allowing the black lace and cloth combination of her now discarded panties to hang from her fingertip in a very provocative way. She tilted her hand and dropped them to the floor, suggesting many delightful promises.

Xerx was unsure if Pepper had fully understood his rapid and distracted comm message, but a few minutes later, he was just this side of not caring.

Artemis glanced toward the hangar bay entrance. The stars were still mostly out, but she could see the band of steadily approaching sunlight on the horizon, appearing just above Siberna Prime's distant skyline. God wouldn't be up at this hour, but the *Shadow Star*'s crew certainly was, loading up *Tiberius* next to *Slayde*, the captain's fearsome-looking Gestalt, and doing final preparations for the trip to Tophanavar. Paige was oddly not with them, overseeing the loading process as she was inclined to do. Instead, she was standing in the observation window of the hab deck. Artemis watched her with unblinking eyes.

The captain looked as if she hadn't had a wink of sleep the prior night, not even with that bottle of dark rum from the distilleries on Columbus she had been gripping like the hand of a lover. Her bleary-eyed gaze was set upon the bustling crew as she leaned against the armored glass, passively watching her crew operate the cables and hydraulics that maneuvered *Tiberius* into the secondary storage frame forward of her own personal Gestalt, *Slayde*: an armored knight in odd colors next to an austere-looking juggernaut, armed to the teeth with the best weapons that M.T.H.I. Corp's R&D could devise.

"Geez, this is high up!"

The voice was familiar, yet nonetheless startling. Artemis spun around, her hand going instinctually to the knives she always kept sheathed on her belt, but then she settled down as she saw Maria, who, in spite of her considerable size, managed to sit gracefully into a cross-legged position near the lip of the open upper loading door where she was perched. Today must have been a good day for her pain index, Artemis supposed, as sitting that way was something that her profusion of battle injuries would have made especially uncomfortable.

"Just what are you doing up here, anyway?" Maria asked. "It's rare that you sit out in the open."

"People watching."

The massive tank settled down beside her. Despite her having been born and bred as an elite soldier for the Second Imperium, Maria had always held a personality completely antithetical to her genetic breeding, which manifested itself as a disarmingly sweet and gentle nature, which had beguiled even the normally standoffish and taciturn Artemis.

"Oh. I thought you'd be napping in the air ducts like usual," Maria said.

"I just wanted to be outside," Artemis replied. The massive tank knew her and her partiality to small, even cramped, hiding spaces well. She gestured toward the crew. "They're nearly done."

"I know," Maria said with an almost cheeky grin. "Why do you think I'm here?"

"Paige has been drinking a lot."

Maria's smile vanished as her gaze shifted toward the observation window without Artemis' guidance. But this time, the brooding figure of Paige was not to be found. The now-empty liquor bottle was still there, though, abandoned on the windowsill.

"She's come here for the last three days," Artemis said.

"That's what's bothering you, little one?" Maria asked.

"She's not happy about this."

Maria suppressed a guffaw. "That goes without saying, I'd think."

"She doesn't want to do it."

"There's a lot more to this than meets the eye, I'm afraid," Maria explained. "I don't know all the details, but Captain Paraska has dibs on this target—something about a family vendetta. If it's who I think it is, then I'd just as easily twist her head off. But a lot of powerful people are interested in this person, including our bosses, who want her alive."

"He should say no," Artemis said.

"It's not that simple, I'm afraid." Maria shook her head. "When they pay for a job, the bosses get what they want. They started the avalanche; us pebbles can only hold on and ride it down." She gave Artemis an affectionate grin before leaning over to plant a kiss on the much shorter woman's forehead. "But don't worry about Paige. Things will work out in the end. I promise you that."

Artemis wished she shared Maria's optimism. But such was the curse of being the pragmatist that she was.

TWO

Kairen grumbled as he strode down the crew quarters' deck of the *Shadow Star*. Although the crew had been fully loaded for almost two hours, the captain was still "indisposed." It was a cute way of saying she had bugged off to her quarters—unless she'd used her spare artificial arm to confuse the sensors again. He'd seen her do this before in order to evade Pip's hacked video feeds when she'd wanted to have some truly private "quality time" with him. But currently, his thoughts were about as far from those pleasures as possible. They were embarrassingly behind schedule, and the *Reckless'* crew was nearly finished with their own preparations. Hadn't Paige said that she wanted to be en route to Tophanavar before Xerx and his crew had left?

"Paige?" He knocked on her door out of politeness, seeing how they shared quarters so often that he could practically consider this suite just as much his home as hers. "You in there?"

There was no answer, but he could hear noises inside, muffled through the door's plastics and metals, even as he placed his ear to it.

Well, if she's not there, then she left the holoscreen on again, he thought.

"Look, I'm coming in," he announced, then allowed himself a moment of cheekiness. "So ... if you're not decent, you're gonna be not decent in front of the whole crew."

When his quip was answered by further unbroken silence, Kairen pressed his hand against the door's biometric panel. As per his emergency access privileges granted by his position as the ship's medical officer, the door slid open to semi-lit darkness and the combined buttery scent of popcorn and cloying sweetness of rum.

The source of the light was easy to see with the images on the holoscreen flashing starkly in front of the couch. Kairen noticed a part of the multicolored quilt he'd bought for her at a bazaar on Dionysus Minor draped over one of the armrests.

"Well, you don't sound like the whole crew... unless you were hoping I'd actually be naked," she said, her tone flat and with just a hint of sarcasm.

"Another time, I think." Kairen stepped into the suite and approached the couch. Looking over the top of the backrest, he saw Paige curled up on the right armrest with her multicolored checkered quilt wrapped around her. A bowl of popcorn was placed precariously on the armrest while an empty bottle of Sergey & Kotori rum lay beside her.

At least she'd decided to get drunk with something top shelf.

Her artificial legs leaned upon the couch like a discarded pair of steel boots, disconnected from her thighs like she was wont to do whenever she wanted to get especially comfortable. Her thighs, now divested of their extensions, were hidden beneath the folds of the quilt. She stared listlessly at the program on the screen, shoveling handfuls of popcorn into her mouth.

"You know, rum will only make you thirstier with all that salt," Kairen began, feeling no less awkward or at a loss for words than he felt walking through the hallway. He then momentarily eyed the program that was currently being broadcast. "Wait, really? *Judge Trudy* is your go-to mope show?" He leaned forward and swiped a handful of popcorn from the bowl.

From beneath Paige's quilt, her hand emerged, holding the remote.

"Did you know that this guy is suing an android for unpaid rent?" Paige said after she'd muted the volume. She was now gesturing accusatorily toward the defendant, whose skin had a bluish tint like most androids and looked like it had been sculpted from plastics rather than flesh. "A. Freaking. Android!" She flung her arms out toward the screen, nearly dropping her popcorn bowl. "Who the hell is going to believe that? Since when do androids never pay their rent? Dickhead!"

Kairen hopped over the couch, then heard a sudden, loud crunching noise as he landed backside-first on a hitherto unseen bag of protein chips. He frowned, fishing the ruined bag out from underneath him, then shrugged it off as he faced Paige directly.

"You know full well why I'm here, Pij."

He supposed it had been his use of his pet name for her that had put a momentary dent in her façade. His remark seemed to shake her from the fence of self-distraction she'd apparently built around herself.

"I know you're just trying to avoid talking about it. But I'm the only one here now. You can talk to me."

Paige pressed her hand to her head as if she had just been overcome by a severe migraine. Kairen stiffened in alarm as a noticeable shiver seemed to run through her body.

"Paige...?"

"Talk about what?" Paige practically fired off the words as if they had been MAG rounds from her mouth. The sudden outburst nearly knocked Kairen from the couch. "That our employers have put me in an impossible situation? That I'll have to screw over a friend in order to just keep the fucking lights on?"

Kairen's insides abruptly became a series of impossible knots, and he felt like he had been stripped naked, then dropped onto a busy street corner on Xiao during rush hour. He opened his mouth, but nothing came out at first. Outbursts weren't uncommon with the captain; she was never one to bottle up her emotions unless on a mission, but perhaps he'd stepped on a particularly nasty land mine here.

"Look," he said, at last finding his voice and somehow keeping it even. "If you don't want to talk about it ... or maybe, have you tried talking with Xerx?" He wasn't one hundred percent sure if it even was the *Reckless'* captain that was the issue, as he was now only going by what he'd overheard Brogan talking about with Ike in the three days since their adventure at the Rickman's pulsar. The least combat-capable of this band of oddballs and bruisers, he had been minding the ship while the crew went off on their mission taking on that horde of Raiders that had attempted a hostile takeover of her friend's ship. But even though she'd seemed fairly san-guine during the party Xerx had thrown in Pit Town as a thank-you not long after, her mood had noticeably darkened afterward. So, what other "friend" could it have been?

"And say what?" Paige said. She now seemed more aggrieved than outright pissed. "'Sorry, love, but your Pirate traditions mean shit to my employers, so if you don't mind stepping aside whilst I turn this bitch into a backdoor VIP, I'd appreciate it?'"

Kairen sighed. At least his guess had been correct. But since he hardly knew the other captain, he was now even more at a loss for what to do.

And yet the crew sent me to talk to Paige, he thought with chagrin. He was definitely going to have words with them later.

"Well... I... ah... wouldn't put it that way," he stammered, trying to think of something comforting to say. He brushed his long fall of dirty blond hair back behind his ear with a somewhat unsteady hand. "I'm guessing he's got dibs on this Doctor?"

"His cousin, actually," Paige said. "But he's too busy being a father now, and his family's picked up the vendetta. If the Pirate King had been closer, it would've fallen to him."

"He can't back out of it?" Kairen asked.

"You must've not been close to your family," Paige said, shaking her head.

"Not really, no," Kairen admitted. "But I think I can see what you mean." He reached out and brushed a stray hair from Paige's forehead. "I can't say I under-stand everything. And I understand vendettas even less.

But what I do see is that this has got you stuck between the old rock and hard place."

"If you only knew."

"I wish I could think of a way out for you," Kairen said, now feeling even more helpless in spite of how much he'd just now learned from the captain. He opened his mouth to say more, but just then, a static crackle from the room's external comm interrupted him as it brought the shrill sound of Pip's unexpected voice barging her way into the conversation.

"Slim Jim's right, you know, Boss. It's not fair to just fuck them over like this. And not to be pedantic, but the lights are kept on by tesseract power distribution nodes. Just saying."

Paige's reaction made Kairen's heart sink into the second circle of hell ... or perhaps the third. He knew that livid expression, and he knew that growl. Usually, it happened when she realized that Pip had managed to spy on them yet again during sex, but even at other times, it was no less frightening.

"Now listen here, you nosy little fucking shit!" Paige's voice was a hissing growl that came through clenched teeth. "Where do you think the money comes from to keep that node running, eh? Who pays for all that fancy VR shit in your room and the high bandwidth subspace antenna so that you can game with your friend aboard the *Reckless*? Who do you think pays for that? And do you have any fucking idea what the company will do to us if we renege on this contract? There's a bloody reason nobody asks those questions!"

Now, it was Pip's turn to fluster. But Paige didn't give her much time for this as she pressed on, while Kairen could only stare, gobsmacked.

"Out of tongue, are you now? Then maybe you'll stop listening in on private conversations that have fuck all to do with you! And since you seem to be listening now, I want you to listen to me as hard as you can. I don't want to hear your voice for the rest of the fucking day, or so help me, I'll disable the fire suppression system in your room and toss a Molotov in there! Am I making myself clear?"

Her question was met with an unnerving silence.

"Good," Paige said, her tone less acerbic, but no less curt. "Now fuck off."

The comm didn't have a sound to signal a terminated connection, but Kairen was quite sure that Pip had indeed fucked well off. Still, he was no less speechless, only staring at Paige, whose fury had quite subsided, and now become a smoldering frown, with perhaps a hint of regret in her eyes.

"Was that necessary?" he said, at last risking words.

"Probably not," Paige said, not setting her eyes on him. She was staring past the silent images on the tank now. "But she—"

"I really don't think she deserved that," Kairen replied, shaking his head.

"I've been too lenient with her," Paige said. She closed her eyes. "That girl needs to learn some damn boundaries."

"Yeah," Kairen said, unable to deny it, despite the captain's outburst. "Feel better?"

Paige shook her head as her response came out in a brittle tone. "Not in the slightest. And I'm no closer to solving the problem."

Now, Kairen understood why Ike and Brogan had selected him for this. Paige was clearly in a vulnerable state, showing a side of herself that she would have never shared with any of her crew, perhaps not even Brogan, who, along with the captain, had borne the wrath of the androids that had sadistically maimed and eviscerated them. These divided principles, however, were a wound of a different kind and one for which she needed a different kind of sympathetic ear, an ear from a person who had shared something intimate with her in a way that was different from battle wounds and bionic replacements. Whether he could give her advice or not was irrelevant.

"I'm sorry," he said after some time of silence had passed between them. He leaned forward and touched her chin. Paige turned his way, and in the holo's ambient light, he saw tears streaming from her one remaining natural eye.

"I wish I had a solution for you," he continued as her face contorted into a grimace. She tried to look away, but his touch on her cheek caused her to pause. No doubt she was ashamed of this moment of weakness and helplessness in front of a member of her crew, boyfriend or not. Her shoulders slumped, and her lip trembled.

With nothing else to say, Kairen pulled Paige to his chest as she heaved perhaps the ugliest sob he'd ever heard. Silently, he gave her all the time she needed to let out her emotions in all their shuddering, wet misery, while he tried to do the only thing he could do, which was to be there for her.

Life in Pit Town woke with the roosters during G1 season. Today would turn out to be especially busy, Xerx expected, as those who would be participating in the exhibition on Tophanavar would be leaving for the distant orbital colony. Others from the minor leagues or those who did not place in the ranking matches, having the luxury of traveling light, had already taken leave and were on their way. No doubt setup crews were already there. Tophanavar's habitat levels were as modern as they came, but the surface of the asteroid upon which it was built was just as barren and airless as any hunk of interstellar rock, with low-G conditions that required trained specialists to prep for Gestalt fights.

The *Reckless* crew was all packed up and ready; all that remained was loading up *Imani*, and they would be on their way as well. Salt and Pepper were installing the low-G mods on the Gestalt in the moments before the move, which gave Xerx time to himself. Neela had run off to the local café to get some decent coffee for the crew while he stood atop the roof of his team's hangar, watching the *Shadow Star* lift off and disappear into the stratosphere.

Paige's sudden departure had continued to vex him, even now. It had only been a few days since he had shared that bottle of whiskey with her in this same spot—just two old friends getting drunk after a brush with death. But after the comm from his cousin Isibar, she became as scarce as a decent meal on a garbage scow. And now, she'd just bugged off without even saying goodbye.

"That's not like her at all," Xerx mused aloud.

"What's not like who?"

Neela, having come up suddenly from behind, startled him. She laughed, handing him a lidded styrofoam cup of coffee from the large tray that he supposed had held enough for the entire team.

"I just saw Paige's ship leave," Xerx explained, accepting the steaming cup. He took a sip of the energizing beverage with the extra sugars and Irish cream that he loved. "She didn't even tell me she was leaving."

"I would imagine that in her line of work, things come up pretty quickly," Neela said with a shrug. "Besides, I'm sure it wasn't personal since I saw them loading *Tiberius*. Isn't Artemis scheduled for the exhibition on Tophanavar?"

"Unfortunately," Xerx said, still stinging from that last match.

"Then I guess you have your answer. They're probably just dropping her off."

Xerx sighed. "I don't know why this bothers me so much," he said, then at last deciding to drop the notion entirely. "Well, all things considered, I'll be glad to be underway. I need to clock a lot of simulation hours; maybe that'll get my mind off this. Has Mobola finished installing that new VR program?"

"I think so," Neela said, taking Xerx by the hand and leading him back to the stairwell. "It's probably why she wouldn't let anyone else touch *Imani*'s systems beforehand. And since Pepper and Var work quickly, I'm sure they're almost ready for us."

As if her words had been portentous, Var's gruff, but erudite voice broke in on the comm.

"Mods finished on the big lady, Captain. We're ready to load."

"Tell Mobola to spin up garrison mode for the hangar bay, and we'll get her in," Xerx said. I want us to be hitting vacuum within the hour."

"Copy that," Var replied.

Xerx smiled as he and his wife hurried down the stairs. "Gotta say that garrison mode was kind of a mixed blessing, don't you think?"

"Now that Mobola knows how it works, it certainly will make storage easier," Neela replied with an eager nod. "We should be able to take on some impressive freight jobs now."

"We'll be able to out-capacity most cargo ships," Xerx said, no less enthusiastic. "We'll have to keep the business discreet, though."

Neela pursed her lips. "That will be the tricky part."

"Small steps, then."

THREE

RECKLESS: HYPERSPACE TRANSIT TO TOPHANAVAR

Pepper suppressed a laugh as he stole a glance at Mobola, who sat with the attention of a college student to the most interesting lecture of her life. She cradled her glass of frothy *amasi*, the beverage seemingly forgotten as she studied the hologram above the coffee table in the middle of the observation lounge's central arrangement of sofas. The image displayed what appeared to be three flat slabs of unevenly shaped stone. They floated above an asteroid that resembled a lumpy, gray potato, with three holes in the exact shape of the slabs carved out of its pockmarked surface. In the middle stone was a round, transparent dome, which capped a landscape within that looked like someone had bored into the rock with a titanic drill. The image then shifted to focus on the landscapes within the dome: corkscrew terraces that were shelves of greenery, gray spires, and rivers that fed into waterfalls and lakes. Two glass tunnels outside ran in opposite directions from the central dome and over a bridge on either side that connected the two slabs and led to a domed industrial complex at the center of each.

"Tophanavar is the result of growing trust between the free worlds of the Alliance and the Felyan Empire," said an accompanying voice-over as the image began to shift away from the asteroids to reveal a single moon. Its surface was concealed by high thin clouds that came alive with irregular flashes of lightning. Panning farther out, a monstrous gas giant appeared with banded clouds of purple and blue. "Hollowed out of an asteroid in geosynchronous orbit around Quandisa, a moon of the gas giant Hyacinth in the Coriana system that borders Felyan and Alliance space, it houses a population of twenty-eight thousand permanent residents, all charter workers, Felyan Imperial subjects, and colonial citizens in project New Eden, the first nanotech terraforming effort since the days of the First Imperium. Thanks to a boon from the Felyan Empress, the human population of the colony currently benefits in the rare sharing of technology between the Empire and Alliance."

Pepper had tried to stay quiet with what he was doing, but the high-pitched ringing of several glasses tapping against each other caught Mobola's attention. She looked up from the hologram, pausing it while she observed the charcoal gray-haired Felyan up to his normal antics. He was pouring a carefully measured glass of Felyan brandy that he'd filched from the bar's usually locked bottom back shelf. Aside from his usual twinkle of mischief, the look in his eyes betrayed well-earned exhaustion from the day's work on *Imani*. He was clean from head to toe from the sonic scrubbers with an especially healthy sheen on his striped skin, but even they couldn't revitalize a person on the inside.

"The captain is going to kill you if he finds you've been in his special stash again," Mobola warned as Pepper placed the decanter back into the cabinet and reset the lock. She recognized the brand as a brand that was unavailable in the Colonies: something his cousin had sent to him from An'Re'Hara. Pepper had managed to bypass the cabinet lock months ago but had been careful not to access it too often.

After a long, groaning stretch, he picked up the glass and plopped in two ice cubes from the nearby freezer.

"Would you tattle on me, then?" he asked before joining her at the opposite end of the couch. He fixed her with a cheeky grin.

"N-no!" Mobola felt a heat worse than noontime summer heat in Pit Town come to her face as she curled her knees tightly up to her chest. Pepper, seeing her reaction, barked out a laugh.

"You're so adorable when I get you unnerved," he said, his voice still shaking as Mobola sulked. Pepper's jokes could be so juvenile. "Besides, the captain will just probably blame Var."

Mobola stared at him, aghast. "You'd throw your own teammate under the bus?"

"Not normally," Pepper said with a shrug, "but after his Dorado scorpion cactus prank from last month, he's got it coming to him." He huffed out a small hiss. "I couldn't feel my tail for nearly a week after, y'know?"

Mobola shook her head. "It's a miracle you all get along so well," she said.

"Who do you mean?"

"You, your father, and Var," Mobola replied. "I guess it's a Felyan thing."

"You've seen us arguing, right?" Pepper raised an eyebrow over an otherwise blank expression. "I mean, we're not exactly subtle."

"A few times," Mobola replied, "but you always seem to get along right after."

"More like we tolerate each other."

Mobola frowned. "I'm sure you'd be upset if something were to happen to either of them."

"Maybe." Pepper sounded almost reluctant, and the realization of this caused a look of shame to flash across his face. "Well, I guess so." He quickly shifted his gaze to the paused hologram. "So, what was it that you were watching?" he asked, taking a sip of his pilfered beverage.

"Just a video clip about Tophanavar that I got off of the StellarNet," Mobola explained. "I've never been there before."

"Neither have I," Pepper said with an abrupt burst of energy. "So, fire this puppy back up. I wanna see."

Mobola unpaused the recording.

"The project is in its fiftieth year with forty years remaining until completion. As such, the Felyan Empress has appointed her most recently born daughter as the future administrator of Quandisa upon completion, sired through human bloodlines as a symbol of unity. Festivities commemorating the birth are ongoing."

The image faded as the playback ended, leaving a somewhat awkward silence between the two.

"I'm sorry..." Mobola said, staring now at the frozen video. "I didn't realize that I'd already watched most of it. I'll start it over—"

"Nah, it's okay." Pepper waved his hand. "I'll look it up later."

He then leaned forward, his tail twitching. Mobola felt goosebumps erupt on the back of her neck. There was always something about the way Felyans smelled; that powdery aroma, while comforting, was always slightly off-putting in a way she didn't understand, and even a little frightening, despite her having known Pepper long enough to trust that he would sooner cut off his own tail than hurt her.

"So, did you catch anything good about the place?" His grin was broad and boyish.

"Ah, well..." Mobola flustered, "I was looking over a brochure before I saw this video. I think you'd, um, like the fact that it's friendliest toward Felyans and hybrids. It scored the highest in race relations, though opinions about the government setup are a little strained, but mostly among humans." She made a weak-sounding titter. "But that's humans under alien rule for you." Realizing to her deep chagrin what her prior sentence must have sounded like, she quickly added, "Not that there's anything wrong with that!" Defiantly swallowing the urge to bury her face in her hands, she continued. "But it's the most tolerant of interspecies relations. Most of the charter colonist families are mixed-species, and—"

"No, I mean places good for sightseeing," Pepper said. "Or rather, places we'd enjoy, you know, together? Something like beaches, parks, zoos, or restaurants? I think I recall hearing of a really nice lookout spot on the Colony's main dome."

"Well, that would be nice..." Mobola began; then her gaze drifted to her right hand, noticing that she'd done it again. Somewhere in the middle of the conversation, she'd absently grabbed the end of Pepper's tail. It was an idiosyncrasy she'd picked up around him whenever she became lost in thought or subconsciously nervous. He never seemed to mind it, but catching herself in the act, let alone seeing the subsequent look of confusion on her friend's face, never made her feel any less like wanting to crawl into a hole to die.

"I'm so sorry!" she squeaked, dropping the appendage as if it carried a disease. She composed herself yet again, in spite of her awareness of the volcano heat, she could feel all the way to the tips of her ears. Suddenly remembering her glass of *amasi*, she took a large swallow of it, ignoring its tartness. "Um... what we both like? Well, it is a popular stopover for space hippie fleets, and they set up shop all the time." She finally regrouped her waning courage enough to look Pepper in his eyes. "They're sure to be there if there's a festival going on. You like going shopping with me, right?"

"Shopping it is then," Pepper said, finishing off the remains of his own beverage. To her relief, he always appeared unaffected in the slightest by her very conspicuous bouts of self-consciousness. Still, it failed to prevent her from feeling like becoming one with the ship's innards whenever she was embarrassed. She watched as Pepper stood up and gave her a curious wink before heading back to the bar. "By the way, did you and Pip ever find out more about the ship? Whether or not the system is an A.I.?

"Oh, that?" Such a practical question momentarily shook Mobola out of her discombobulated state. "I let her know about it, but she hasn't had much time to work on it with me. She did say that the system is unexpectedly complex. And that's saying something for someone who used to live inside a ship's systems. She said it's complex enough to the point that it wouldn't surprise her if it was an actual A.I.."

"Guess we were both on to something, then?" Pepper said. "Glad I was helpful."

"I went on a deep dive once during a diagnostic, just to scan the memory archives," Mobola said. "It's ... big."

"How big?"

"I don't know how to answer that question, really," Mobola said with a shrug. "Systems are extensive if they have a lot of data archives, but the system—the structure of the thing, I mean—is, well ... big. I wish I knew how else to describe it. Maybe Pip might be able to help when she has a chance."

"I wish I could interface with the system the way you two can," Pepper said, his tone shifting to a wistful one, with perhaps a touch of jealousy. "As it is now, I only can use a VR setup like I did the other day. It really brings out colors, you know."

"I never thought of it that way," Mobola said, becoming mindful of the gray-haired Felyan's bright smile. It was somewhat silly, with his pronounced canines, but in a way that was also handsome. And again, this invoked a spike of that old self-consciousness.

"Yeah," Pepper said. "I never noticed how you turn the most adorable shade of red when you're nervous until then."

Pepper expected a reaction, but the abrupt sound of rushing footsteps, accompanied by the deck's entrance door sliding open, then closing, took him quite by surprise. He turned around to see that Mobola, as he'd figured, had beaten a surprisingly discreet and very hasty retreat.

"I thought human girls were supposed to like compliments," Pepper mused, crestfallen, as he dumped the remaining ice into the sink drain and set to cleaning the now empty glass. A moment later, the door slid open once again. He turned back around, expectant, and then nearly groaned in frustration as Salt appeared. His father was glancing back the way he came, with a look of combined confusion and annoyance.

"Trisi's Love! What crawled up that spaz's butt?" Salt exclaimed, his light gray tail twitching. "If she'd run into me any harder, I'd have needed a pressure wrench to unstick her!" He then eyed Pepper as he slowed down to a halt, and his tone became deceptively flat. "I should've known. Scared her away again?"

"More like she scared herself away." Pepper passed his glass through the flow of water from the faucet, then wiped it off with the nearby towel. "I wasn't even pushing anything much. All I did was talk about Tophanavar."

"And...?" Salt inclined his head.

It was now Pepper's turn for his face to grow hot.

"And … I might have mentioned how cute she looked when she was nervous."

Salt hissed, and Pepper groaned.

"Here we go again."

"The girl's afraid of her own reflection," Salt said as he made his way over to the bar's main shelves. "Why you want something like that, I'll never know. And I hope you haven't forgotten that we have a job to do. I don't need you two running off to do Creator-knows-what when we get there."

"Ever known us to do that?" Pepper said, suppressing his own urge to hiss. "Mobola's a professional, Dad. Were we running off to Creator-knows-where when we learned how the heart of this ship beats?"

"Yeah, yeah. Whatever." Salt heaved a sigh as he ran his fingers along the selection of libations on the bar's shelf. He then paused and sniffed the air. "Hey, you been swiping the captain's special stash again?"

"Maybe." Salt exercised his best poker face, but the older Felyan merely shrugged.

"You're gonna get strung up by your tail one day when he finds out, and I'm gonna laugh when he does it," Salt said, pointing his way.

"At least I'd die happy." Pepper tried to sound annoyed, but inwardly, he was impressed at his father's uncanny ability to single out brands of liquor on a simple sniff. Var was the only other Felyan he knew who could do it, and he envied them both for it. He covered his momentary surprise with a carefree shrug. "'Sides, he hasn't used the stuff in ages. Better I turn it into pee than let it sit around and slowly fossilize."

Salt made a gruff chuckle. "Okay, then, smartass. I'll be sure to tell him that right before he pulls the rope. With that attitude, he might attach it to a winch instead."

"So, I'll donate to the temple when we get to Tophanavar," Pepper replied, a bit more tersely than he'd intended. He'd had all the energy in the world to speak with Mobola, but dealing with his father reminded him quickly of how tired he actually was.

"Oh, speaking of temples," Salt remarked as he made his own beverage selection, "I was talking to Var after we finished work. He let me know that he has an uncle who works with the local honor guard for the high priest on Tophanavar."

Pepper's frustration melted away into a puddle of complete confusion over his father's words. Salt had never approved of things between him and Mobola, even though there technically wasn't anything between them. Still, he hadn't exactly been secretive about how smitten he'd been since the day they'd met on that refugee transport from Mandela I. In fact, it was probably just Mobola who didn't realize his feelings. But with all this in mind, he didn't think that his old man would have ever been this blatant about removing him from the *Reckless*.

"That's a nice gesture, Dad... I think," he said, "but I'm not exactly interested in changing careers."

"That wasn't the reason why I said that, you goof!" Salt poured his drink and slammed the bottle on the bar, rolling his eyes. "I'm talking about his daughters. He's got a big family and a lot of girls who aren't mated. I could introduce you to one of them. Hell, even a hybrid would be less work than you-know-who."

"Stop, Dad," Pepper said with adamant finality. "Just stop. We've had this conversation before; it always turns into an argument. And the answer is still no."

"Dammit, boy!"

Here we go again, Pepper thought as he watched as his father threw his hands into the air, a look of disgust wrenching his face.

"How much longer are you going to keep chasing after that girl?"

"She has a name," Pepper replied, his tone that of forced calm.

"That doesn't change the fact that you wouldn't know uninterested if it jumped up and bit your tail clean off."

"Really, now?" Pepper said. "'Cause my nose tells me different, old man."

"Oh, please," Salt drawled as he settled onto the stool across from him. "When she's with you, her scent shifts around just as much as her mood."

"It's not my fault that humans aren't always honest with themselves," Pepper gestured back toward the entrance door, "or that it sometimes takes them awhile to get their feelings sorted out. I hope that's not your problem with her. Otherwise, I'd have never pegged you for—"

Salt launched himself from his stool in a move that took Pepper completely by surprise. He leaned forward and looked him straight in the eyes. A low growl rumbled in his throat.

"Watch it, boy."

Pepper froze. He hadn't heard that sound since he was a child. And yet, the same as in his childhood, it still managed to shut off any hostility. Then, just as quickly as his father's fury had awoken, he settled back down on the stool. He seemed eerily calm when he swallowed back part of his drink.

"Look, you didn't hear this from me, but the charity match is just a front," Salt said. "It's not the real reason we're going to Tophanavar."

Pepper's anger had settled at his father's words, and he now gave him his undivided attention.

"You heard about the scientist that screwed around with the captain's cousin, right?"

"The pup killer?" Pepper said, recalling the story that Xerx had recounted to them during their misadventure. "Who hasn't? Ah... you *are* talking about the one the captain mentioned during our little run-in with that blue-haired chick, right?"

"That's the one." Salt nodded, his tone grim as he continued. "And the captain has it on good authority that she's headed for our stop."

"And I wasn't told about this why?" Pepper asked, unable to help feeling more than a little insulted that he had not been privy to this.

"Because you weren't part of the plan," Salt said. "You, Mobola ... even Var doesn't know about this."

"Really?" Pepper said. Then, after a second, a question hung on his lips. And he was unable to suppress the notion that he would not like what his father would say in response to it. "And your role in this is..."

"I'm going to flush the bitch out," Salt replied. Pepper was certain his father could see the color fade from his face, down to his stripes.

"So ... he's got you acting as bait?"

"Now don't let your stripes fall off," Salt said. "Your old man's worn many hats in his life. I can take care of an amoral psycho if the need arises." He emptied his glass in one swallow.

"But why you?" Pepper asked.

"I'm the best for the job, I guess." Salt made a vague shrug. "Well, I volunteered actually. You see, I know the captain's real reason for doing this."

"Real reason?"

Pepper sat down on the adjoining barstool.

"You did *not* hear this from me, understand?" His father's words came out with an unusual level of severity. "He kinda spilled it one night at the bar after I won half of his wallet in a poker game. I don't even think he knows that I know; he was pretty weepy-eyed and talked too much. I guess maybe something brought back an old memory? But the deal is that the Doctor and the kidnappings hit too close to home once."

"You're not talking about Neela, are you?" Pepper said, a burgeoning pit of horror growing in the corner of his mind. "They don't have any kids."

"No, not them," Salt replied, "but a friend of his. Name was Will Spars. Had a Felyan lifemate, from what he told me, name of Kialas. They'd just had a kid, their first. They moved to the homeworld soon after, and that was when the kidnappings began. Kialas was worried the whole time; then their worst fears were realized when their kid disappeared from their yard. Kialas saw who it was and chased him through the city while Will got the local peacekeepers involved. I guess she became more trouble than she was worth because he found her dead in an alleyway, her throat slashed. Hara'Kya claws."

"What Hara'Kya would even do that?" Pepper blanched at his father's mention of the barbaric act. No Hara'Kya had attacked another Felyan in that manner for centuries. And none would ever think to do that to a human... unless it was a matter of life and death.

"These were crazy," Salt said. "Dissidents who made a deal with the devil to 'purify' society of human influence. And the Doctor gave them a promise to give them their wish. According to the captain, it was that kidnapping that broke Will. He never was the same. Then he offed himself a few weeks later."

"Shit..."

"So you see, the captain's got a real personal bone to pick with this one, and I don't blame him," Salt said in conclusion.

"Neither do I," Pepper said. In spite of his drink, he suddenly found his throat very dry.

"But there's a further point to this," Salt said, his gaze now shifting away from his son. "If only one human can commit this kind of treachery, and do it using our own people as pawns, then can you truly trust yourself with one as your lifemate?"

Pepper's sympathy vanished as his stomach turned into ice at his father's implication. And it had been about Mobola, no less: a girl who was about as harmless as a stingless panako worm. Besides, it wasn't Salt who knew her. And he had no intention of spilling the beans about something so intensely private as the past that she'd shared with him, especially if he was going to show this kind of prejudice against humans. His momentary loss for words at last alleviated itself as his expression fell into a dark scowl and a spilling over of seething fury.

"You know, Dad, I hope you never slip up and end up in some human's pants," he said at last, throwing down the towel he had only just now realized he had been squeezing in a manner that would have choked out the innards of something living. "And consider this: if that's what you truly believe about humans, then why in the fuck do you work for one?"

Unable to stomach another lecture and refusing to allow the older Felyan to say anything more, he turned and stormed off.

"Thanks for the history lesson, though," he said, leaving his father alone.

FOUR

TOPHANAVAR: COLONIAL ENFORCEMENT HQ

Rati handed his lifemate a cup of hot Felyan *veeja*. The earthy scent of the beverage refreshed his frazzled nerves almost as much as its rich almost-chocolate flavor that had nearly subsumed coffee in the colony for sheer popularity. And it had an added effect of soothing the nerves in a way that nothing else could—a fact that he was immeasurably grateful for.

"Let me guess," Rinkya said. "The chief said to forget about it, didn't he?"

"Is it that obvious?" Rinkya groaned as he led the way back to the garage. "Creepy goth girl is the strongest connection we've had to the disappearances yet. The only difference with her is that the guy she's associated with hasn't turned back up, sick as my little brother's sense of humor."

"Which one?" Rinkya teased.

"Don't you start," Rati replied, but a slight grin betrayed his formerly sour demeanor. "You didn't grow up with a steadily growing number of siblings like I did."

Rinkya sighed. "No, I didn't. And you're right about that Sarah person."

"At least someone agrees with me," Rati said.

"Someone has to be on the same team," Rinkya replied. "Might as well be me."

"Now that makes me feel better," Rati said. "At least the chief didn't take us off the case entirely. But I've never seen him so inflexible."

"Wait. He *didn't* take us off the case?" Rinkya said, pausing in her tracks. Rati, who led the way with her hand in his own, stopped only when he felt the sudden resistance, then turned around. He eyed her questioningly at first, then, gauging the glimmer in her eye, caught on. Without a word, he gestured with a nod of his head toward the route that led back to their car and said nothing else until they were seated.

"You know, I didn't get it until you put two and two together," Rati said.

"Like you said, can't be too careful," Rinkya remarked, shrugging her shoulders.

"So the chief wants us to keep at it?"

"I would hope so. Alliance military's looking for her as hard as we are. If the Doctor's not already here, she'll be coming soon."

Rati smiled. "I love it when we're on the same wavelength."

"So what do we know?" Rinkya asked.

"Not much. Just what the Alliance military sent a couple of days ago. The Doctor's on her way. But we're getting mixed signals with these disappearances and illnesses."

"Right. I got that much. I just wonder how this Sarah person factors in."

"I'm not sure." Rati leaned back in the driver's seat and let out a sigh after taking another sip of his *veeja*. "I'm kind of wondering if we were even barking up the right proverbial tree with her. And with the Queen's damned royal immunity, there's not much we can do. Have we got anything else?"

"We can go and inspect the protocols at the spaceport," Rinkya suggested.

At this, Rati lit up. "Spaceport? Shit! I totally forgot."

Rinkya's large, green eyes blinked once, questioningly. "Forgot what?"

"Xerx."

There was a blank look on her face for a moment before recognition hit her. "Your cousin?"

"Yeah, he's supposed to be here today with the Gi exhibition. I forgot all about it. And Dad let me know that he'd be looking for the Doctor himself. Something about a vendetta?"

"Vendettas?" Rinkya frowned. "I didn't think your family went for stuff like that."

"It's a pirate thing," Rati explained. "Dad retired; Cousin Iriid's the king, so he can't just piss off and do it himself, so Cousin Xerx is the only one left. He'd have some info on it."

"Looks like we might have a bigger lead than we thought, then," Rinkya said, daring to let hope back into her voice.

"Yeah, but it can't hurt to hedge our bets," Rati said, punching in the car's start command and feeling the engine whine to life. "Let's go to the traffic control first, then hit up the Gestalt crews for my cousin."

"Sounds like a plan," Rinkya said and smiled.

TOPHANAVAR: TERTIARY CARGO HANGAR BAY

Xerx was not sure if it was the fact that this hangar, part of Tophanavar's vast terraced caverns, seemed like being inside the maw of some big space monster or if it was the simple unfamiliarity of his surroundings that put him so ill at ease. He wondered if Alexa and Salt, standing across from him, could decipher his emotions. Alexa had arrived soon after they had landed, and that was at least a plus. She was, after all, not only a fellow Gestalt pilot, but as his cousin Iriid's wife, she was his representative here for the Pirate Worlds. Her help would at least make for a clearer conscience on his part.

His gaze swept from the Pirate Queen back to Salt and then back to the cavern's bustling activity of ships docking and unloading their respective Gestalts and pit crews. There was *Tiberius*, whom he'd fought to that tie in the last tournament match. And then there was *Hunter*, a true monster of steel, built like an armored wall, piloted by his friend Tyger Ral, who had conveniently—and most likely, futilely—vanished among the bustle of pit crews and pilots the moment he'd heard that the *Wraith* had been incoming. No surprise there; Alexa would most likely be bringing with her the intense sexual appetite that came with her frequent heats, and Tyger was among her favorite playthings to sate that itch.

Last, and definitely least, there was *Khan*, resembling a five-story upright jungle cat on steroids, piloted by Radic, the resident asshole. Instead of practicing or helping his crew, he was, as expected, reclining in his foldable chair, being waited on hand and foot by his scantily clad, all-female entourage with the biggest shit-eating grin plastered on his very punchable face.

The conversation about today's plans was winding down, and Xerx brooded over the fact that he would be sending one of his own crew on a mission that he was most likely better suited for. But here and now, still busy calibrating *Imani*'s systems for tomorrow's match, that was out of the question as he sat, half-settled into the spherical, detached cockpit unit, the goggles of its VR set resting above his eyes like an unusually thick pair of sunglasses.

"Never realized how tight your arse looks in an I-suit." Alexa gestured to the skintight pilot suit that Xerx wore with a bemused look. "I can see why Neela married you. You know, I have a spare hour or two if you need help getting out of it."

"Never let Neela hear you say that," Xerx said, considerably less amused by her quip than she was. Of course, Alexa had made sure his wife was out of earshot for such a remark. Neela wasn't the jealous type, but she and the Pirate Queen had never been terribly friendly with each other. Perhaps it was the fact that he might have just as easily become another one of her "boy toys" if he hadn't been happily married. Regardless, the two had enjoyed merely cordial relations, which hearing Alexa make such blatantly lascivious comments would certainly not have improved.

"Tyger would love it, though," Salt added at the edge of a guffaw. But at Xerx's lack of gaiety, Alexa narrowed her eyes.

"Well, this isn't like you at all, Xerx love. Usually, you're in far better spirits before a mission, especially one that I've done most of the legwork on."

"I just don't like having people worry over me," Xerx confessed.

"I talked with Iriid last night," Alexa replied, crossing her arms over her ample breasts. Xerx noticed her discreetly scratching at the green scales that ran down her shoulders. They were far less lustrous than normal: a sign that she would be shedding soon. "So, thus far, you have two cousins, a wife, and at least two crew members worrying ... if I'm not mistaken. Live with it."

"I wouldn't mind being worried over once in a while," Salt grumbled. "Pretty sure that son of mine doesn't care."

"I wouldn't bet on that," Alexa warned. "In fact, it seems he cared enough to tell someone, as I overheard Mobola telling Neela about your recent fight."

"Dammit!" Salt made a hiss that sounded like sandpaper, after which Alexa gave a loud, high-pitched cackle.

"You're actually surprised? Even I know your son tells that girl everything."

"Gotta have to have a talk with that boy," Salt muttered and threw on his jacket. "He's gonna be the death of me, I swear."

"Seems you should be thankful you have somebody to worry about you," Xerx advised.

"And to argue with," Alexa added. She then gave a wistful sigh. "That makes me miss post-row sex with Iriid—some of the best hammering I've ever had."

"Okay, first of all, too much information," Salt said to Alexa. "And can we just get on with this?" His terseness took both Xerx and the Pirate Queen aback. Xerx began to wonder if it was Alexa's sexually charged sense of humor or simple anxiousness that was causing his impatience to get the better of him. "The sooner we catch this bitch, the sooner none of us have to worry about things going to shit."

"You doubt my source?" Alexa said. "It's a bit early in this plan for things to go tits up, sweetie."

"Gotta side with Salt on this one," Xerx said in an apologetic tone. "Knowing your source, the intel had better be sound. These disappearances you told me about don't sound like the Doctor's M.O. if you ask me. It's too sloppy."

"*Et tu*, Xerxes?" Alexa placed her hand dramatically above her left breast. "You do wound me to the quick. Have I ever been wrong before?"

"Considering Sarah got herself nailed by the local cops, I'm a little less than enthused this time around," Xerx said.

His response caused a glint of worry to spark in Salt's expression. "Wait. Arrested?"

"You say that like it's unusual for her," Alexa remarked dryly. She then led the way in the direction of the hangar entrance, where her valet was waiting. "In fact, her bail has been posted for a full day. I was about to go and pick her up when your captain gave me a call." She waved to Xerx, then patted Salt smartly on the backside. "Ooo! Tight buns! Well, it's on to the hunting now."

Xerx watched as the two headed off to their respective missions, still unable to suppress his growing feeling of guilt that he was involving one of his crew in something he should have been handling alone.

"Stop feeling guilty, *Kidege*," he heard Neela say, her voice coming from the direction of the ramp that extended from the cargo bay of the *Reckless*. "I know how you think."

"It's supposed to be a *personal* vendetta," Xerx said.

"Salt is resourceful," Neela assured him. "He should be okay. And Alexa has been in just as many scrapes as you, if not more. Besides, these preparations are important."

"I've been preparing the whole trip." A ghost of prior restless nights aboard the *Reckless* running simulation after simulation passed through Xerx's mind, making him feel a tiny fraction of that remembered exhaustion. "I'd rather be cleaning my guns and polishing my knives."

"You did that too," Neela said. "And I've never seen them so clean or shiny."

It was the first time that Xerx had laughed all day.

"Ah, now I see that my husband's sense of humor has returned!" Neela said with a jovial sigh. She leaned forward and pecked him on the cheek. "There is hope for you yet."

"So, you're gonna be my program runner this time?" Xerx said, preparing to settle into the cockpit. He pulled the VR goggles down over his eyes. "I thought Mobola wanted to do that."

"She will." His vision returned as Neela lifted the goggles back onto his forehead. "But first, I came to let you know that we have company."

"Company? Where?"

With a grin, Neela gestured back toward the open door to the *Reckless'* cargo hold where two Felyans in black police uniforms now stood at the edge of the ramp, speaking to each other. At first, he didn't recognize them and had been about to ask Neela what two blues wanted with them, but then he realized who they were. They were both hybrids, and both people whom, with the exception of videos and pics, he hadn't seen in a very long time.

"Is that who I think it is?" Xerx asked, then stood upright once again.

"Does he look like anyone else?" Neela said teasingly.

Xerx removed his goggles. "I don't know. I've never seen Rati with a goatee before. Wasn't he like, five when we last visited Izz?"

"It suits him well, I think," Neela said. "And yes."

"That would make them ... twenty now?"

"Twenty-two," Neela corrected.

"And ... now I feel old."

Though Rinkya and Rati were hybrids, they were clearly separate *kya*. Rinkya was a child of the more feral-looking Re'Kya with tan fur, dark brown stripes, and long blond hair, while the much taller Rati, his cousin Isibar's son, was of the more humanlike An'Kya, like his mother, Cala. Rati had black hair, a black tail, and tanned skin with dark stripes. Hybrids could grow facial hair, and, as an expression of pride in their human heritage, most of them did. Rati was no exception. Neela had been right; it looked good on his little cousin. Both wore blue and black trench coats with an official-looking silver shield embossed upon the left shoulder and breast.

"When did they get here?" Xerx asked, crawling out of the cockpit.

"A few minutes ago," Neela said. "I was speaking with them aboard the ship while you were talking with Alexa and Salt."

Xerx's grin broadened as he called out to the taller of the visitors. "Rati! That you, kid?"

The young man turned, blinking a set of eyes as green as Xerx's. He grinned somewhat shyly as he took Rinkya by the hand and headed their way. Xerx climbed out of the cockpit and met them halfway along with his wife.

"Cousin Xerxes?" Rati said, shaking Xerx's offered hand. Xerx laughed and pulled him into an open hug.

"You're not a kid anymore," Xerx said. "No need to be so formal; just call me Xerx. Though 'Zee' might be easier." He broke away from the hug, then inspected his cousin from head to toe. "I remember when your mom brought you to Siberna to visit; you couldn't even pronounce it."

"You kept calling him 'Jerx,'" Neela said with a tiny snort.

"You never said that, *Li-ah*," Rinkya said to Rati, her voice shaking with her own laugh. Rati turned a slight shade of red.

"Rinkya?" Neela shifted her attention to Rati's life-mate, who nodded. "I remember you, though I don't know if you remember me."

"I do, a little," Rinkya replied. "But I was pretty young."

"Just a pup," Xerx said, shaking his head in wonder at how much time had passed from the last time he'd met them in person, as rambunctious children. "And I guess I owe you two an apology. I wish I could've gotten over to An'Re'Hara more often, but GI and work kept me busy. Nothing else has brought me this close in years."

"No worries," Rati said. "Dad told us about it. We watched your fights all the time, and I still got all your birthday presents."

"And the commemoration gift for your mating announcement," Neela said. She gestured to her husband. "Xerx and I picked out those bracelets."

"And we love them," Rinkya said. "We still wear them on special occasions."

"Glad you came by," Xerx said. "I was planning on calling you up, but not until tomorrow," He shifted his gaze to Neela. "Did you call them?"

Neela shook her head. "It appears your cousin gave them a heads-up."

"No surprise there," Xerx remarked, then pointed back toward the cockpit. "I was about to get started on the VR sim for the match tomorrow. I can get you pit access if you'd like."

Rinkya frowned, her fluffy ears drooping. "We couldn't get off for it."

"Yeah, no rest for the wicked," Rati said, equally deflated.

"With the festivities following the announcement of the administrator's birth, we've been working doubly hard on just keeping things together here," Rinkya added.

"And then there are the disappearances."

This, Rati mentioned in a more reserved tone, making a not-so-subtle suggestion that there was more to say. His tail twitched nervously, the same as whenever Salt or Pepper had something to hide.

"What is it?" Xerx said.

"Not here," Rati replied even more confidentially.

"I have a conference area in the rear of the cargo hold." Xerx removed the VR goggles and returned to the cockpit, placing them into the cockpit seat. He then gestured back toward the *Reckless* before leading the way with Neela. "There's so much noise outside that no one could hear it if they wanted to."

As they made their way inside the cargo hold, Rinkya scanned the area, her expression shifting from fascinated to confused. She stopped in her tracks, then stepped back outside the ship, gazing upward, and then ran back inside, her look of puzzlement only deepening. Xerx and Neela stifled their mutual urges to chuckle at the sight of it.

"You know, if I didn't know better, I'd say that this place looks bigger on the inside than the outside," she said, eyeing *Imani*, standing upright and still locked in place, with the ceiling high above. Sure enough, from the inside, it appeared to reach higher than the top decks of the ship.

"That's because it is," Xerx said, at last allowing himself a guffaw.

"We had the dubious fortune of learning that this ship was full of surprises during our maiden voyage," Neela explained. "A freak accident triggered something called 'Garrison Mode.'"

"Long story short, it can manipulate space inside the ship," Xerx said, then grimaced at the memory it evoked. "Almost got lost in the damn thing."

"That's ... amazing," Rati said, looking stuck for anything more significant to say, but it seemed to be enough for Neela, who was quite proud.

"Oh, it certainly is, now that we know how to operate it."

They reached the corner that Xerx had indicated: a long fiberglass table next to *Imani* but set behind a partition of metal shelves, overflowing with tools and various technological odds and ends. Xerx settled into one of the metal chairs, kicking his feet up onto the table as he was wont to do. He waited until Rinkya, Rati, and Neela sat down as well.

"So I gather this is about the disappearances?" Xerx asked.

"Probably so," Rati replied. "I think you know where this is going, though."

Xerx was almost certain that he did.

"Your dad told you about what happened on Icona?"

"Bingo," Rinkya said as Rati removed a holo-projector from the pocket of his trench coat. He switched on the ring-shaped device, and a three-dimensional, full-color image of the Doctor's face appeared: delicate, almost androgynous features framed by glasses that appeared nearly too big for her face and a thick crown of neck-length, ink-black hair. Above it floated the words, "WANTED, DEAD OR ALIVE: DR. SELENE HAYASHIBARA" along with a bounty that was comparable to GI prize money payouts. "And there's a lot more going on here than you realize."

There always is, Xerx thought, observing the holo carefully before his cousin put it away. "Care to share?"

"We got orders through the grapevine, straight from the colonial administration, from the Alliance council," Rati said. "In fact, this is so hush-hush that I could be fired for just talking to you about it. Probably even spaced."

"In that order," Rinkya added.

Rati leaned forward in his seat, resting his chin on his folded hands. "The Alliance has learned the Doctor is on her way."

"Wait, she's not here already?"

Rati shook his head. "Not yet, but something strange is going on, and I'm pretty sure she's behind it."

Xerx mulled this over. This was certainly new. The Alliance intel really wasn't much of a surprise, to be honest; they had their own ways and means, and the Doctor's reputation preceded her.

"The disappearances," Neela mused aloud, and Rinkya nodded.

"They follow her M.O.," Rati said.

"But she's on her way," Xerx said, shaking his head. "Not here, not yet?"

"That's the weird part," Rati said. "As I said, the crimes follow her M.O."

"I disagree," Xerx countered, recalling his conversation with the Pirate Queen. "Even if she were somehow able to make people disappear without even being there, why leave victims just lying around? She's shown herself to be cleaner than that in the past."

"Because they're not dead," Rinkya answered, to Xerx's surprise.

"They show up later, alive," Rati added, his tone grim for what would have otherwise been good news. "They're sick as hell, and doctors can't tell what's happened to them. And none of them remember. The reason the brass thinks that it has to do with her is because this same sequence of events happened on Halo Meridian a couple of years back. But it stopped as soon as the authorities there got curious. All they uncovered was an abandoned lab in the orbital habs. It looked like they'd been scrubbed clean of any evidence at first, but a few trace DNA sweeps found a match with the Doctor. What she had been making there, however, is anybody's guess."

"But that still leaves the two-ton elephant in the room," Xerx said. "It doesn't explain how she could've done all this here, yet without even being here. You sure you don't have a copycat?"

Rinkya shrugged. "That isn't off the table."

That was the last thing that Xerx wanted to hear. As unlikely as it seemed, this whole scenario being the actions of some nut job who'd somehow idolized that psychopath would leave both him and his cousins back at square one.

"You don't believe that yourselves, do you?" Xerx said, more hopeful than certain.

"I think that we aren't being given the full story, to be honest," Rati said. "There's something here that we're not seeing, especially since the Alliance sounded so damn sure about it. Despite her not exactly being here yet, they seriously think that she's using, or plans to use, Tophanavar as a test bed for her latest antics."

"The spaceport authorities have been in contact with the Alliance military, and they say she's not here yet," Rinkya remarked. "But it would make sense if she actually was here. Small wonder she wants this place; it's remote enough. And the festivities right now make for good cover. They've got us doing investigations but with orders to be as discreet as possible."

"They want her," Rati said. "Bad."

"Not as bad as I do," Xerx remarked with a grim smile. "But yeah, something doesn't fit here. As much as I'd prefer that you don't get involved in this, I know that it's too late for that."

"Way too late," Rati said, then gave a sad-looking grin. "I said that Dad told us everything about Icona. And I mean *everything*. Even..." He swallowed and looked away, hiding a sickened expression. "Even about the children." He then hesitated yet again before adding the last part. "And your friends."

Xerx's expression darkened for a moment. Quickly, he shoved down the reflexive rage that threatened to well up from within at that painful memory, seeing Will and Kialas' happiness transformed into ruin in the matter of a few minutes. It should have been ancient history, but the pain had never truly dulled, even after all these years. Perhaps it was just as well; he needed fuel to carry this vendetta to its end. Still, he wanted to have words with his cousin for spilling something so personal. But sense quickly overrode his emotions. Rinkya and Rati would have good reason to need to know this part of his past.

"I'm sorry," Rati said, his voice quiet.

They'd seen his face, Xerx figured, after that remark about his friends—God rest their souls. Both he and Rinkya now looked as if they had just stepped on a landmine.

"It's good," Xerx assured them, shaking his head. This seemed to set them at ease as he then focused back on the business at hand. "Why else do you think I gave you this heads-up?"

"We'll certainly be keeping our ears to the ground," Rinkya said, then raised a stern hand before Xerx could interject. "Rati and I talked it over before you guys arrived. We're not pirates, but we're family."

There was a long pause before Neela at last spoke up, eyeing Xerx with a bemused look.

"It looks like you will have more help with this than you want."

"And with nothing that I can do about it," Xerx said, his voice almost a croak. He rolled his shoulders, trying to ease the tension from the increasing burden he felt. This was the last thing he wanted, but he wanted to make a potential enemy of his cousins even less, and he wasn't about to by trying to order his own family off the case—not that he actually could.

"If you do this, then ... just be careful," Xerx said after some time, musing futilely over any way that he could talk his cousins out of this. "I don't want to have to be responsible for either of you losing everything, or worse, because of me."

"We're big kids," Rati assured Xerx with a confident grin, shared by his lifemate. "We can manage this."

FIVE

"This place reminds me of home," Salt observed.

"Really now?" Alexa said. "How so?"

Salt made a surprised noise, raising an eyebrow. "You've never been to An'Re'Hara?"

"Not since my days on the 'Wizard with Rico," Alexa replied, referring to her surrogate father's ship, the *Pinball Wizard*. "And Felyans don't trade much with pirates. I don't think their guilds trust us."

Salt pursed his lips, mulling over this fact. Felyan trade guilds were notoriously selective about whom they did business with. The general consensus was that pirates were, by nature and reputation for following their own code of conduct to the exclusion of local system laws, bad for business. If the rumors were true, the Pirate Clans did manage to snipe a rather lucrative contract from one Felyan trade guild on Zynj years ago. And though the Empress didn't shed many tears over losing the business of that colony of racist ingrates, it didn't exactly improve relations between An'Re'Hara and the Pirate Worlds.

"I see," he replied in a reserved tone. "Well, let me explain. The architecture is mostly Felyan. We tend to construct in a way that works with the local topography. You know, keep it as organic as possible."

Alexa nodded, rubbing her chin. "Efficient use of the inherent space, like using tower blocks as support columns for the level above. Clever."

The main highway itself wound around the edge of the levels, and Alexa started out following the road as it spiraled gently downward, myriad off and on ramps allowing access to and from each level as they narrowed before culminating in a deep blue reservoir at the bottom.

"A guy like me could feel right at home here," Salt said with a soft laugh at the passing sights: a strange mix of the organic architecture created by Felyan engineers and stark, concrete shapes of the human settlements in between.

"I think that was the point," Alexa said. "Felyans do slightly outnumber humans here, after all."

"Mostly due to hybrids being born," Salt said. Alexa could detect a vague, yet nonetheless annoying undercurrent of hidden bitterness in his voice. "Humans still classify them as Felyan. But it doesn't surprise me; we're near the border, after all. So, how'd your sister know that this place we're headed to is where we'd find our target?"

"She didn't," Alexa replied.

Salt's expression turned blank. "Then how do *you* know that this is the place?"

"Profiling," Alexa said as they headed farther into the shadowed portion of the level, where the lights dimmed as they passed beneath the massive shelf above. Their surroundings now reminded Salt of downtown Siberna

Prime at night, where neon lights and streetlamps kept everything in a perpetual twilight. Most of the buildings were human design.

"All the establishments were bars and lounges in neighborhoods with a high human-to-Felyan ratio," Alexa said, explaining further. "Plus, the establishments were in or around an area called 'Risstown,' known for its pleasure houses. The target isn't exactly making their M.O. a secret. In fact, if I didn't know better, it's almost like they want to be caught."

"So I'll be 'casing the joint,' as the human saying goes?" Salt asked.

"Indeed." Alexa pointed her finger like a gun at Salt, making a firing gesture. "That reminds me—did Xerx give you a firearm?"

"He didn't need to," Salt said. "After the shit that went down aboard the ship, I sleep with one." He vaguely indicated the waistline at the back of his pants, where he kept the MAG pistol holstered and safely hidden.

"Good thing, then," Alexa said as the valet pulled up beside a building lit up with neon-bright holos. It seemed conspicuously well-kept in contrast to the state of its surroundings, which had perhaps seen better days. "I heard this neighborhood can be a little ... dodgy."

They stepped out onto the sidewalk, and Salt sniffed the air. Alcohol. Nearby restaurants. A few pleasure houses perhaps a block away; that scent was unmistakable. Aside from things looking somewhat old, it did not give off the air of danger that Alexa had warned about. But of course, there were areas of Pit Town that were just as deceptively innocent looking. Though none of the establishments there had such a non-threatening, if not revoltingly cute name.

"The Purring Princess?" Salt said, staring blearily at the sign, his tone flat. "Really?"

"Don't let the name fool you," Alexa said. "I heard it's got quite a seedy clientele."

Meanwhile, Salt could only stare at the hologram that was the building's sign, half in doubt, the other half questioning the judgment of the wily Pirate Queen.

"Besides, this was the place that my sister suggested. So, it's as good a place to start as any."

"I think your sister might need to get off her meds," Salt said with a snort. "This name makes it sound more like a pleasure house—not that I'm complaining."

"Are you always this grumpy?" Alexa observed as she passed through the automatic doorway at the entrance. "It's a bar ... mostly. And it's run by Felyans."

"What do you mean 'mostly'?" Salt said. He cast an unquestionably suspicious look at Alexa, who maintained her own expression of defenseless innocence that was as transparently false as the shifting advert holos that had stood out against the building's brick façade.

"I'm sure you'll understand once you get settled in," Alexa said. "Just enjoy yourself and keep your eyes open. I'll be coming back soon enough. After all, I have someone to pick up." She gave a shrewd grin. "*Two* someones, actually."

Salt put two and two together. "You mean your boy toy? How'd you even know Tyger would be here?"

"I have my sources," Alexa replied, "cloaked sources, but sources, nonetheless. You think that someone in my position would really be able to wander about without someone looking over their shoulder?" She rolled her eyes as Salt remained silent. "Frankly, I think it's all rather unnecessary, but Iriid insists. Still, I've found a few good uses for them."

"And you're sure that my being here actually has to do with the mission?" Salt asked. He could not help but feel like he was being used as a personal bloodhound by the Pirate Queen.

"Of course," Alexa said. "We're in the right place."

"Where your fuzzy sex doll happens to be?"

"A happy coincidence." Alexa shrugged her shoulders. "And I'm serious about that. Now, if you don't mind, I have a pissed-off sister to pick up. Go get a drink and make yourself comfortable. And if you find anyone suspicious, remember what your captain said."

"Yeah, yeah, no solo actions," Salt replied, deciding against questioning her motives any further. "I got this."

"No doubt," Alexa said, slipping back into the valet and blowing him a kiss.

Now alone, Salt made his way inside. The light was dim, but not to the point where seeing would be difficult. Curtains of dark crimson, purple, and blue greeted his eyes, serving as partitions between tables and couches where an already decent amount of clientele was seated. They were an even mix of humans, Felyans, and hybrids, drinking, laughing, and smoking strong-smelling herbal mixtures from hookah-like apparatuses. A small crowd was gathered around the bar at the far end of the room, attended by a Felyan and two human bartenders.

Salt scanned the lounge and found him. That fur-lined coat was unmistakable, as he was the only Re'Kya, hybrid or otherwise, who would wear one. His hair was dark and slicked back, and he wore a well-coiffed goatee: all just as much of a trademark as his coat. Tyger Ral, the GI champion himself, was sitting in a shadowed corner, deep into what he did best: storytelling. He was recounting one of his grand adventures before a captive audience, regaling several female patrons, and was as deep into his story as his listeners seemed to be, thankfully oblivious to everything else as Salt made his way to the bar, not sure of what to do next. His attention flitted from the remaining clientele back to Tyger and his smitten audience. The sight brought back recollections of his conversation with Alexa, which caused his mind to drift back to his son and his irritating obsession with his human crewmate.

"Humans…" he said in a huff. "What do we see in them?"

"What does who see in humans?" asked a soft voice in front of him.

"My idiot son," Salt said, only moments later realizing that had been replying in Felyan to whoever had been speaking to him in like language. "Why do we have to fall for humans more easily than our own kind?"

He lifted his head to see that the person he had been speaking to was the bartender: a Re'Kya Felyan who was a fair sight prettier looking than she had seemed from a distance. A cascade of blonde hair flowed over a face and shoulders of orange fur with dark brown stripes. The tips of her ears and muzzle were slightly graying, but in spite of her age, her pale blue eyes were as lively as someone half her age.

"Ah..." Salt began, startled at the unexpected sight before him. But he quickly became aware of his flustered look as well as the scent of mild embarrassment that was, interestingly enough, not coming from him.

"Well, I'm glad to see that I still have that effect on men," the bartender said. It was at that moment that Salt became aware of the very stupid-looking grin he'd had plastered on his face. At what had now become his own momentary embarrassment, the bartender laughed.

"What'll it be?" she asked a moment later.

"A little bit of my dignity back," Salt replied. "Plus an absence of drama in my life and a son who takes my advice." He gave her a sly grin, attempting to regain some of that dignity himself. "And your name, if you don't mind?"

"It's Ti'Niya," the bartender replied. "And while I can't supply the rest of what you want, I can supply you with something that'll make you forget about it all." She gave a wink as she reached below her and brought up a large, unmarked bottle. At first glance, the liquid inside seemed clear, but in the contrast of the lounge's subdued ambient light and the harsher track lighting above the countertop, it shimmered in a shifting rainbow of hues.

"Pretty name," Salt said. "Almost musical." He noticed that his remark had flattered her somewhat by her expression after she'd brought up the bottle. "Hey, is that what I think it is?"

"If you're thinking it's *asak*, then you'd be right," Ti'Niya said.

"Trisii's love..." Salt murmured as she poured the pungent liquor into a whiskey glass. "I haven't had that since my days with the space gypsies." He took the glass she offered and watched as she poured herself a significantly smaller amount.

"A little taste of home, then," Ti'Niya lifted her glass and touched it to Salt's. "We've been getting some big orders for it lately."

"Is that out of the ordinary?" Salt asked.

"A little," Ti'Niya replied, scratching her nose thoughtfully. "It just might be the celebrations. Oh, by the way, have you seen the pics of the Empress's new daughter? Cute as a button, as the humans say. The Alliance diplomat to the Empire is the father. It's said that he and the Empress actually fell in love, so much so that she thought about abdicating just so she could have him as her lifemate. Isn't that romantic?"

Salt could only make a noncommittal noise. It was common knowledge that part of the Empress's duty was to bear heirs to govern the Empire through every Kya, and though there was no law against producing hybrid heirs, she was the first of the direct royal line to do so. He might have been against this, but he chose to stay quiet and drink his *asak*. He swallowed the liquor with its heavily citric aroma, weathering its bold, almost sour punch in his mouth and its subsequent smooth warmth as it went down his throat.

"Good stuff," he said, nodding as he exhaled, "just like I remember. You got a good supplier."

"Well, if I ever see them, I'll let them know," Ti'Niya said, settling on her elbows and grinning at the compliment. She purred with delight as her tail swished back and forth—something that Salt was aware of to the point where he felt the tingle of a blush break out on his skin as he looked her way.

It all came to an end, however, as the bartender's gaze shifted to their left, where a sudden, high-pitched titter broke into their conversation. Ti'Niya's purr transformed into a hiss. Salt's surprise became confusion as she scowled and then stalked away. He turned to the source of the laugh... and into a scent that was like a chemical cosh to his brain.

Her eyes were a striking mix of blue and gray, almost to the point where they glowed. Her face was framed by a cascade of hair so black it was almost like a shadow. At first, he thought it was a white stole that was wrapped around her neck until three liquid black eyes opened, then blinked his way below a set of two long, slender antennae, revealing the fact that it was a pet panako worm.

"You made her purr," she said in a soft voice that was confusingly androgynous. "How adorable."

Even her breath held the scent that accosted Salt with her nearness. But if it was what he thought, it was far too strong. The Felyan aphrodisiac was used to enhance intimacy but in the bedroom only, not worn like perfume, like some humans liked to do. But it was as if this woman had bathed in it. She was human, but he could not help but become aware of his pants becoming significantly tighter. The woman returned the silly grin that had formed at the sides of his mouth with a much more seductive smile of her own.

And now, a wreath of darkness was slowly clouding his vision.

"You know, it's probably best not to eat every person you take a dislike to," Alexa said.

"Oh, come on, that's not true, and you know it," Sarah replied. "After all, I didn't feed on that white-haired witch friend of your husband's." She crossed her arms and leaned back in her seat, clearly grateful to be out of that cell, though once she relayed her story, Alexa felt like placing her into a smaller one. No intel was worth the trouble her tenacious sister would always seem to find her way into. Still, it was amusing that she thought that she could best Kumiko, who could perhaps tear her into component molecules. But she had no reason to bring that evasive and antisocial girl into this. She cast her sister a withering look that instantly destroyed the playful expression on her face.

"Don't give me that look; the guy was a lowlife," Sarah pleaded. "He wasn't even part of the charter. He was a ghost. No chip ID, just some transient from the wrong side of the Tantagel DMZ, trying to make a quick cred off of girls' arses. Thought he could strong-arm me into working for him. I worked him instead." She gave a wry grin.

"Did he stay crunchy in milk?" Alexa said, her tone flat and humorless.

"Funny," Sarah said sarcastically. She put a hand to her chin, and there was a dull click as she cracked her jaw, revealing black gums and tongue; she then licked her prominent canines as she opened her mouth wide. "In all honesty, I was lucky to have eaten him so fast. I've never distended myself so much in one sitting before."

Sarah inflated her cheeks and made a bulging motion with her arms across her belly. "You'd have thought I was pregnant; his bones nearly pierced my skin from the inside."

Alexa looked at Sarah, eyebrows raised. "I'm sure it was sheer hell for you. I'm amazed you managed to break him down so fast. Were seconds on the cards?"

Sarah fixed her sister with a sour look. "I'd have thought you would be more understanding about my condition, Mrs. 'a-shag-a-day-keeps-the-doctor-away.'"

"Do not make this about me," Alexa warned. She would have none of Sarah's bullshit attempts to flip the argument. "You really need to learn subtlety; this could have made things much harder for us."

"Actually, I lucked out," Sarah said, her tone hinting at a secret she was all too delighted to hold back. Sarah tapped the side of her head. "I got some useful information after I processed his brain."

"Really now?" Alexa raised an eyebrow, her demeanor now in intrigue mode. "Care to share, or are you going to keep fucking about?"

"He did know a bit about what's been going on in that neck of the woods," Sarah said. "He's the reason I was able to put two and two together after all: the disappearances, the unknown chemicals in the victims, their lack of memory. He was a middleman for one of the places we've gotten the most recent reports from."

"Well, then, Salt should be right on the money," Alexa said, "provided he's able to sniff out the proper amount of trouble."

"If you had gotten me out sooner, you wouldn't need to send in someone else," Sarah protested.

"You shouldn't have gotten in trouble in the first place."

"It won't make a difference."

"And why's that?"

"Because she's only been sniffing out humans or hybrids," Sarah said. "At least thus far."

"Why only those?" Alexa asked, feeling a slight twinge of worry that Xerx had had him go on a mission that was destined to be a bust.

"How should I know?"

"You didn't get any reason from your last snack?" Alexa said.

"He wasn't that clever," Sarah said. "Sadly, if I'm honest, it was like eating a shi—a poop sandwich."

"Even an idiot can have useful information." Alexa sounded far less sanguine now, despite her usual amusement at her sister's constant attempts to avoid swearing.

"I really don't know, actually," Sarah said, giving a tired shrug. "That's just how the victims have turned up. I can tell you if our target has been there and how recently, but I'm sure Salt can do that too. He is a Felyan, after all."

"Jealous, are we?" Alexa asked, noting the somewhat sour tone in her sister's voice.

"No, just hungry. It's been a while since I last had a legit meal."

"Well, that I can rectify," Alexa said. "Once we pick up my dessert for the night, we can hit a sushi bar. The StellarNet shows one not too far away with great reviews."

"You're buying?" Sarah asked.

"You have any money?"

Sarah held her tongue.

"The words are..."

"Thank you, Queen Alexa," Sarah recited like a kindergartener who had just learned a sentence by rote.

"Your information was good," Alexa said, now with a genuine smile. "Xerx and I may be able to nail the bitch."

"You'll nail anything with a pulse," Sarah quipped.

"Oh, fuck off, dear sister," Alexa quipped back. She held up a clawed middle finger, at which Sarah laughed.

"There is one more thing," Sarah said, her demeanor having quickly transformed back to complete sincerity, "something that I didn't even dare send your way before you arrived."

"Oh?" Alexa sat upright.

"It should be hitting your private account right about now." Sarah tapped her head, indicating her own unique set of bionics that allowed her to encrypt and transmit data in her own ways. Only a moment after she'd completed her sentence, Alexa's tablet pinged, and she brought up the now-decrypted file. It was safely stored from prying eyes in her royal priority inbox, which only someone with her unique DNA signature could read.

"Well ... this complicates things, doesn't it?" she said, frowning. "Are you sure they can do this?"

"I was able to tap into the network," Sarah replied. "I didn't believe it at first until I saw it all myself. So, you're right. It does muddle things up somewhat. And it makes the mystery that much bigger."

"And you got this from that one little runt you turned into a kipper?"

"No, just from some drunk guy I nibbled." Sarah gave a cheeky grin. "Seems he was a former techie who worked with our prey once but got kicked to the curb back on Halo Meridian. Don't worry; he's still alive. Think of it like a hors d'oeuvre."

"You're bloody incorrigible."

Sarah followed Alexa inside the Purring Princess lounge.

"Is this guy really so important to pick up after the info I gave you?" she asked.

"Must be really good to not itch for a good drilling every month," Alexa said, growing somewhat tired of her sister's barbs against her libido. "I, on the other hand, don't have that luxury." She then gestured toward the corner where Tyger still sat, prattling on amidst a sultry cloud of smoke.

"He doesn't look like much," Sarah observed, "more like a space hippie than a champion Gestalt pilot."

"He's a man of, ah, many talents," Alexa said, unable to stop a grin from appearing at the side of her mouth.

"And you left him here with no one to look after him?"

"I have my guards keep tabs on him. Keeps me from having to root him out."

"So where are they?"

"Right there," Alexa said, gesturing toward the area where Tyger sat, still oblivious. "I've had them here for over an hour, actually."

Sarah sniffed the air. "Ah. Tanks. Incognito?"

"The best 'cognito' to be 'in.'"

"Diffraction cloth?"

"Of course."

"How can he not smell them?"

"You've clearly never seen Tyger get really into one of his yarns," Alexa said as she removed a bottle of perfume from her purse. She applied a generous amount to her neck and cleavage, then stalked over to where Tyger sat. Alexa glanced back and suppressed a laugh at the sight of Sarah wrinkling her nose at the cloying scent of the *riss* she'd mixed into the perfume's bouquet of floral essences.

Tyger's concentration at last broke as she approached him, coming from an angle that she assumed would be out of his peripheral vision.

Damn, she thought as Tyger froze mid-story. Perhaps it was the perfume that gave it away? Few humans mixed the powerful Felyan aphrodisiac with such things, finding the scent off-putting outside of a censer.

Tyger's look of relaxed ease became that of tension and poorly disguised anxiousness as he dropped the pipe of the hookah. He said something to his entourage of ladies, and they quickly scattered, seemingly more disappointed than angry.

"Oh my, did I interrupt your flow?" Alexa asked in a voice that was butter-soft. Tyger, now behaving more like a cornered animal, started to back away—until he bumped into what appeared to be an invisible wall behind him. It quickly rippled away as the diffraction cloth powered down, revealing a tall, muscular woman. Another woman wavered into visibility beside her, both standing nearly half a meter taller than the startled hybrid and sporting the same monochrome hair and skin. Alexa smiled with pride. Her bid to allow the Pirate Clans to take in deserters from the Second Imperium's militia had certainly not been for naught.

"You weren't thinking of leaving so soon, were you?" Alexa said, allowing the full force of her body's growing ache to seep into her voice. "Must you make me play hide-and-seek with you? My girls had such a hard time finding you for a change."

"Finding ... me?" Tyger said, at last speaking. He glanced furtively at the two bodyguards, who now blocked off his only route of escape, then sputtered out a high-pitched and very uncomfortable-sounding laugh. "Why would you need anyone to go looking—"

"Oh, don't be obtuse," Alexa said, pressing her voluminous chest against him to the point where it nearly squeezed out of the neckline of her green blouse. She made certain that Tyger's eyes, now twice their normal size, would go right where she wanted. He was a skilled pilot like her, and a renowned storyteller, even if he did exaggerate. But with women, he was almost tiresomely predictable, if the current condition of his pants against her thigh was any indication.

Plus, it didn't hurt that *riss* worked fast.

"And don't make excuses about practice time," the Pirate Queen said. "You're last on tomorrow's roster. I made sure of it."

To her chagrin, that admission almost broke her spell upon the hapless hybrid.

"Wait. You... you did what?"

"Executive privilege," Alexa said. "Besides, it puts you in a better position. You get to fight me."

Tyger's demeanor shifted once again, showing actual interest. "You seriously did that?"

Alexa grinned.

"Now, we have all the time we need. You go with the girls and make yourself comfortable. I'll be along later."

"Okay…" was all that Tyger could say and in the dumbest-sounding voice imaginable. At least he knew when to give up the fight. She'd make it up to him later by trimming her claws.

"I do such nice things for you, now don't I?" she asked.

"Y-yeah … nice."

"Well, that didn't sound terribly enthusiastic," Alexa said, her expression turning into an affected look of disappointment. "You know how much I enjoy your company, and with Iriid always away doing Pirate King shit, I do get so very lonely." Covertly, she moved her hand down to his very eager-feeling bulge in his groin. She then made a gentle squeeze that caused Tyger to jump in place. "So lonely … and so very horny!"

She hopped forward and planted a tiny kiss at the end of Tyger's nose, and that was that.

"Now off you pop," she said and snapped her finger at the two tanks. "Ladies, if you please? I'll be along later to pick up where we left off."

"So, all done now?" Sarah said, coming up from behind as the guards led the besotted Tyger off to the waiting valet they'd discreetly parked a block away. Not waiting for her sister to reply, she grinned. "Excellent. Sushi time!"

But to her consternation, Alexa's attention was already drawn to the lack of Salt's presence. A more thorough evaluation of the lounge clientele revealed his glaring absence.

"Shit," Alexa murmured as she quickened her pace to the bar. Sarah followed behind.

"What's wrong *now*?" her sister whined.

"Salt isn't here," Alexa said.

"Oh, him," Sarah said and pursed her lips. "Why do they call him Salt, anyway? Because of his salty demeanor?"

"Not the time," Alexa replied testily. "Did you see him when we came in?"

Sarah shook her head. "Not to my knowledge. Maybe if you'd have been paying attention to that instead of your 'itch,' you'd—"

"Sarah! Focus. Check the restrooms. He hasn't changed much since you saw him last. Light gray hair and tail."

Alexa arrived at the bar where she was met by the orange-furred bartender.

"I, ah, overheard your conversation," she said. "I suppose you're looking for the grumpy one who came in here earlier?

"You know where he is?" Alexa nearly leaned over the counter, her eyes wide.

"Yeah, he took off to the back rooms with some human girl," the bartender said. Her tone of voice sounded disappointed, almost hurt, as she gestured to an alcove that was partly obscured by a black curtain. A payment kiosk sat directly beside it with a dispenser at the bottom.

"Looks like a love hotel key terminal," Alexa said.

"It ... kind of is," the bartender admitted with an expression as forlorn as the tone of her voice. "We need the extra income. It leads to the back rooms for, ah ... privacy."

"So the old bloke buggered off into the rooms with a client?" Alexa said, speaking more to herself than to the bartender at first. "That's not like him. What did she look like?"

"Black hair, gray eyes. She had a panako worm ... and, ugh! She smelled like..." The bartender wrinkled her nose. "Gave me a headache just to be around her."

"Smelled like what? *Riss*?" Alexa asked. The bartender nodded.

"Interesting," Alexa mused. "Do you know which room they're in?"

"Not our business. No cameras and they're swept for bugs nightly. Everybody vacates come morning. You can either wait until then or..." she shrugged. "You're welcome to go back there and look for him. But I doubt anyone who bothers to answer the door will be willing to talk."

It was at that moment that Sarah joined her. "No one in the restrooms. Unless you count some classy cow who sounds like she's dropping a planetoid. So, we're done here?"

"That won't be necessary," Alexa said to the bartender. "I won't need to knock on every door." She then turned to Sarah and heaved a sigh, which she could tell her sister understood by her discouraged expression.

"I'm afraid we'll need to postpone dinner for now, dear. I'm going to need your help. And yes, I know I'll owe you a planet for it."

BRIDGE OF THE *SHADOW STAR*: TOPHANAVAR PARKING ORBIT

Paige viewed the grainy surveillance images on the screens in front of her, frowning as she scanned the timestamps on each image, all sharing the exact same date and time, within a few seconds of each other. All of them unmistakably, impossibly, displayed the same person, Dr. Hayashibara, each at a different location in the colony.

It was like the cameras were haunted.

Taking a step back from her MSO dais, Paige folded her arms and sighed. Putting a finger to her chin, she turned to her left and opened her mouth to speak, but immediately stopped herself. Instead, she stared guiltily at the empty pilot seat normally occupied by Pip.

Having settled down after her outburst on Siberna, thanks in no small part to Kairen's consolation, Paige had meant to take some time out in order to reconcile with her diminutive crewmate. Maria had approached her a few hours ago, sharing her concerns that Pip appeared to be overdoing her fitness regime. To the surprise of no one, Pip had been keeping a very low profile since the incident, mostly avoiding any situation that would find her in Paige's presence. Miranda was more than capable at her job, but she was no Pip, possessing her speed, but none of her enthusiasm, style, or finesse. And now, the captain found herself missing the near-constant prattle. Moreover, the lack of "Money for Nothing" blaring over the comm as the hyperdrive engaged had made the jump almost boring.

Paige sighed and dropped her hands to her sides. She turned to her right where Miranda sat at the copilot station. The introspective tank was studying the images closely, as if at this point in time, nothing else in the universe existed.

"I'm gonna take a break, Miz," Paige said. She didn't wait for a response; Miranda was unlikely to provide one anyway. She had a prodigious intellect and a tactically brilliant mind, but she was also autistic and interacted on her own unique terms. To the uninitiated, she could appear aloof, sometimes rude, but to the crew of the *Shadow Star*, she was simply being herself. Despite her almost solidly logical nature, Miranda was sometimes incapable of abstract thinking, and so Pip, a tech tank with a naturally inquisitive mind, was needed here more than ever to solve this puzzle. It was time to mend fences.

The bridge doors slid shut behind her, and Paige set about the task of tracking down the tiny woman. Fortunately, she did not have far to look. As she stepped out onto the Deck-1 observation gantry, Paige heard the rhythmic sound of feet pounding on deck plates. Across the hangar bay, she spotted the distinctive monochrome skin. Clad in a tiger-striped, cropped compression vest and gym shorts, Pip jogged along the portside gantry toward Paige. Support sleeves covered her knees and ankles, and compression bindings adorned her thighs. Pip was a light shade of gray as opposed to the paper-white skin of her fellow tanks, and a thin sheen of sweat covered her exposed limbs.

Looking up for a moment, Pip's eyes met Paige's, right before she quickly looked away. She then picked up her pace, heading in the direction of the access ladder. Paige followed, watching as Pip made her way across the hangar bay floor and into one of the open garage bays along the starboard wall. Inside was a make-shift gym with a few improvised training machines.

Paige entered and watched as Pip grabbed a towel from atop a small storage unit. She brushed a few strands of sweat-soaked hair behind her, then dabbed her face with the towel. Forcing down all her appre-hensions, Paige swallowed, then addressed the dimin-utive tank.

"Can we talk?" she asked tentatively.

If Pip had heard her, she gave no indication as she discarded the towel and clambered onto an upturned storage box. Paige reined in her flash of anger at being ignored, choosing instead to watch as Pip reached as high as she could and then, with a quick jump, grabbed a pipe above her head and began a series of pull-ups.

"Look, I know I was harsh the other day," Paige said, undaunted, "but you need to remember the responsi-bility I carry. As captain, I'm responsible for the welfare of my crew."

Paige stumbled over the words, not really convinced about what she was saying, while Pip continued her pull-ups, making a puffing sound as lifted herself toward the ceiling. Biting back her growing frustration at the tank's sullenness, Paige continued to speak.

"Regardless, I need you to return to your duties," she said, making a second futile attempt to put her thoughts into words. "I need your skills to check some footage for me, okay?"

Pip responded with a simple "uh-huh" and carried on.

Unable to contain herself any longer, Paige let out a snarl. "For fuck's sake, Pip! Would you at least look at me?!"

The outburst made Pip flinch mid-flow, and she let out a yelp as her left arm appeared to stiffen. She hung from the pipe by a single hand, teeth gritted and her left arm clutched to her breast. Slowly, her hand slipped from the pipe. Paige was already in motion to catch her, but she was unable to prevent the tiny woman from bouncing off the crate. Her left arm took the brunt of the impact as she dropped to her knees and slid into position, Pip falling otherwise safely into her prosthetic arms before she hit the floor.

Paige came to a stop against the crate and slumped onto her rear. She could hear sobbing coming from Pip as she cradled her close to her chest. It might have been the pain in her arm, but Paige wasn't so sure. Pip was small and lean, yet she had an insanely high pain tolerance. Paige felt a wave of emotion welling up inside, and she felt the sting of tears forming in her organic left eye. She heard Pip take a shuddering breath.

"I'm sorry," the diminutive tank said. Her voice was hoarse and shaky.

Paige brushed her hair behind her right ear and sniffed.

"Oh, why can't you understand? You're my little girl, Pip. I just want what's best for you."

"Wait, what?" She felt Pip stiffen.

Paige paused and looked down. Pip's black eyes met hers.

"Are you saying you're, like, my mom?"

Paige felt warmth spreading across her face, and she bit her lip. She broke eye contact and looked sheepishly around the room. She then turned her gaze back to Pip.

"Ice cream?" she asked.

From the outside, the Purring Princess appeared business as usual. Inside was a mass of confusion. While Rinkya and Rati were near the bar interviewing a number of patrons, Sarah drifted quietly toward the entrance that led to the private rooms. In her arms was a small bag filled with clothes. Ignoring the police barricade holos, and especially the Felyan duo, whom she certainly did not want another run-in with, she sauntered down the seedy-looking corridor.

She stopped at room 4, where the door hung slightly ajar, then pushed it fully open with her foot. Aside from the newly applied organic components that made it into a murder scene, its furnishings were fairly basic and mostly tasteless; garish wallpaper adorned the walls with sepia-toned silhouettes embossed into their red surfaces. The room was dominated by a large, white bed, and a small desk by the door was set with a comm and a holo emitter.

Sarah eyed the bed, resisting the urge to dive onto it and shove her face into the blood-soaked sheets. A door at the far side of the room opened, and Alexa stepped out of the bathroom. Before Sarah, Alexa stood naked, running a white towel through her scarlet hair. Her scales appeared a semilustrous green from the shower, and the bony ridges down her spine were a deep dark red. She gave Sarah a wide grin.

"Thanks, sweetie," she said and nodded toward the pile of clothes her sister had brought. "Just set them down on the desk, would you?"

Sarah took a step toward the table, then wobbled as her high-heeled shoe slipped slightly on a puddle of viscera. She wrinkled her nose and glowered at Alexa.

"Did you need to make such a mess?" she said in an acid tone as she set the bag of clothes down on the desk. Alexa, in turn, placed a hand on her hip and matched her sister's expression.

"This from the one that murders people and stuffs them in the fridge for a snack whilst living in their flat for a month?"

"I only did that once!" she retorted; then with a sideways glance at Alexa, she tried to hide a grin. "The second one had a chest freezer; it was much more convenient."

Alexa rolled her eyes.

"Are you going to get dressed or what?" Sarah said, fidgeting slightly. "I'm tired of that red bush of yours drawing my eye."

Alexa snorted and approached the table, where she opened the bag of clothes. As she began pulling her underwear on, Sarah wandered around the side of the bed and stared down at the dark-haired woman's corpse, torn open from neck to abdomen, with various organs littered around it. Sarah had tried to catch her panako worm, but it skittered away through the open door in the earlier confusion. A pity. She had always wanted a pet.

"Geez, even I'm not that messy, Sister dear."

"I had to be thorough." Alexa continued to face away from her as she fastened her bra. "She definitely wasn't Hayashibara, but damn, the work is good! I couldn't find any trace markers from the artist anywhere. It's even better than Imperium tech."

Alexa pulled a tight white T-shirt over her head. The word "BITCH" was written in green boldface all caps across the chest. Upon noticing it, she looked at Sarah, nonplussed.

"Funny."

Sarah looked at the floor and let out a quiet giggle. "I thought so."

Alexa then gestured toward the corpse. "Do me a favor; be a darling and have a chew on her brain. Maybe her memories can tell us something."

"It doesn't work like that!" Sarah snapped with a scowl. "She's been dead too long. I'd need some left-over brain activity to work with. Plus, I may be synthetic, but that doesn't make me your slave!"

"No, your bail debts do that," Alexa replied. Her tone was nonchalant but nevertheless carried a familiar venom to her sister.

"You wouldn't dare hold that over my head, would you?" Sarah fixed her with a spuriously charming grin, but her confident demeanor quickly dissolved as she awaited a reply that never came. Instead, Alexa cast her a very telling, yet otherwise silent sideways glance as she pulled a pair of golden bracers from the bag.

"Anyway, how is he?" she asked as she slid her bracers onto her wrists.

Sarah folded her arms and looked away. She clicked her tongue.

"Well, say it," she said.

"Xerx said that they've put Salt under for now, but he should recover."

"Any idea what she used on him?"

"One of the doctors speculated he overdosed on *riss*, but tox screens aren't showing it," Sarah said. "At least that's what they say. Whatever the chemical was, it was in the sweat and vaginal fluids on the sheets, and in such high concentrations, it was like someone filled a bug bomb with the stuff." She absently rubbed her nose and sniffled. "It's still making my sinuses itch."

Alexa noticed Sarah appeared uneasy, unusual for her. Her sister was normally calm to the point of psychopathic; for her to be on edge meant something was up.

"What is it?" she asked tellingly.

Sarah sighed and let arms fall to her sides. "Xerx is pissed, Alexa. I mean, *really* pissed. I think he might do something stupid."

"Then we'd best catch up with him," Alexa said on the edge of a gentle growl. She pulled on a pair of black scale-patterned leggings.

"What about the police?" Sarah asked, indicating the condition of the room. "This isn't exactly subtle, is it?"

Alexa shot her a sly grin and headed for the door. "Diplomatic immunity has its perks. Now hurry up. We've got a hospital appointment."

"So, the way I see it, these definitely can't all be her at once."

Paige half-smiled as Pip talked, seemingly none the worse for wear, despite her left arm being heavily strapped by Kairen. After settling their differences, Paige had taken her to the Med deck. Kairen had said nothing, but Paige saw the glint in his eyes at how the two seemed to be on good terms again. Her only concern was the casual way in which Pip waved her spoonful of ice cream around as she spoke. Fearful of potentially wearing the tiny woman's dessert, Paige reached out and steadied Pip's hand.

"Okay," she said, "so there's no evidence of tampering with video logs. What are we looking at? Prosthetics?"

Pip shook her head and placed her spoon on the table next to three empty tubs of ice cream. It always surprised Paige that for such a small person, Pip had the appetite of someone damn near Maria's size.

"No, the facial construction is too good. We're looking at doppelgangers and really expensive work at that." She pursed her lips. "Or..."

Paige narrowed her eyes, trying to understand Pip's thought process. "Or what?"

Pip appeared almost embarrassed for a moment, then spoke again. "Or they're imperfect clones. That would explain the slight variations at least."

Paige leaned back in her chair and rubbed her chin. Pip clearly felt a bit stupid for suggesting such a thing. The monster that the Second Imperium had created by militarizing cloning tech was such that the very idea of using it for their own means was shunned by just about every respectable biological and pharmaceutical company in the Alliance, despite the potential medical benefits. But Paige had the sneaking suspicion that it wasn't as absurd a possibility as it seemed.

"You might be on to something there, Squeak," Paige said, not believing her own words. Pip shot her a sideways glance at the nickname. Paige knew her pilot wasn't overly fond of it, despite the fact that Brogan had started it.

"We know Hayashibara is an expert in biology and genetics," Paige continued, "and she was in cahoots with the Imperium, so it's not beyond the realm of possibility that she's created doubles, enacting her dirty little schemes."

Pip nodded, clearly deep in thought. She locked eyes with Paige.

"Have you decided what to do with Xerx?" she asked. Her tone was tentative, as if fearing another tirade from her captain.

Paige paused for a moment and put a hand to her chin. She snapped her prosthetic fingers as an idea came to her.

"Is there any way to tell between these 'clones' and the real Doctor?"

Pip shook her head. "Only the ones who deviate the greatest from her baseline genetics. But otherwise, no, at least not visually. What've you got in mind?"

Paige leaped to her feet and started heading for the door. She pointed in Pip's direction as she moved. "Get me the *Reckless* on the horn! I've got an idea."

Pip nodded and placed a hand on the implant above her right ear.

Alexa made her way quickly down the sterile white corridors of Tophanavar's B-level main hospital. Ahead, she could see Xerx pacing back and forth through the glass doors at the end. Sarah followed behind, keeping a discreet distance. She hated hospitals; for her, it was a pit of temptation. She could smell the blood and meat lurking behind every door, despite the thick scent of antiseptic hanging in the air. Sarah bit down on a finger as the feelings washed over her. She hadn't always been like this. In the beginning, she was a compliant and curious soul. But something in the technology used to create her began to whisper within the silica pathways of her synthetic mind. She began sneaking out of the facility and seeking out victims, initially feeding only on their blood. As time went on, the whispers grew into shouts, and Sarah found herself consuming the entire bodies of her prey. Alexa could be tough, but she had always sought to help her no matter what trouble she landed herself in. For that, Sarah was eternally grateful—not that she'd ever show it.

Alexa quickened her pace as they spotted Xerx accosting an orderly, grabbing his uniform and clearly raising his voice. She pushed the door open and strolled into the reception area, taking care to appear calm and relaxed. Sarah sidled in behind, quietly making her way around the edge of the room.

"Zee, sweetheart, do leave the poor man alone," she said. "I'm sure he is doing everything in his power to keep Salt comfortable."

Xerx glared across at Alexa and released the orderly. The frightened man glanced her way with wide, yet hopeful eyes, and Alexa nodded her head toward the door. Not requiring a second invitation, the man quickly departed.

Alexa held Xerx's gaze as she strode slowly toward the center of the room. "I seem to have arrived just in time before you made a proper ass of yourself, eh?"

There was no humor in her voice. Alexa could see the seething rage behind Xerx's olive-colored eyes. Without his wife here to drag him back to reality, Alexa quickly decided she would have to perform that role instead.

Xerx drew a deep breath before speaking in a low rumble. "You denied me a kill, Lex. This was my promise to Izz and mine alone to execute!"

"Oh, don't be so dense." Alexa rolled her eyes and gently shook her head. "It wasn't her at all; the shuttle is still a day out. Sarah and I did a thorough examination."

"Every part," Sarah said, continuing to prowl around the edge of the reception room. "No organ left unturned." She then approached a row of chairs lined up against a wall with a large window set into it. A number of fake cheese plants dotted the corners. Seated in one of the chairs was Pepper, hands clasped together, staring at the floor. He looked up sharply as Sarah passed him by. She flashed him a brief, fanged smile and then moved on, leaning herself against the empty reception desk, stretching out her fingers, and studying her ebony nails as Alexa broke the tension.

"So, how is he?" she asked. There was an edge to her voice that was clearly not lost on Xerx.

"They said he's critical, but the signs are looking good," Xerx said, his words a low mutter. In response, there came a snort from the corner of the room. All eyes shifted to Pepper, his lips curled into a near-snarl.

"Oh, I hope he gets better all right," he said, stretching and placing his arms behind his head. "I can't wait to hold this one over his head. All that bullshit about me and humans he gives me; then off he goes, listening to *his* little man ... and with a human woman, no less! Yeah, I'm *so* gonna enjoy this."

"You need to show your father some fucking respect, boy!" Alexa shot back, giving the younger Felyan a venomous look. "Maybe if you pulled your head out of your arse for long enough to actually speak to your old man instead of just dismissing his opinions, you two would get along a lot better. Now, grow up!"

Pepper wilted in the chair like a whipped puppy. Even Sarah gave a start at Alexa's sudden outburst.

"Woah, Lex!" Xerx suddenly moved between Alexa and Pepper. "Just who do you think you are talking to him like that, huh? He's a member of my crew!"

"And last I checked, you are a subject of the realm to which I am head of state!" Alexa barked. "Tread carefully."

Xerx stared at her for several seconds, tense as a dog that was ready to bite. But soon, he exhaled, then, with visible reluctance, took a more deferential stance, looking away.

"She must have agents working for her," he said, shifting the subject, speaking tersely. Then abruptly, he seemed to gain a renewed audacity. "I'm gonna find them and make them pay, dammit! Stay out of this, Lex; you have no right to interfere."

With no warning, Alexa grabbed Xerx's lapels and pulled him in close, the worn blue denim making a popping sound as her claws pierced the material.

"I have *every* right! Or have you forgotten? I am your Queen, Alexa Montrose, Dutchess of King's Knight and Lifemate to Iriid Rhoma the First. And *you* will show me the courtesy I deserve! Are we clear?"

"Wait!" Xerx, all anger evaporated at the sudden show of force, raised his hands, his expression stricken. "You're pulling rank on me?"

Alexa bared her teeth. "You're damn fucking right I am! You're angry and irrational, and if you won't listen to reason, then perhaps you'll take note of a royal command!"

Alexa held her gaze on Xerx, her blue eyes appearing to have glowing orange flecks within.

She heard the sound of someone clearing their throat, and Alexa saw Sarah over Xerx's shoulder, fixing her with a nervous expression and making a finger motion toward her eyes. Alexa nodded and took in a deep breath. Closing her eyes, she released Xerx, who staggered a step back and dusted himself down, his pride slightly wounded, but more contrite. Alexa turned away for a moment, then placed her hands on her hips.

"Xerx, honey," Sarah's voice was soft but seemed loud in the sudden silence. "Aren't you scheduled to fight in a couple of hours?"

Xerx gave a slow nod. "Yeah, but there's no way I'm gearing up when I'm hunting the bastards who set up Salt."

Sarah stood up straight and appeared to acknowledge Xerx's words with a simple "hmm" before she continued speaking, an almost predatory grin now on her face.

"If the itinerary is right, you're slated to fight the *Khan*. You get yourself off to the stadium and take out some of that pent-up rage on dear, sweet Radic whilst Alexa and I take care of the intel side of things." She then gestured dismissively toward Pepper. "I'm sure the pup here can keep an eye on dear old dad for a tick."

Pepper sat up and began to protest but was silenced by a sharply raised finger from Sarah.

Xerx sighed, and his shoulders slumped. "I guess you're right," he said before pointing at Sarah. "Just try not to eat anyone."

"Oh, ye of little faith." Sarah walked past him and put an arm around Alexa's shoulder.

"Also, maybe you should schedule some sack time with your wife to blow off some of that steam," the Pirate Queen added. "Come along, sister dear; we have work to do."

SEVEN

What passed for night through the dome of Tophanavar bathed the colony in a faint pseudo-twilight created by the glow of the miniature towns on the higher terraced levels. Deep inside the level-3 streets and alleyways lay the Marksman's Arms, an otherwise nondescript drinking establishment located in a quieter part of the level. Normally the sounds of socializing and singing could be heard from within, but not tonight, as muffled noises of an altercation filtered out through the doors.

With a mighty crash, Paige came flying backward out of the pub's large front window, landing in an awkward heap. Gingerly, the *Shadow Star* captain rolled onto her back, shards of glass crunching as she moved, shattering under the rigid alloys of her prosthetic arms and legs. As she raised her head, a hooded figure leaped through the broken window and sprinted down the yellow-lit street. Hot on her heels, Maria appeared, barreling through the window frame, tumbling with surprising grace for her massive size. She sprang to her feet and tore after the shadowy figure. Next, Ike stepped through, gave Paige a nod, and then gave chase himself. Only Brogan stopped a moment to look down at his captain.

"You all right?" he asked, genuine concern in his voice.

Paige snorted and met his gaze. "Never mind me, Jay; I'll be fine. Get after the others!"

With a nod, Brogan turned on his heel and hurried after his crewmates down the street. Having had time to catch her breath, she brushed off the remaining glass shards from the steel of her prosthetic arms and body armor, then rose to her feet, and hurried after her crew. She'd just caught sight of them in time to witness Maria launch a thunderous spear tackle into her target. The figure seemed to fold in half like paper, and the pair hit the road with a force that made her genuinely surprised that it didn't make cracks in the asphalt. It made Paige think of a strange organic car crash, sliding several meters across the ground. Maria stood up, barely seeming to register the torn skin along her left arm. Ike approached and pulled a nanospray from his belt pouch, quickly seeing to the massive tank's wound while she gazed at the figure lying motionless in the middle of the street, miraculously not dead. Paige gave a nod to the others and dialed up the comm built into her left arm.

"Pip, sweetheart, it's me. We've got her. Make the call."

Xerx stalked along the boarding gantry high above the Gestalt hangar floor, tugging at his interface suit, a black one-piece with a large neon purple "X" across the torso. It clung to him like a second layer of skin, designed to allow a seamless connection between the machine's systems and the pilot's neural interface implants. Having to wear such tight-fitting garments had failed to improve his mood. Not that he would have minded if it had only been Neela to enjoy the view, but otherwise, he felt like an idiot, and it left very little to the imagination in certain parts.

Another tug and he paused to look out across the cavernous expanse that led from the pit complex to the arena. Far below, the bustle of the various crews preparing their fighting machines echoed around the vast chamber. There was a loud rumble as a hauler rig approached from the far end carrying the Gestalt *Tiberius* on its vast trailer pan. *Tiberius'* iridescent armor plates were covered in scratches and gouge marks but otherwise appeared intact.

Arty must have won again, he thought. *No surprise for the pink-haired menace.*

Xerx turned to continue along the walkway and saw Artemis walking toward him. *Speak of the devil ... or rather think...*

As usual, she eschewed the walkway in favor of the railing, arms outstretched for balance. She was dressed in her own interface suit, though hers was dark green with a stylized "A" symbol in hot pink and her trademark black-and-white striped left sleeve. A rare smile crept across her face, and she seemed to be studying the gigantic ceiling spars above them. Looking down through the grated floor panels, Xerx grumbled out loud.

"God forbid you actually use the walkway like a normal person, huh?" His complaint sounded almost petty, so he paused to consider his situation.

"Who are you talking to?"

Xerx almost jumped out of his skin. Perched right next to him, almost at his eye level, was Artemis. Too busy with his thoughts, he had failed to see that she'd cleared the distance between them in the space of time where he'd become lost in thought.

"W-what?" Xerx stammered, struggling to get his words out. "No one. Just ... thinking out loud. You shouldn't sneak up on people like that, anyway!"

Artemis cocked her head to one side and fixed her trademark unblinking, green-eyed stare his way, making him begin to shift uncomfortably.

"I don't sneak," she said. She then jabbed a thin finger into his shoulder. "You weren't paying attention."

Xerx frowned. She had a point; he had been operating on autopilot since Alexa had torn him a second hole to shit out of. Now he was certain she hadn't blinked since they'd started speaking.

Her impassive expression became a frown that mirrored his own. "You're not happy," she said. Her expression of the obvious was more of a statement than a question.

"That's putting it mildly, *La Muerta*," Xerx said, using the nickname Isibar had once given her as an inside joke. He sighed, his shoulders sinking. "Salt's in the hospital; someone drugged him with something nasty; then Alexa killed our primary lead when she rescued him. So, yeah, I'm pretty pissed about it all, if I'm honest, but Lex put me in my place. And to be fair, I was kinda being—"

"A dick?"

Artemis' blunt response took Xerx by surprise but was ultimately accurate. He grinned in spite of himself.

"Heh, yeah, a dick. I was ready to lose my League license by no-showing just to go after these people."

"That would have been stupid."

That was certainly the understatement of the year. It always surprised Xerx how forthright Artemis could be, and yet her tone remained strangely neutral. He had expected her to understand his point of view, given her history.

"Yeah, Alexa made that abundantly clear. But I'm facing off against Radic, so I suppose I get a chance to let off some steam there."

Artemis blinked, then let out a juddering giggle that made Xerx almost laugh out loud himself.

"He does make a good punching bag occasionally," she replied. Xerx heard the barest hint of emotion in Artemis' voice. He knew all too well that she enjoyed putting their cocky rival in his place just as much as he did.

There was a loud clang, followed by the sound of huge industrial motors winding up. The pair watched as the maintenance crews began raising *Tiberius* back up to its feet.

"Guess that's my cue," Xerx said, again studying the damage that crisscrossed *Tiberius'* body. "Looks like you guys took a beating out there."

Artemis shrugged. "You should see the other guy."

Xerx shook his head and grinned, holding his hand out to Artemis, who reached forward and shook it.

"Stay bad, girl." Xerx released her hand and slapped the pink-haired woman on the shoulder.

"Mmhm." Artemis smiled, stood up on the railing, and turned back toward the direction she was headed. Xerx continued down the walkway and through the access door to the cockpit prep area. Across from where he stood, he studied the hulking form of *Imani*, his personal Gestalt. Umbilical lines fed into various points across its body, transferring fuel, power, and data as a crew of humans and Felyans prepared it for the startup procedure. Unlike most GI teams, Xerx was both the pilot and owner of his fighting machine. He believed it gave him a stronger bond between himself and her A.I., allowing them to interact on a more effective level than others. Below him sat the spherical pilot's pod, access hatch open and ready.

He climbed inside, nodding to the two official GI crewmembers waiting on either side. The cockpit was not exactly spacious; the seat was molded to his exact body shape, and a thick sparred safety cage surrounded him. Xerx clicked his boots into the footrests, and the crewmen reached in, assisting him with his safety belts in the cramped space. The harness was secured, and the men retreated. Xerx pulled the control console down from above his head and attached it to the connector unit in front of his lap. Several lights blinked on and began to turn green in sequence. He gave a thumbs-up to the crewmen, and they cleared away from the pod as a final piece of the cage was lowered and secured into place with a muffled clang. Then the hatch closed, and he heard the bolts thump into place.

For a moment, he sat alone in the dark, illuminated only by the green glow of the console lights. Xerx then felt a jerk as the pod was lifted and moved toward *Imani*'s open chest cavity. He leaned back and engaged the neural connectors in the chair, which attached to points near the top of his spine. He heard the familiar dull scrape as the pod slid into place inside *Imani*'s chest. There was a second jolt and then a click, and Xerx's dark, claustrophobic world suddenly came to life. Holo displays lit up the space before him, and a timer bar began climbing, denoting the progress before *Imani* was fully operational. Xerx closed his eyes and let out a long sigh, puffing out his cheeks as he did so. He was still upset, but his brief chat with Artemis had helped dissipate much of his anger.

An incoming message icon flashed up in the bottom right corner of his display. He selected it and rolled his eyes as the grinning face of Radic appeared in front of him, his voice smug and like nails on a chalkboard as he delivered his message.

"Greetings, comrade! I thought I would wish you luck in our imminent confrontation. You're going to need it!"

Xerx bristled as he felt his choler rising once more. Radic was still talking, but he'd lost interest in what the cocky asshole had to say. Xerx cut the transmission and hit the FLOOD button. Ports around the edge of the pod opened, filling it with the breathable shock protection fluid. Xerx relaxed himself, suppressing the natural fear of drowning that came with submersion, and prepared himself. In tandem with the surprisingly airlike, oxygen-rich mixture that filled his lungs, the artificial mind of *Imani* became active and merged itself with his.

Time to relieve some stress, they thought, and Xerx hit the STARTUP confirmation on his console.

Alexa leaned back against the bar of the sushi shack she and Sarah had stopped at. It was open to the street, and she sighed as she watched the crowds bustling in front of her, the hypnotic sight slightly curtailing the aching need to feel a certain sweating hybrid pumping away between her legs. That would come eventually, though ... as would she. To her right, Sarah hunched over the counter, stuffing sushi rolls into her mouth with remarkable speed despite using chopsticks. Alexa rolled her eyes in Sarah's direction and leaned her head toward her.

"You'll make yourself ill eating like that," she said. "And maybe you might even consider chewing at some point?"

Sarah scowled back at her and swallowed a sushi roll loudly.

"I'm hungry," she replied testily. "Unless you'd prefer I find a tasty hobo to feed on?"

"Kindly fuck off, sister dear." Alexa turned her attention back to the street, making a two-fingered hand gesture at Sarah. "Anyway, hurry up. I want to find the one we tracked onto this level sooner than later."

Sarah snorted and turned back to her food. Alexa ran a hand through her hair and shook her head. "I'm going to head off and see if I can find out anything," she said. "Call me when you're done, okay?"

Sarah nodded a barely noticeable reply, and Alexa stood up. As she stepped into the busy street, she was immediately barged into by a figure in a white hooded coat. Alexa turned to apologize and locked eyes with the stranger. Recognition flashed across her face.

"Selene the Second, I presume!" she barked.

The woman looked at her wide-eyed and made a run for it.

"Oh, for fuck's sake! She's done a runner!" cried Alexa, setting off on her heels and yelling for Sarah to catch up. Sarah launched herself from her chair, threw some wadded-up notes onto the bar, and made after them, stuffing a handful of sushi rolls into her mouth. Alexa dodged and pushed past the crush of people as they moved toward a nearby transport hub. As she broke through the throng, Alexa spotted her quarry dive down a nearby alleyway. Giving chase once again, she flew around the corner and stopped abruptly. Before her stood the Doctor twin, smiling. Her black leather trench coat fluttered wide open, shamelessly revealing sheer red lingerie as if nature itself had been working with her in some impromptu career as a flasher. At that same moment, a wave of dizziness overcame Alexa and clouded her thoughts with an overpowering fog of naked lust. Being sexually heightened wasn't unusual for her, but this was different: powerful and all-consuming. All she could think about now was taking the woman standing across from her, pushing her deeper into an alleyway, and fucking her brains out. And this woman seemed more than willing to accommodate her. Alexa was only barely aware of her soft voice speaking seductive, cajoling words as she took her by the hand

and led her deeper into the alley, then being pressed up against the wall behind a large dumpster—not exactly the most romantic venue, but she was too far gone to care.

The woman began to kiss Alexa on the lips, and the Pirate Queen eagerly reciprocated. She felt the smooth, deft touch of her hand as she reached down inside her waistband. Alexa's eyes rolled back inside her head, and she grunted in delight.

"Are you enjoying yourself?" the woman's voice dripped with seduction. "We concocted this recipe just for you."

Suddenly, Alexa's eyes snapped open, and she fixed her with a glare.

"She was until you stopped," came a voice from behind.

The Doctor twin whirled around in surprise as Sarah approached, almost sauntering up to them.

"Nothing annoys her more than working her that hard and then denying her a good orgasm. And believe me, before you came along, she was already horny as an open-legged pleasure girl."

Sarah pursed her lips and clicked her tongue, her eyes moving slowly from left to right and then fixing on the woman. "But in all honesty, that's not my business. I'm here for a different reason."

The Doctor twin stuttered, trying to find something to say. Sarah sniffed the air and wrinkled her nose.

"Ugh! Whatever this stuff is you're playing with, it sure doesn't smell very nice." She nodded her head toward Alexa. "You doing all right there, sis?"

"Excellent now." Alexa nodded, the fog still clearing from her thoughts. Slowly, she felt her lust being subsumed by anger at this audacious bitch who had nearly made her fuck in an alley: something she hadn't been desperate enough to do since before she'd met Iriid. "But would you mind, you know, assisting me? Assuming you've got your breath back, of course."

"What are you talking about, you mad bitch?" The Doctor twin looked between the pair of them, exasperated. Suddenly, Alexa grabbed her from behind and held her arms fast.

"Oh, it's nothing much, sweetheart," said Sarah, sounding as innocent as she could. "Just a penny for your thoughts."

The Doctor twin reeled as Sarah's jaw made a dull crack, and her mouth opened impossibly wide, revealing jet-black gums and tongue. The woman struggled, now desperate, as she realized what was about to happen, but Alexa's hold was too strong. Fangs extended from Sarah's upper jaw, and she pounced. Her mouth had become wide enough to encompass the twin's scalp, and it convulsed as Sarah's fangs pierced her skull.

Sarah swam in a sea of darkness—not quite pitch black, but a strange gray twilight pierced by shafts of sunlight. As she moved forward, inky black tendrils overtook her, leaving smoky trails that spread out and swallowed the light. Images began to form around her: people, places, events. Slowly, the scenes began to take shape, and

Sarah took control of her victim's mind, sifting through memories like papers in a filing cabinet.

Sarah followed the clone—the closest word to what it really was—as it arrived on Tophanavar, heading for the transport hub after clearing customs. Sarah skipped forward past several uneventful sequences, at last pausing as she noticed an odd sensation in the back of her mind, like an itch that she couldn't reach. She felt like she was being watched, a common feeling for her when she fed on a victim's memories.

Sarah turned her attention to where the clone was heading. It appeared to be an industrial complex near the outer wall on one of the lower levels. Sarah watched as the clone met with others of her kind in a secluded spot near the atmosphere-processing plant. Sarah noticed a series of auras flowing around each clone, each a different color. Concentrating as hard as she could, Sarah drew on its memories, learning that the aura was visible only to them and represented a different pheromone mix designed to target different individuals and generate a number of different reactions in the target. The clones had been discussing their designated zones and where they were likely to find the people with whom they had been tasked with making contact.

Sarah felt she had learned all she needed and was prepared to withdraw from the clone's mind when something abruptly drew her attention. Each clone appeared to have a faint "string" winding away from them and fading into nothing a short distance away. Studying her own victim, she discovered the same thing, manifesting as a trail of light leading away into a cloudy haze. She decided to see where it led, plunging into the gloom. Black tendrils surrounded her, winding around the trail and obscuring its glow slightly. The tendrils pulsed with silver light, making circuitry patterns across their surface as she traveled along. The strange trail of light and the mass of twisted darkness had an eerie familiarity to her.

Suddenly, the light expanded and became blinding before clearing, giving way to a sight that gave even her the chills. She realized she was connected to the mind of another clone and stood before it. It was Dr. Hayashibara herself, grinning like some kind of psychotic demagogue.

Time to leave, Sarah thought before retreating as fast as she could, the world around swirling in a sickening kaleidoscope of motion and color.

Sarah's distended jaw released the head of the now-dead clone, and it fell unceremoniously to the floor. She blinked as her eyes reverted from a deep black to their usual icy blue, like storm clouds receding from a clear sky. Alexa looked at her quizzically as Sarah's jaw popped itself back into place.

"You okay?" her sister asked.

Sarah nodded, rubbing her jawline and flexing her lips. She appreciated the sound of genuine concern in her sister's voice. She looked straight at Alexa and clicked her tongue.

"We have to reach the others quickly," she said. Her tone was urgent, but she could see Alexa needed more before she could act. "The clones—they're all connected. The Doctor knows everything; she's been observing us through them the whole time. They're her eyes and ears."

"Shit," Alexa hissed, the curse coming out almost inaudible.

"Words out of my mouth," Sarah said as she started walking. Alexa followed closely behind, leaving the corpse where it lay. It would perhaps be a day or so before the stench would attract anyone to it, but Sarah's DNA signature was nigh untraceable.

"How can you be sure?" Alexa asked as they headed back into the street.

"There's a link. It's difficult to describe exactly without being able to show you; however, there's a familiarity in their makeup."

"What do you mean?"

Sarah stopped in her tracks and looked directly at Alexa.

"The technology used to create them, Lex. It's the same as what your father used to create me, and it doesn't give me a good feeling. It felt ... I don't know ... malevolent."

"Explains a lot about you," Alexa said without humor.

"Quite," said Sarah, unfazed by what she was almost certain was an implicit insult. "Now, we need to reach the others before they get their hands on another one!"

EIGHT

"I need caffeine..." Rinkya groaned to Rati. Sitting beside her lifemate in the maglev, she struggled to stay awake as it shuttled them up to the hangar bay level. Pulling long hours was par for the course in their line of work, but with the Pirate Queen sticking her fingers in every pot in Tophanavar's seedier dives and right into their investigations with her damned diplomatic immunity, things were quickly becoming more complicated: a series of deaths by seemingly the same culprit that seemed to vanish, even from security feeds, almost as if someone had been hacking them. But she had no doubt that the lusty redhead whom she'd seen at several crime scenes seemed to not only know something, but also appeared to be hot on a trail that they hadn't zeroed in on yet.

So why had she called them?

"You want to get off at the next stop?" Rati asked. He was looking out at the passing scenery, unfazed by lack of sleep. Of course, he was freakishly active at night, her exact opposite. They complimented each other in this way, as well as many others, so neither her mother nor

Rati's parents found it any surprise when he'd at last asked her to be his lifemate.

"There's a coffee shop I know about on the next level, and it's close to the maglev, so we can hop on another train to get us to the hangar without wasting much time."

Rinkya shook her head, yawning. "No need. I've got a better idea. I'll hit up the Pirate Queen for coffee when we get to the hangar. She's been a pain in the tail since she got here, her sister even more so. I swear she gave me the stink eye back at that bar."

"Wouldn't be the first time a person of interest thought they'd pulled a fast one on us and gave us the finger," Rati said.

"Well, either way, I figure a coffee is the least the Queen owes us."

"Petty revenge," Rati said, surreptitiously nuzzling her cheek with a soft purr. "That's my girl."

"Not while on duty, *li-ah*," Rinkya reminded her lifemate. Still, she could not suppress a giggle, which she hoped would not attract the attention of other passengers. With a sigh, Rati put a stop to his affections and reclined in his seat, looking back at the scenery as the maglev spiraled up the colony's terraced levels in the artificial night. His actions having woken her up somewhat, the ensuing silence gave her a moment to muse over the situation, where she soon discovered something she hadn't previously thought about.

"How did the Queen even know who we were?" she asked, sitting upright.

"She and Cousin Xerx are longtime friends," Rati said without any hint of reflection. "I'm sure she knew about us. I noticed her glancing our way during a couple of our investigations, and I could've sworn she even smiled once," he shrugged. "And she's married to the Pirate King, our cousin. So she's basically related to us. Make of that what you will."

Rinkya hissed softly as a chill ran through her back. "How can you make something so innocuous sound so creepy?" she asked.

"It wasn't me," Rati replied. "The Queen's reputation precedes her. You know, I heard she keeps a hybrid on standby for when—"

"Too much information," Rinkya said with a finality that rendered her lifemate silent. "Y'know, I thought she was trying to get ahead of us back in the investigation at the bar at first, but now I'm thinking I might've been wrong to think we were rivals in this."

"Maybe that's what she wanted us to think," Rati said. "Maybe we're just a concession; maybe Xerx asked her to get in touch with us. For all we know, he could've been badly hurt in the last match."

Rinkya frowned, feeling a different kind of frustration over missing the match that Xerx had traveled so far to attend. "I hope that's not the case."

"You and me both, *li-ah*. But this is a lot to think about either way. Hell, this might just be a game to her. Lead the blues on, with a little extra fun on the side."

"You don't think she'd be that petty, do you?" Rinkya asked, stirring in subdued horror at that prospect.

Again, Rati shrugged. "They don't call her the 'Dragon Bitch' for nothing. But we'll know when we get there."

"You don't feel like we're going against the badge, though?" Rinkya asked, a tinge of worry creeping into her thoughts. "She did tell us to tell nobody about this."

"It won't be the first thing we've done off the record," Rati said. He flashed her a gentle smile, which set her somewhat more at ease. "I'm sure it'll be okay. My only worry is that this will be a big waste of time."

"Well, as you said, we'll see when we get there," Rinkya remarked, returning her lifemate's grin.

They stepped off the train onto the empty platform. The transit on Tophanavar was automated, running 24/7, even when there were no boarders, and the lack of proper security on some stops made for the occasional issue, which was why travelers at night rarely went alone. But as Rati neared the escalator with his lifemate, the approaching footsteps he heard and familiar scent gave him pause to wonder about the sanity of this particular would-be assailant.

"You hear it too, don't you?" Rinkya said in his ear.

"One person. Got some balls to come after two people, especially two blues with their badges out," Rati said.

The path was open, with now-closed ticket kiosks and vending machines lining the wall to the right in set intervals, forming niches between them for hiding places. But this person hadn't counted on a Felyan's wider field of vision, removing herself from her hiding place once she supposed she was out of view. Her steps were light in such a way that perhaps a human might not have heard her, but again, Felyan hearing was keener, even with hybrids.

"Female," Rinkya whispered, leaning into his shoulder, but surreptitiously removing her pistol from its holster. "Smells like—"

"One of *them*," Rati said, scowling as he drew his own sidearm. He wrinkled his nose at the scent he'd recognized from the victims in the hospital. Similar to *riss*, but different. And not in a way that made him lose his faculties to the horniness that usually came with it. This was unnatural. Nasty.

"You ready?" He whispered to his mate.

"Always."

They both stopped. The footsteps stopped at nearly the same time, then shuffled away.

"You might as well come out," Rati announced, raising his voice to a tone that could be heard above the PA system's automated arrival and departure announcements. "Dunno why you're following a couple of officers, but I'd advise you to knock it off."

The blues turned around, keeping their weapons holstered, but their hands firmly on their handles. The station still appeared empty, save for the ubiquitous elevator music and litany of announcements.

"We know you're hiding between the vending machines," Rinkya said. "Come out, or we'll come in after you."

A high-pitched tittering laughter rose from exactly where they expected as a lithe, black-haired figure emerged from the alcove, dressed in a blue trench coat. Beneath was a tight-fitting blue ensemble that left little to the imagination, along with thigh-high black leather boots. They recalled pictures of the infamous Dr. Hayashibara, and she only bore a passing resemblance to the actual thing, as if she'd undergone the kind of cosmetic surgery that only StellarNet stars could afford.

"Creator, she stinks..." Rinkya said, growling, her ears flattening. "Like *riss*, but nasty!"

"Yeah," Rati said, his nose catching a renewed whiff of the odor. She was nearly fifty feet away, and yet it smelled like she'd bathed in the stuff. "You think she's trying to knock us out like what happened with the others?"

"I'd rather not find out," Rinkya said.

"What's the matter?" The woman sneered. Rati caught her mocking grin as she began sauntering forward. "You'd think I carried Pazuzu ticks or something from how you're keeping your distance."

"Stay where you are!" Rati barked.

"But we just met," the woman replied in a playful tone. "Don't you want to get to know me a bit better?"

"I do believe the man said to stay put," Rinkya snapped as she produced her gun from within her jacket. "Now back away."

"I'm unarmed, you know," the woman said. "Or would you prefer to frisk me?"

"The hell is wrong with this psycho?" Rati said.

"Only way to find out is to get closer, and I think that's what she wants," Rinkya said.

"Yeah, not doing that," Rati said.

"Doesn't look like we're gonna have a choice," Rinkya said, as once again, the woman tried to close the gap between them.

"Stay. Where. You. Are!" Rati roared, drawing his own pistol. "I don't want to have to use this!"

"But it looks like you're not going to have much of a choice," the woman said. She kept her distance at first, walking sideways toward the platform, but Rati noticed that she was subtly making a wide, circular path their way instead of a straight line. "You see, my benefactor needs people like you. And since there's no one else around, you'll do."

If Rati hadn't seen what he saw himself, he never would have believed it.

"*Li'ah*, look out!" Rinkya wailed, pushing him out of the way. In the flurry of movement, he caught a glimpse of what had happened, as the woman moved with a speed that defied nature. Outside of the unnatural *riss*, there had been no scent of bionics on her, yet she'd covered the entire fifty feet in less time than he could blink, carving a path between himself and his lifemate. And that was all the time it took to toss her into the kiosk across the way, and her pistol to go skidding across the ground and onto the tracks below.

Uttering several oaths in Felyan that would perhaps have had him excommunicated from any temple, Rati scrambled to his feet and aimed his weapon at the woman. But she was far quicker, on top of him and gripping his wrist with a force that he'd never thought could be possible.

Worst of all was the *riss*-like scent, now dizzying as, like a lover, the woman pressed herself against him, opening her mouth as her face hovered above his own.

It was at that moment that a memory of his training kicked in, his commanding officer holding him in a chokehold, forcing a concept that one could do more in a state of peace, and that fear was a choice. And choosing to take action rather than be afraid was at least one thing that he'd always been good at.

He stopped his breathing, stopped struggling, going limp, finding peace.

The woman had not expected that, applying force against him where he had been fighting back moments before. Now, limp and loose, she lost her footing and tumbled forward. This gave Rati enough time to do what was needed.

The shots fired into the woman's stomach, exiting right beside her spine. For a moment, the woman froze in place, then after several gurgling, shuddering breaths, fell on top of him like a sack of hammers before she lay still. Summoning his strength as his lungs burned for air, Rati shoved the lifeless woman off of him before rolling away. Quickly, he discarded his jacket, which he hadn't doubted was now covered with her vile scent before gasping in several breaths. The *riss*-like stench was still everywhere, but it was far from overwhelming, like the woman had perhaps intended it to be. Next, he set his sights on Rinkya, who stood propped up against the now-damaged vending machine, holding her shoulder.

"Are you all right?" He said, staggering her way. "Do you need an—"

"I'm fine," Rinkya said, standing upright and wincing against her arm and side. "Just knocked me senseless is all." She nodded toward the doctor's lifeless form. "I'm just glad to see you got the bitch."

"Yeah, I did," Rati said. "But now we got a ton of paperwork to do and—"

Yet another thing happened that Rati would not have believed if he hadn't been there. And it happened just as the electronic beep signaled the arrival of a new train.

The woman leaped to her feet, moving as if there had never been three holes pierced into her body and most of her blood now lay in a puddle on the floor. As the train approached, speeding through the maglev tunnel, she jumped into its path, landing on the tracks the instant it came across. Both blues stood in paralyzed silence, watching the horrific sight. If the train's impact hadn't pulverized the body, the superheated plasma that the railing generated would have incinerated anything that was left.

"So much for an autopsy," Rinkya said, holding the back of her hand against her small muzzle. And yet, as gruesome as that joke had been, it was true that they would be taking care of far less paperwork. Still, there was nevertheless a lot that needed to be done now, as Rati commed dispatch and reported the incident.

Imani was light on her feet in this diminished gravity. As asteroids went, Tophanavar relied on artificial gravity augmenters to keep things satisfactorily anchored to the ground for human and Felyan standards of comfort. For Gestalts, it made impacts sufficiently ... impactful, like the right hook he'd just landed on *Khan*'s kisser—if the big hunk of metal had possessed lips.

Probably a good thing they can't kiss, Xerx thought, watching his opponent's machine stagger back from the unexpected love tap, barely avoiding a deep ravine that marked the edge of the massive crater that was the combat zone. Radic would have probably spent about as much time making out with his own Gestalt as he did balls deep in his skank du jour.

And this train of thought disobligingly brought him back to the situation with Salt, still weighing heavily on his mind and conscience. Alexa had been right, but his inability to help nevertheless rankled him. True, he could not have possibly known that he'd sent his own crewmate into this kind of danger, but he should never have underestimated what the Doctor could do. Now, because of this, his own cousins were so mired in foot-work and paperwork that they might not be of much use now. And he still did not know if this was a good or bad thing.

Xerx realized, almost when it was too late, that *Khan* had taken a flying leap instead of vanishing from his line of sight like a ghost. Noticing the lidar readout in the nick of time, he ejected *Imani*'s blade and thrust upward into *Khan*'s hulking mass while at the same time side-stepping the area of impact, causing a glancing blow which, though failing to leave a dent in his Gestalt's ablative armor, caused his own teeth to rattle uncomfortably. He watched as Radic's Gestalt landed on all fours, nanofluid and coolant leaking from its damaged belly onto the surface of the asteroid. Xerx cut off any retaliation with a smart blow to the damaged area of *Khan*'s belly, knocking him onto his back like a turtle that had been flipped over with a stick. Visualizing the loudmouthed pilot rendered silent and his prize Gestalt wounded left Xerx with a feeling of gratification that was not unlike the aftermath of sex.

"The crowd really liked that one, *Kipenzi*!" he heard Neela say over the comm. "Emotional feedback gauges are off the charts!"

"Radic's groupies are gonna have a bad day," Xerx remarked, holding *Imani*'s knife at the ready. The wound did not look like a game-ender from the outside, but his sensors showed that he'd nicked some of the power couplings on *Khan*'s primary core. The dark patch surrounding the damaged area and black puddle on the asteroid's otherwise pristine surface was proof that he didn't have long to last before his onboard computer set off an emergency shutdown. If he kept fighting, Radic might still have a chance at winning, but he had a rapidly shrinking window of opportunity. Or if Hell felt like freezing over, he could signal a submission to the judges.

As per Radic's predictable pride, *Khan* crawled to its feet, swaying as if the hulking machine's pilot could actually feel just how punch drunk it ought to be. Razor claws ejected from the Gestalt's fingers as it fixed him with his multiple eyes, all red as a demon's. Arcs of blue lightning sputtered from the knife wound as he reared back for a massive slash.

Oh, he's mad, Xerx thought with sadistic delight. This had worked to his advantage. Radic's blind rage would now make him ignorant to everything but an all-out attack.

Radic's slow preparation for the strike left an opening the size of Siberna for Xerx to rush in and use his knife to sever the cables in his outstretched arm. A shower of sparks and electrical arcs spilled out from the wound while the momentum from *Imani*'s bulk took Radic by surprise. Xerx quickly stabilized himself, jamming *Imani*'s foot into the ground as the two Gestalts spun around each other, his quick act of anchoring himself keeping his Gestalt from falling over along with the opposing machine and, at the same time, ripping the knife from the wound. This widened the cut, rendering *Khan*'s arm useless. *Khan*'s splayed position granted Xerx the opportunity he needed to straddle the machine with *Imani*'s other foot, pinning down its other, still-functioning arm. *Khan* struggled against the inevitable, straining itself against *Imani*'s weight.

Imani's knife was raised for the final blow to the power core, Xerx's eyes on the shifting target reticle, waiting for a good moment for a perfect strike not marred by *Khan*'s incessant struggling, when an unexpected voice broke into the comm channel. His surprise at how anyone could have hacked into it vanished into slight annoyance at his recognition of the familiar squeaky register.

"Hi, this is a collect call for Xerxes Paraska from his favorite cute and intelligent cybernetic genius. Do you accept the charges?"

"Kinda ... busy here, Pip!" Xerx replied before his wife could admonish the diminutive tank. He gritted his teeth at the mental and physical juggle of staying atop the floundering Gestalt. "In fact, how the hell did you break the League comm encryption?"

"Puh-leeze!" Pip drawled. "I've had takeout menus that were harder to navigate than this antique. You know, the hardest part was locating your comm signal.

Do you know how much data traffic you guys generate? I've never seen so much telemetry for something this size; it took forever for me to—"

"Get. To. The. Fucking. Point!" Xerx said, struggling to maintain his balance against *Khan*'s increasingly more potent attempts to unhorse him from his position. Risking that very outcome, he slammed *Imani*'s fist square into the Gestalt's sensor-filled head, nearly losing his grip on the blade in the process. He was certain he would be covered in beads of sweat if not for the fluid-filled cockpit. "And this had better be goddamned important!"

"Fine, fine," Pip said, as if someone had just taken away her laser pointer while playing with a particularly energetic kitten. "Paige says hit the *Shadow Star* when you're done. We got one."

A thrill of victory fired through Xerx's synapses at Pip's words, renewing his focus and senses, just as *Khan*'s defense faltered. The targeting reticle flashed with an established target, and Xerx brought the knife screaming into *Khan*'s armored chassis, piercing down into the power core.

But his thrill came with an undercurrent of fury, powered by a resurgence of the memory of all his recent frustrations: his friend's injury on what was to be a simple mission; Alexa yelling at him in the manner that she did; even the strange, yet poignant insights of Artemis, among many other things this journey had thrown at him. Xerx saw red as he let the momentum of the blade tear deeper down and toward its target, opening the furrow for leverage.

As the haze of fury settled, Xerx stood there, holding the orb of *Khan*'s cockpit in his hand, fluid pipes and circuitry dangling from between his fingers.

"*Kipenzi!*" Neela's voice crackled into the comm as instantly, the judges' words appeared on his screen.

"MATCH COMPLETE. POWER CORE BREACH; COCKPIT REMOVAL. WINNER: *IMANI*."

For a moment, Xerx was left in the muffled silence of his own cockpit once again. His fury seemed so far away now, though he knew that Radic's emotions emanating from that tiny cockpit would be enough to power a sun.

"Looks like Alexa and I are more alike than we know," he murmured.

"Retrieval teams are inbound," Neela announced after a significant lapse of time. "So I guess your next stop will be the *Shadow Star*?"

"You heard the tiny lady?" Xerx said.

"Comms go both ways," Neela replied.

"Then you know I'm needed."

"Shall I come with?"

"With Salt out, you and the team will have your hands full with *Imani*," Xerx replied, though in truth, he desperately wanted Neela with him. She was his grounding force, but it looked like he would have to do without her for now. "I can take care of this. It's good news, after all."

Waiting at the top of the *Shadow Star*'s boarding ramp was Paige. Xerx noticed her arms were folded across her chest and a subtle tap of her foot, as though she had been impatient for his arrival.

"Hey, Chook, I hear you pulled a Dragon Bitch just to get here sooner," she said.

Xerx winced at the words. They seemed unusually terse despite Paige's affectionate term for him, born many years ago on a drunken night out. He had been regretting his decision to pull the cockpit pod from *Khan*'s chest. It wasn't an illegal move, but it was considered unsporting due to how expensive the damage was to repair.

She motioned for him to follow, and they headed toward one of the portside service doors that led from the hangar deck and into the outer corridors. Xerx looked around at the passage: a major contrast to the clean gray lines of the hab decks he was familiar with. Exposed pipework and cables ran along the walls and below the grated floor. To his right, panels were covered in a number of hydraulic warning signs and safety notices detailing the functions of the *Shadow Star*'s monstrous landing gear. Everything was lit by small, caged lights set at regular intervals in the ceiling. They took a right turn and came to a stop outside what Xerx surmised was a small storage room. Unlike the doors on the hab decks, this was a heavy industrial hatch mounted on thick hinges and with a large wheel in the middle.

"What is this? Your private sex dungeon?" Xerx joked. He flashed Paige a grin, and she chuckled.

"Not my scene, frankly." Paige placed a hand on the wheel and began to turn it. "Although if you're into kink, you might want to have a chat with Maria. She and Arty are a right motley couple."

Xerx shivered; something was off in Paige's voice. Her delivery of her normally humorous quips had a subtle, yet noticeable edge to them. He couldn't quite put his finger on it, but his friend just seemed to have an undertone of aggression to her. Although he had to admit the mental image of the two lovers wasn't unpleasant, he didn't need to know any more about their relationship than that.

Paige finished turning the wheel, and the bolts released with a dull clang. She pulled the door open and stepped inside. The room was a dirty white, lit by stark strip lights down the center of the ceiling. In the middle of the room sat a figure in a long coat, hands handcuffed behind its back. It looked down at the floor, and its long dark hair obscured the face. A table ran along one side of the room, and Xerx noted the presence of Pip, the *Shadow Star*'s crackerjack pilot and general know-it-all whose interruption had nearly cost him the match earlier. She leaned back on a simple chair, feet on the table, eyes closed and bobbing her head to a faint tune emanating from the headphones covering her ears.

Xerx felt a presence behind him and realized that Paige's childhood friend and number two, Jason Brogan, was standing to one side of the doorway. He was wearing his traditional bandana and goggles that hid his prosthetic eyes. His face, as always, was impassive. Xerx often wondered and, at the same time, shuddered to think about what it would take to make the man angry.

Brogan gave him a subtle nod, and the corner of his mouth flickered in a brief smile.

Paige walked over to where Pip was sitting and leaned in close. Quickly, she grabbed one side of Pip's headphones and pulled it back before letting it go again. The headphone made a slap sound against the side of the tiny woman's head. She jumped, making a high-pitched yelp and grabbing her left shoulder, nearly falling out of her chair. It was then Xerx noticed that her arm was bound in compression bandages and held in place with a grav sling. Her dark eyes glared up at Paige as she slowly removed the headphones and placed them around her neck. She tapped a button on the right speaker, and the faint sound of music switched over to silence.

Paige snapped her fingers at Pip. "Okay, Squeak. Mush, the adults are here now."

Xerx watched Pip's lips squeeze together as if she were holding back a return comment. But then the diminutive woman simply turned and quietly stepped out. Something about the whole scene annoyed him; he'd never seen Paige behave in such a manner toward her crew. True, sometimes they had arguments, but they were as much a family as they were shipmates. He sighed and rubbed the sides of his head. His whole skull felt like it was starting to ache. He looked up again as Paige turned her attention to Brogan. "Jay, if you wouldn't mind just waiting outside?"

With a nod, Brogan stepped through the hatch and out into the corridor. Paige then turned to Xerx with a weird grin.

"Right, let's get to work, shall we?" she said and stalked over to the figure in the chair, which Xerx could more clearly see was a woman, though most of her facial features were still obscured. Paige grabbed her hair and pulled her head back. As her hair fell back, her face became visible. The woman drew in a sharp intake of breath, and her eyes fluttered open.

Xerx was stunned. Aside from the deep graze that swept across her left cheek and temple like road rash, this clone did indeed look exactly like the other one, "Selene" that Alexa had eviscerated in the hotel room. And yet, somehow, she seemed different. He couldn't put his finger on it, but something just didn't seem right about the person in the chair.

And why was his head aching so damn much?

"This is her?" he asked, sounding underwhelmed. "You're sure?"

Paige let go of the woman's hair and placed her hands on her hips.

"What's that supposed to mean?" Paige's left eye twitched, and a sour look crept across her face. Her tone was accusatory as she jabbed a prosthetic finger in Xerx's direction. "I didn't have to do this for you, you know." She jabbed a finger at the clone. "I could just follow my orders and intercept the real Doctor when she arrives, but for the sake of your 'honor,' I thought this was a good compromise. All you bloody pirates and your so-called Code just get in my fucking way, forcing me to choose between my friends or my future!"

Xerx's initial shock combined with the ache in his head, and he bristled with a seething anger. It was no real surprise to learn that she was being paid to round this psychopath up for some amoral corporate bigshot, but who the fuck was she to talk to him like this? He wasn't just some two-bit raider from a backwater clan world. He was related to the King! Damn it, the King was his cousin, and he would be damned if this corporate bitch was going to disrespect him like this.

"Excuse me?" he said, matching Paige's gesture of pointing fingers. "Who do you think you are talking to me like that? We had a mark on this bitch long before your corporate masters wanted to get their dirty little claws into the genuine article! But you just want to let your corporate overlords pull your strings and make you dance! Neither I nor my cousins are concerned about this secondhand copy's secrets; fuck what she knows! Just kill it and make the universe a better place!"

Paige clenched her fists and gave Xerx a venomous stare. "We are puppets to no one!" she hissed.

Xerx opened his mouth to answer when the sound of quiet laughter made him pause. He looked at Paige, and then both turned to the clone, who shook in a conniption fit, her gaze steadfastly holding onto them.

"Oh, please continue," she said, still tittering. "I could watch you both argue all day. It's almost sweet to hear you actually be honest with one another for a change."

Paige cuffed the clone across the face with the back of her hand. "Who the fuck asked you to speak, huh?"

Unfazed by the steel components of Paige's fist, the clone continued to chuckle, leering as she licked the blood from the cut at the edge of her lip. "Oooh, so angry! So forceful! I can see why she chose you for this test."

Paige looked confused. Her anger momentarily extinguished, she looked questioningly at Xerx who shared a similar expression.

Suddenly, there was the sound of a commotion outside in the corridor. Xerx could hear Brogan arguing with someone with a very familiar voice.

Alexa?

"I'm serious, Jason. Sweetheart, move out of my way. We need to get in there now before they tear each other apart."

Brogan made a response, but Xerx couldn't make it out. There was a clatter, and Brogan stumbled backward through the hatch and fell on his back. Through the doorway stepped Sarah, arm outstretched.

"She said move," the dark-haired woman announced.

Sarah then stepped aside, and Brogan rolled over as Alexa followed, MAG pistol in hand. Her blue eyes shifted from Xerx to Paige, then settled upon the clone, to whom she raised the pistol. Without a word, she pulled the trigger and sent two rounds into her head. Brain matter and blood spattered across the far wall, and the body slumped forward.

Both Xerx and Paige turned to face her, mouths agape. Before either of them could speak, she lowered the pistol and raised a clawed finger to silence them.

"No questions," she said. "Outside. Now." Her voice carried an undeniable force of authority that Xerx obeyed. Paige started to argue but was again silenced by Alexa with a growl and a flash of her sharp teeth.

"Don't. Fucking. Argue," she said, her tone quiet but with a threat of growing impatience. "Do as I say, both of you. Outside, down the ramp, and clear your heads.

I will explain everything when you're both in a better state of mind to understand. You were played. That's all you need to know right now."

Sarah shared an awkward smile with them as they left with Alexa and then approached Brogan. "Sorry about that, dear," she said, offering a hand to help him up, "but the matter really was rather urgent. No hard feelings?"

Brogan snorted and took her hand, another thin smile creeping across his face. "You're stronger than you look."

"There's more to me than meets the eye," she replied, pulling the big man to his feet with a strength that belied her smaller stature. Brogan stretched his back and gave his prosthetics a quick check over.

"So, you're a synth, right?" he asked.

Sarah cast him a suspicious eye. "What of it?"

Brogan shrugged, then smiled. "Do you drink?"

"Find out later, honey," Sarah replied with a wink. "I've got to go and assist she-who-must-be-obeyed first."

Alexa paced back and forth at the foot of the boarding ramp. Sarah had caught up after her brief chat with Brogan and stood quietly nearby. Xerx was crouched down near the lip, sucking in a lungful of air, and Paige sat on the base of the ramp's lowering mechanism, one knee raised, arm perched on top supporting her chin. Alexa was desperate for a cigarette, but she'd promised Iriid she would quit. Nevertheless, she'd kept an emergency stash back aboard the *Wraith*, but of course, they might as well have been on the other side of known space.

"So, let me get this straight," Paige said. "These clone 'Doctors' are all just part of a wider experiment?"

"That's correct," Alexa replied. "First, she knew we were coming, somehow. So she targeted specific individuals first: Salt, you two, me... There are likely many more."

"But why us?" Xerx said, looking up from his perched position. "Seems a little too specific just for a test."

Alexa smiled. "I think it's a personal thing. After all, we all share a strong link to the man who exposed her illicit actions on Icona. It doesn't take a bloody rocket scientist to figure she would want us out of action. Not only are we a coherent threat, but we have the resources to put a huge dent in her operations."

Paige leaned back against the huge hydraulic piston behind her. "But why Tophanavar? The place is out-of-the-way and a lot closer to the Felyan Empire than I imagine she'd be comfortable with. There's not exactly much here strategically, assuming she's still operating for the Second Imperium."

Alexa shook her head. "No, she's been rogue for some time. Her experiments were too much, even for them."

Paige nodded. That went without saying, considering how the news of her atrocities had forced even the Felyan Empire to undo centuries of progress to reinstate the death penalty specifically for her. "Pardon me for asking, but how did you come across all this information exactly? We've been trying for months to learn anything of the Doctor's operations, and all we got was that she was coming here."

Alexa snorted out a humorless chuckle.

"The clone we encountered was very forthcoming in the end, although she ultimately didn't survive the extraction process."

Paige looked at Alexa quizzically. "Extraction process?"

"I ate her brain," Sarah said, raising a finger.

Xerx didn't think Paige possessed the capacity for turning green. It was almost hilarious.

The *Shadow Star* captain shook her head and blinked. "I'm sorry. You did what?"

Alexa shot Sarah an irritated look, but Sarah merely flared her nostrils and continued speaking.

"Let me put it another way. I extended my canine proboscises and pierced the skull, thereby allowing me access to the brain matter and then subsequently interact directly with the clone's consciousness and memories and real-time neural processes." She shot Alexa a sarcastic look. "Better?"

Alexa gave her a subtle flash of her eyebrows and turned back to Paige. "Basically, Sarah was not only able to discover what the clones' purposes are, but also that they have a direct neural link to the Doctor herself."

Alexa measured both captains' expressions of awed realization, then looked over to Xerx. "So, as you can see, we've been played for fools. All of us."

"In short, all of you have been targets for Hayashibara's experiments," Sarah explained further as she came to Alexa's side. "Each clone has a targeted pheromone output designed to trigger certain behaviors within their chosen subjects. Both of you were subject to a rage-inducing compound. With Salt and my darling sister here, we think it was something akin to *riss*, but a lot stronger. And not only does it heighten sexual desires, but it also turns those affected by it into her personal meat puppets."

Sarah gently slapped Alexa on the back and grinned. Alexa bared her teeth, then took in a deep breath.

"We're fairly certain that the pheromone experiments are the forerunner to something much bigger, a demonstration of some sort."

Xerx looked up.

"And the colony is the lab," he said distantly.

"Back up a second." Paige raised a palm, frowning. "You said the Doc has a direct neural link to the clones, in real time?"

Sarah nodded. Paige's frown deepened.

"How?"

"Well, it's somewhat complex." Sarah bobbed her head from side to side and tilted her hand slowly. "More than just an embedded subspace link, almost like she's physically connected to them. Are you aware of quantum entanglement? 'Cause it's a bit like that."

Xerx looked at Sarah blankly, but Paige was nodding.

"I have some idea of what you're describing," she said and started to pace slowly. "So we have to assume that the mad witch has been watching the whole time and has a good idea of what awaits her when she arrives."

Paige trailed off, deep in thought. Xerx stood up as he saw Rinkya and Rati approaching. Sarah followed his gaze and sneered.

"Is my presence still required, dear sister, or may I excuse myself before Tweedledumb and Tweedledumbass join in?"

Alexa shrugged. "By all means. I'm sure Paige won't mind if you want to go and wait in the Obs Lounge."

Sarah hopped and clapped her hands. "Do you have sushi, perchance?" she asked Paige.

"We have a protein resequencer," Paige said, gesturing in the direction of the *Shadow Star*'s loading ramp. "It's got sushi on its presets, but it's never been good at replicating raw meat, so it'll probably taste like crap." She gave an ambiguous grin. "Knock yourself out."

Sarah let out a little whooping cheer and jogged up the ramp. Xerx rose to his feet and greeted the pair as they came to stop under the *Shadow Star*'s immense form.

"Boy, have we got a story for you," said Xerx.

"Us first," said Rinkya, placing a hand gently onto Xerx's chest.

Xerx's gaze swept over Paige and Alexa and then back at his cousins.

"What is it?" Xerx asked.

"Outside of the run-in with somebody that looked like the Doctor..." Rati began.

"You saw one of those things too?" Xerx said, all at once half fascinated and half terrified by the news. "Are you okay?"

"We wouldn't be here if we weren't," Rati said, giving Xerx a cocky half-grin that looked uncannily like the kind he would sometimes flash Neela's way. "You need to remember I'm a big boy now, cousin."

"She tried to gas us with whatever that *riss* stink she was wearing," Rinkya said. "But Rati filled her with holes."

"Then she got up again," Rati continued, then suppressed a smirk at Xerx's reaction.

"She *what?*"

"Then she offed herself."

"And gave us a headache of paperwork," Rinkya said. "But outside of destroying the evidence through self-deletion, that's kind of a problem that solved itself. We have something else to let you know about."

"Which is—?"

"The Alliance."

Rati stepped forward. "The task force, they've arrived."

"Well, fuck." Alexa, who had been listening in during the conversation with Xerx, sighed loudly, placing her hands on her hips. "That puts a crimp in things."

All heads turned toward the Pirate Queen as she began to recount her story for the latecomers before they began to speak of plans.

"Looks like it's time to get moving on our end then," Paige said and gestured to the two blues. "A moment, you two. Can you help get me a moment with the colony administrator?"

"We can get you to him," Rati said, suddenly appearing less confident. "But even he doesn't hop when we say."

"He's king of his particular hill," Rinkya added with a shrug.

"Worth a try anyway," Paige said. "When can you do it?"

"Right now, if you want," Rati said.

"Excellent." Paige then commed the bridge. "Pip, you and the others mind the fort while I'm gone."

"Will do!" Pip replied. "We promise not to blow too many things up."

"Funny," she said flatly after switching off the comm. "Lead the way."

NINE

"**I** wish you'd wake up, Dad."

Pepper sighed, flipping listlessly through the schematics files on his tablet. Mobola had found some recovered blueprint fragments from pre-war mainframes that had luckily contained declassified designs for Imperial military vessels. They were incomplete, but they provided excellent insight into the workings of key systems aboard the *Reckless*, sparing him the need to gut them. And they had been just fascinating enough to assuage his discomfort, at least for a time.

Even the captain hadn't given him a tongue-lashing like the Pirate Queen had. That woman was downright frightening.

"That Queen Alexa almost made me need to go back to the ship for a change of pants," he said, about as much to himself as to his father. He sniffed once, then perhaps realized that he would need to return to the *Reckless* anyway to get cleaned and dressed. He hadn't had a proper bath or shower since he'd gotten the news of Salt's accident, and he and Mobola had spent the better part of the prior day doing shakedown analyses on *Imani*'s systems before the big game.

"Weird, but she reminds me a lot of Mom, the way she scolded me … like when I'd done something that really pissed her off," he said, continuing to attempt what passed for conversation with the older Felyan's sleeping form. He hadn't woken up since the incident at the bar, and the doctors had been of little help after they managed to stabilize his condition. He'd been hit with some kind of chemical; the smell of it still hung on him despite everything the doctors had done to get it off and put the ventilators in the room at maximum. It gave Pepper a slight headache at first, but it was wearing off now, slowly but surely.

"I hoped you'd have woken up sooner because, to tell the truth, I really wanted to let you have it, after what the cops said," Pepper said, continuing. He swallowed against a dry throat as he spoke on. "I mean, I never thought you'd... Well, I mean, with a human. But then that redheaded queen with the shark's mouth put the fear of the Creator in me. Getting scared within an inch of your life makes things clearer, that's for damn sure. And I realized that you were used. And by the Doctor you told me about to boot."

He twisted the end of his tail in his hands as he struggled to muster the humility to say the words that came next.

"So, yeah. Now I guess I feel like..."

"You feel like a total clown for doubting your old man's integrity?"

Pepper gave a start and turned in the direction of the gruff voice. His father lay there, eyes closed, but there was a distinct, very present, and very satisfied smile on his face. The older Felyan shook with a faint chuckle, and Pepper at last smiled back, a flurry of combined consternation and relief flooding into his extremities.

"So, when does this end?" Salt asked. "When you cut off your tail in shame?"

Now, here was the hard part. And Pepper suddenly found himself unable to look his father in the eye.

"Well, at least when I ... apologize," he finally said, feigning picking at the fur of his tail.

"Okay, who are you, and what the hell did you do to my son?" Salt said. "And I might not have been fully awake when you started this conversation with yourself. So do tell. Why do you need to apologize, anyway?"

Remembering that his father hadn't been awake for any of it, he recounted the events after his arrival at the hospital, and even after swallowing a mass of pride that he imagined was big enough to choke a horse, he admitted his altercation with Alexa and her verbal undressing.

"So the Queen used your balls for dice, eh?" Salt said after a thoughtful noise. "Can't say that I blame her. But at least you got a bit of humility shoved into you." He paused and then smiled once again, more warmly this time. "And I accept your apology."

Pepper sat down in the chair beside the bed, now feeling less unsettled. "So, how are you feeling? You need me to call a nurse?"

Salt shook his head. "Had better days, but I think I'll be okay. How long was I out, anyway?"

"Only a day," Pepper said.

"Well, all things considered, I've been awake long enough to put two and two together about that black-haired bitch who squirted me with that *riss* stink that made me black out."

Pepper sat bolt upright. "Wait. So, it really was *riss*?"

"It was like when humans try to hide their scents under all those perfumes and shit," Salt said, his expression falling into a disgusted frown. "Its initial smell was just nasty. But underneath it all, yeah. I'd know that smell anywhere." Absently, he sniffed at his wrist and hissed. "It's still on me, looks like."

"Docs couldn't get it all off," Pepper explained. "They had to bring you here in hazmat suits, then immerse you in an organic solvent solution for several hours to just bring the smell down to levels that didn't make everyone within fifty feet of you get cramps or priapism."

"Damn," Salt said. "So it affects humans?"

"That's why the docs didn't think it was *riss*."

Just then, the entrance door, which had been partially open earlier, swung open fully, bumping loudly against the doorstop. A human doctor hurried in, a look of complete excitement on his face.

"Look, I'm sorry for disturbing you," he said, adjusting his glasses after the noise of the doorstop had caused him to start. "But I couldn't help but overhear your conversation. I was looking over your case ... especially that goop we had to dissolve on you." He made a quick check of the holo on his wrist before his gaze fell straight on Salt. "Are you saying that it really is *riss*?"

"Sure is," Salt replied, nodding. "It's hard to tell, but all the additives didn't fool me." He and Pepper were somewhat taken aback by the doctor's sudden appearance, but Pepper supposed that the doctor's zeal meant that this was something big. And he was not disappointed when, at his father's response, the doctor spun around in place, making a high-pitched noise, right before stopping himself, suddenly self-conscious.

"Sorry about that," he said, suddenly in much higher spirits. "But you just won me a bet."

"A ... bet?" Salt asked.

"Yeah. You're not the only patient who got wheeled into a hospital with that stuff sprayed on him, you know. These cases have been going on for the last few weeks. A few have had pretty severe reactions to it. I don't want to scare you, but we've had at least one death."

"I hope you're not saying—" Pepper began. The doctor vigorously shook his head.

"Oh, no, no, no. We've been able to put together a process for cases like this, and we purged your dad's system of the stuff before anything worse than being a horny puppet took hold." The doctor gestured toward Salt. "I'm gonna go out on a limb and say that you don't remember what happened after you got a dose of the stuff, do you?"

Salt shook his head. "I remember the woman. I remember the smell, and I remember seeing her. After that, it was lights out—wait. Did you say 'horny puppet'?"

The doctor's self-consciousness returned with a vengeance, in a way that reminded Pepper of Mobola when she believed she'd committed some imaginary faux pas or let her lips reveal her heart too much. Then, with the look his father gave him, he began to understand how she most likely felt in those moments.

"I'm sorry," the doctor said. "I gather you weren't informed as to how you were found?"

"Not yet," Salt said, still suspiciously eyeing Pepper, who could do little else but shrug.

"I hadn't gotten to that yet," he said. "But it's pretty embarrassing."

Salt settled back into the bed and sighed. "If it was anything like *riss* ... I can imagine." His frown deepened into a scowl. "And it was ... with that human?"

"I wasn't there," Pepper said, "but the paramedics told the captain you'd ... well..." He gesticulated in a very telling way. "several times." Most likely until exhaustion."

"Shit..." The older Felyan practically wheezed the word. "Well, at least I know why you were apologizing."

"Yeah, the Queen scared the moral high ground into me," Pepper admitted; then he switched his attention back to the doctor. "So you guys seriously didn't know it was *riss*?"

"The chemical configuration was a hodgepodge of compounds, with biosignatures from organic components blending into one another to the point where sensors just gave us the blue holo of death. But I figured it had to be *riss*. No one believed me, though. No matter how strong the concentration, it just doesn't have any effect on humans. This stuff was ... well, you know what BTS is?"

Salt shrugged, but Pepper nodded. "It's mostly a problem in the Imperium and border worlds, but I've heard of it through some space hippies from around Halo Meridian. They call it 'sex candy' there."

"Yeah, it's like *riss* but has worse side effects. It's a purely artificial substance, though. This stuff was almost totally organic, just like *riss*. But if your dad's nose is correct, then they may give me the green light to order some different tests from the lab."

"Wait, you're saying that no other Felyans could smell it?" Salt asked.

"I couldn't," his son reminded him, to which Salt made a reluctant grunt.

"None of our Felyan staff could either," the doctor said. "Neither could the hybrids. But they did talk about some who had a more sensitive nose than others. It's supposed to be very rare, though. But if you say you can smell the difference, it might just give me the leverage I need to get the tests okayed. Before, it wasn't a high enough priority; now, they're going to have to listen to me."

"Well, I'm glad that I could be of help," Salt said, nonplussed and still reeling from the blow to his pride, the discovery of his nonconsensual tryst with a human, but visibly pleased with the doctor's turn of fortune. "Is there anything else you're going to need from me?"

"Not for what I have planned," the doctor said, approaching the opposite side of his bed. He switched on a monitor above and studied it for several seconds. "I just came by to check on you. And it looks like you're doing okay. Slightly elevated blood pressure, but that's a side effect that we knew about. It should go down with the meds we put in you."

"Well, as humans say, any day above ground is a good one." Salt's quip elicited a groan from his son, but the doctor gave a small chuckle.

"That it is," came another familiar voice from the doorway. Pepper craned his head to look past the doctor toward the doorway and saw Neela, who had briefly visited earlier along with Mobola and had to return to the *Reckless* for the match. Both wore smiles on their faces, seeing the healthy and awake state of the older Felyan in the hospital bed.

"Finally back with the living, I see?" Neela said. "We were beginning to worry."

"Awake, and hoping they'll put some pants on me soon," Salt said. "At least Felyan hospital frocks have 'em." He then narrowed his eyes, looking past Mobola with momentary confusion on his face. "Hey, Var didn't want to come by?"

"Oh, he did," Mobola said, glancing back toward the door. "But the captain needed him back at the ship for a post-match checkup."

"And he was not happy about that," Neela added.

Salt gave a sigh. "Yeah, the big guy was probably pissed as hell. I'll make it up to him somewhere with an open bar soon as I get out of here."

Neela then turned her attention to the doctor. "Well, he's speaking normal, it seems. Will he live?"

"I'm afraid so," the doctor replied with a mischievous sideways grin. He shut off the monitor, then made his way back to the door. "I'm gonna hurry and see if I can get those tests greenlit," he said, taking a quick look back at Salt. "I'll let you guys know."

After the doctor had taken his leave, Neela cast a shrewd look at Pepper.

"So, should I be worried about these tests?" Neela asked.

"Not so much," Pepper said and explained the conversation they'd just had with the doctor: a story to which both Neela and Mobola's eyes grew ever wider.

"Well, Xerx is certainly going to want to know about this," Neela said at the conclusion of the tale. Her expression then shifted into an even shrewder one, focused on the younger Felyan. "As for you, should I be impressed or ashamed that I thought that this is the last place that you'd be?"

"What's that supposed to mean?" Pepper asked, himself not sure if he should be amused or annoyed at the question.

"I'm just happy to see that he's with his father, as much as they fight," Mobola said, clarifying things.

Even Mobola threw me under the bus, Pepper thought with chagrin. Nevertheless, he was in better spirits, despite this embarrassing moment of piercing insight spoken aloud.

"I heard Alexa had given you quite the chewing out," Neela said.

Those words wiped the smile clean off his face.

"I can see why the captain married you," Pepper said in a flat voice. "Your insight is like a MAG round to the kneecaps."

"He is looking after his father," Mobola said, coming to his defense.

"Oh, I never assumed he didn't regret whatever he did to piss her off," Neela said, her expression in no way judgmental. She approached Salt's side on the opposite end of the bed and took his hand in hers.

"Not that I'm not happy to see you two coming in to check on my old man," Pepper said, stealing a brief grin at Mobola, whom he figured hadn't noticed, "but I'm just as surprised at seeing you here as Dad is at seeing

Var absent. Isn't the captain working on some big case? Won't he need all hands on deck?"

Neela shook her head. "You underestimate my husband's resourcefulness," she said. "He has help with his cousins, along with Alexa. And Paige is here."

"She *followed* us?" Pepper said.

"She ... had similar motives for being here," Mobola said. "Pip explained it to me when they broke radio silence. It seems to have been a bit of a moral conundrum for her, at least at first. But long story short, it got resolved."

"Looks like I'm a bit of a fifth wheel here then," Pepper said, speaking more to himself than to anyone else.

"Now don't go getting any big ideas." Neela set her gaze upon him in a way that reminded him of a vague fire behind her almond-shaped eyes. It was uncanny how she could remind him of a strict teacher or disapproving mother sometimes. "You are exactly where you need to be. In fact, you need to call my husband and report on your father."

"He's..." Mobola began, her timidness reasserting itself. "Well, he's not been in a good mental place."

"Or maybe I should call him myself," Salt said, sounding just a bit annoyed. "I'm in a hospital bed, but not an invalid, you know."

"Not in a good mental place?" Pepper gestured to the holoscreen on the wall across from the bed, broadcasting a muted rugby match on Haven. "Coulda fooled me with how he spanked Radic during that match."

"He knows how to channel his frustrations," Neela said, coming to the opposite side of the bed, where the doctor had been. "And what about you two? Have you reconciled?"

"More or less," they both said in unison.

In truth, however, Pepper did still hold on to the tenuous desire to make sure that his dad never lived this down. But he suppressed the initial inclination, recalling his humbling receipt of that verbal undressing and bullwhipping by the Pirate Queen. Still, for all the flack his father had given him over his closeness with Mobola, it nevertheless was quite tempting. But common sense had a better hand, he supposed, as he acquiesced to the understanding that vindictiveness would be about as helpful as his dad's frequent snide remarks toward him and his friend.

"I'll try to be the bigger man," he said.

"Well, now, who are you, and what did you do with the real Pepper?" Neela said, a wry smile at the side of her mouth. Mobola laughed softly in the background.

Just then, the door opened, and a Felyan that Pepper had never seen before—one with deep orange fur and a striking cascade of blonde hair—stepped into the room. She was middle-aged, judging from the speckles of paler orange and a bit of white about her muzzle, visibly older than Neela, perhaps about his father's age. But his father seemed to know her, judging from the way he straightened up at the sight of her, then adjusted the bed to a reclining position, all the while grinning from ear to ear.

"Ti'Niya?" Salt breathed and was met with a similar smile from the woman, who quickened her pace toward the bed. Salt reached out his hands and grasped hers.

Pepper could hear their mutual purring and suddenly wished to be as far away from that bed as possible.

"I'm sorry," Ti'Niya said, turning back around to face the others. She gave a slight bow, her tail swishing with discomfort. "You probably don't know me." She inclined her head toward Salt. "And to be honest, I barely know him. I work as a bartender at the Purring Princess. "I saw what happened to him, and I was concerned."

Neela narrowed her eyes, her look reflecting the same startled suspicion as Pepper. Even Mobola seemed equally nonplussed. Small wonder, that, Pepper mused. They were both thinking the same thing he was. And the gazes they threw her way were making this stranger about as far from comfortable as she could possibly be.

"I... I know w-what it looks like," the woman continued, her words now coming out in a slight stammer. "This doesn't really have anything to do with me, but he and I got to talking; then this human girl butted in, and he wandered off with her, looking like a zombie. I was concerned, and ... one of the paramedics was a friend of mine, and I know it's unethical, but I asked him, and he owed me a favor. Just ask him. He'll vouch for me and..."

She was visibly shaking now, Pepper noticed, standing stock still; even her tail had stopped twitching. She was staring at the floor wide-eyed, avoiding everybody's gaze, which was probably nowhere near conducive to making her feel comfortable.

The room was silent, and this did not seem to make the woman any less self-conscious.

"I probably shouldn't be here," she said. She then turned stiffly back toward the door.

"People, you're making my friend uncomfortable," Salt admonished.

Now, it was Pepper's turn to feel awkward. And he could see the same emotion in Neela and Mobola's faces.

"You're right," Neela said. "We were being rude, and we apologize." She approached Ti'Niya and took her hand as Salt let go. "I am Neela Eweke Paraska." She then gestured toward Mobola and Pepper. "This is Mobola Kufi, and that is Kyorinya Renyu. We call him Pepper, like we call his father Salt. You say that you saw what happened?"

"I'd like to know the full story too," Salt said, then gestured toward Pepper for his comm.

"I didn't know what happened after I saw him leave with that woman," the Felyan woman said. "I'd gone on my break at the food stand down the road at the time." She gave a shy grin. "I was a little upset about his leaving; he seemed so nice, and we hit it off well. And then that smirking bitch just swooped in and led him off. But when I got back, I'd just missed the excitement. My boss told me what happened as they carted him off."

"Why didn't any police stick around to ask you about it?" Mobola asked.

Ti'Niya made a soft laugh, smiling at Salt, who reciprocated with a look of gratitude as he toyed with the comm to make the call to Xerx, who would almost certainly like to know about this development.

"My dear, in the neighborhood I work, people getting drugged and mugged isn't exactly new. You see that and worse sometimes. But even then, I'd heard rumors about what had happened at work having happened to other people elsewhere on the colony."

"Well, it would be a help to us if you told us every-thing you know," Neela said. "We have a ... personal interest in what happened."

But before she could continue, Salt interrupted, sounding miffed.

"Hey, Neela, the captain's not answering his comm. Did something happen?"

Paige studied the room she now stood in. It was sur-prisingly small for the office of the Tophanavar station administrator. Considering this was meant to be the place where all important station business was decided, it was, in Paige's opinion, an archaic mess.

Pinned to the walls were paper hard copies of var-ious work schedules, inventories, status reports, and any number of requests. The small desk in front of her was similarly cluttered with a small computer terminal at one end.

Behind the desk sat the kind of man Paige loathed dealing with. He was a small, overweight man with a thin mustache and a leering smile. The type of smile that made Paige's skin crawl. Combined with his wrinkled shirt and poorly presented tie, he had the demeanor of a man who was lord of his little kingdom and enjoyed wielding the power it granted him.

Wrestling with her remaining patience, Paige folded her arms and tilted her head to one side. All the while, the man had kept her waiting while he typed on the keyboard of his terminal with pudgy fingers.

"I wish I could help you; I really do," he said, finally looking up from his terminal. He leaned back in his chair in a manner that was anything but apologetic. "But the orders came directly from Alliance command. No one gets in or out of the port until the Task Force has completed their mission, simple as that."

Paige rolled her eyes and sighed. When she spoke, her tone belied the set tenseness in her jaw.

"You're no doubt aware of whom I work for. We have the same mission and are one of the largest military contractors for the Alliance. Surely we can come to some sort of arrangement?"

She already knew the answer. This was a man who wasn't intimidated by status, and in truth, she hadn't really wanted to play the corporate card, but he'd left her little choice.

The creepy smile returned.

"Would that I had that kinda power, why I'd let you mosey on in there and help yourself."

Paige let out a frustrated grunt.

"You're the *pro tempore* station administrator," Paige said, reminding him of the tenuous nature of his position, despite the fact that the Felyan Empress' newborn daughter would not be taking the reins for many years yet. "What do you mean, you don't have the power?"

He gave her a wide-eyed look. It was about as genuine as the designer watch he wore on his wrist.

"Little ol' me? I run the day-to-day of this place, but if the Alliance Senate or Empress says jump, I just say, 'How high?'"

He arched his fingers and spared a quick glance at the terminal screen.

"Shuttle's about four hours out now, so I suggest you head on back to your ship before we lock everything down, or maybe just enjoy the delights the colony has to offer. Operation shouldn't take more than a few hours."

Paige bristled, but it was clear this man was enjoying the exchange more than she cared to admit.

"Fine!" she growled before she turned toward the door. Clenching her fist tightly, she punched it as hard as her prosthetic limbs would allow.

The massive bulge appeared in the metal of the door before it slammed open—its proximity to Rati's face nearly shaving his beard off. Shrieking a Felyan curse, he staggered back as the door swiped dangerously in front of him, pummeled by the force of Paige's fleur-de-lis decorated steel arm. Not giving him or his partner a second look, the *Shadow Star* captain charged off in a rage, like a rhino who had just taken a blow to the gonads.

"I'll be billing your company for that!" the Administrator shouted back. His threat caught the woman's attention in a particularly bad way, the two blues noticed as she whirled about, murder in her eyes.

"Be sure to bill them this while you're at it!" she screamed back, flashing a very prominent middle finger toward the open doorway before spinning back around.

"*¡Pequeño bastardo oficioso,*" she snarled in Espyan. "*Espero que se te obstruyan las arterias!*"

"Are you okay?" he heard Rinkya say, before her hand gently turned him around. She brushed his hair away from her face, her ears flattened with worry before lengthening again with relief—which was a mutual relief to him with what it entailed. Scowling in the direction in which the woman had stormed off, she hissed, before Rati recovered from his momentary shakeup. Without a word, he took her by the wrist and headed back down the hallway, following the woman.

"What are you doing?" Rinkya whispered. "She didn't exactly look talkative, you know."

"Yes, but I think it's safe to assume Paige needed something she could only get here," Rati replied, settling down after the sudden bluster.

"And that the Admin didn't give it to her," Rinkya concluded. "Want me to go talk to him?"

"That's not a good idea," Rati said. "Changing that man's mind has worse odds than pulling an inside straight in a Dorado casino. Besides, I don't feel like faking my way through that kind of a verbal minefield."

"Then maybe we'll have better luck calming the captain down?" Rinkya said.

"Probably."

Both blues turned the corner and spotted the captain, no longer moving at a furious stride, but with slower, more thoughtful steps. Hopefully, some of her anger had blown off; Rati did not look forward to being at the business end of a cyborg, sidearm or not.

"I gather it didn't go well?" he called out. Paige stiffened and then paused, turning around, her expression souring as she noticed their uniforms.

"How observant," the *Shadow Star* captain said icily. "Don't worry about the door, by the way. My company will pay for the damages; I'll send them a report later today."

"Screw the door," Rati said. "I'm pretty sure the old bastard deserved it."

At this, Paige seemed to relax somewhat. Seeing her realization that he was on her side gave Rati some cause to lower his own guard as he smiled.

"I'm going out on a limb here, but I imagine the Admin was less than forthcoming? Even though you're looking into the situation here? The disappearances and sicknesses? Trust me, I know how you feel. He only answers to the big heads, so even our investigation isn't enough to make him cough up."

"Locked out yourselves, eh?" Paige said, shaking her head. She stared back in the direction they'd both come from and sighed. "And here I was, hoping you might be able to pull some strings with me in the mix. But seeing how you're Xerx's cousin, I guess it can't hurt to have you in on our work."

"That sounds like there are some caveats to this," Rinkya said warily.

"Well, now, that all depends," Paige replied. She crossed her metal arms and grinned in a very telling manner—a manner that told Rati that he would both like and hate what she had planned.

"I don't know if it's a good idea to have a pair of blues working with me on this going forward, but then again, it might make my methods going forward more … legitimate."

"What did you have in mind?" Rinkya said, sounding more enthusiastic than Rati felt.

"I plan on making a more … direct approach."

"And what do you mean by 'direct'?"

Paige leaned back against the wall, her grin turning into an almost predatory thing.

"First, I'll need you to go back to the precinct," Paige said.

"Why?" Rati asked, still not mollified by her answer.

"Plausible deniability," Paige said. "You can let us know if anything develops while my crew does their magic—specifically things in the hangar."

"Don't tell me you plan on—"

"I didn't say a word about what I plan to do," Paige said in a way that both suggested there were big plans afoot in her mind and yet a severe sense of restraint from giving them more intel than they would be willing to keep. "All I need is any notification from your end if there's any local law enforcement involvement in the vicinity."

"There's always a contingency of police in situations like this," Rinkya said.

"But if the Alliance military is involved, they tend to do the lion's share of the work. More blues are called in only if shit hits the fan."

"How can you be sure that we won't just turn you in?" Rati said.

"*Li'ah!*" Rinkya whispered reproachfully.

"You're Xerx's cousins," Paige said. "And I know you're just as much loyal to your family as you are to the force. And if you know your father and your cousin Iriid, you know that loyalty ties run deep among even the family of pirate bloods." She gave a grin that bordered on arrogance. "I think I can trust you to do the right thing."

Rati slowly nodded, the realization of what Paige's plan probably entailed dawning on him. There was no denying the clones behind the attacks were a clear and present menace to the colony, and right now, it was looking more and more like breaking the rules would be the only way to get things done.

"It's better than nothing," Rati said after a conflicted moment of internal debate, followed by a look at his lifemate's ready-to-go expression. "I think we can keep you posted."

TEN

"I'm thinking this puts a hitch in our plans, cousin?" The entire crew was now staring at the holoprojector on the table in the center of the *Shadow Star* observation lounge as the schematic showed the mass of police forces spreading out through Tophanavar's main spaceport, along with the contingent of Alliance border forces, which had arrived mere minutes ago. The blue dots moved around the map, almost mechanical in their precision. Rati, who, with his lifemate, had joined the retinue soon after their episode with the Doctor clone, glanced at Xerx, who stood beside Paige, both their eyes fixated on the holographic display slowly rotating in front of them. Neither of them seemed pleased.

"Maybe not," Xerx said, "but it's gonna make things a lot dicier."

"It's lucky you're in my company then," Paige said.

"Chatter on the public bands is giving some bullshit about a suspected outbreak of Columban Ebola," Pip announced from her seat. "I've tapped the military bands, but they're silent. Like they know someone might be listening."

"The nosey one is right," Rinkya said. "They're using a quarantine as an excuse to keep the place locked down."

Alexa gave a snort. "Columban Ebola, though? That shit would rip through a colony's environmental systems as soon as they opened the doors."

"Any orbital colony with decon protocols that wouldn't prevent an outbreak in a spaceport ought to be shut down," Paige chimed in with a look of disgust. "You'd think they would have been a bit more creative than that. C.E. is nasty, but there's easy treatment for it these days."

Xerx rubbed his chin. Pip was right; this was indeed bullshit. It was standard procedure for ship medics to submit logs of any treatments for infections upon arrival, and any ship carrying a potential pandemic was immediately quarantined in orbit. Orbital colony guidelines about this were doubly stringent for obvious reasons.

At that moment, the entrance doors parted, and Sarah sauntered in carrying a plate of reconstituted sushi in her hand, cheeks full of the food she had already been scarfing down on her way back. She paused and eyed the two Felyan officers as if for the first time, then swallowed the mass of food in her mouth in a manner that would have been severely uncomfortable for any other human, if not deadly.

"Hey," she said to Rati. "Why exactly aren't you out there with them?"

"We're off duty," Rinkya said, answering for her lifemate, who had been too busy fixing the woman with a look of immediate dislike and suspicion to respond.

"And the ones involved now aren't just any blues; they're enforcers." Rati was unable to keep the lack of courtesy out of his voice. "Like SWAT units in the Colonies. We're not called for grunt work like that."

"We get the info; they go for the glory," Rinkya concluded. "So the brass doesn't know we've been helping you."

"I see. So bad news for you if they found out, then." Sarah gave the pair a sly look and grinned, baring her fangs. "Not that I would say anything, of course."

"No, you wouldn't." Alexa's voice cut through the room, matched with a "don't you fucking dare" expression.

"Hey, Captain!" Pip called out, drawing everyone's attention to her look of concentration, which quickly changed to dismay. "We might have a problem."

"Which is...?" Paige prompted.

"New chatter on the military lines. They say they lost contact with the shuttle pilots."

"Did she kill them?" Alexa asked, breaking the brief, confused silence that pervaded the room after Pip's announcement.

"I'm not sure," Pip answered. "Best I can figure, based on what they're saying, is that it was a commercial shuttle coming in from Bartholomew VII. They arranged to have one of their agents pilot it instead of company boys without the Doctor knowing." The diminutive tank shrugged. "Maybe she did, and killed them both?"

"Let's not assume just yet," Paige said, "but this does make things worrisome." She turned to Pip. "Any info on whether the shuttle has changed course?"

"Nope. They say it's still on approach vector. It should be landing within the hour."

"Curiouser and curiouser," Paige said under her breath, but she appeared otherwise unperturbed: a state that did not go unnoticed by Rinkya, who stood across from her. Her tail twitched with interest as she spoke.

"So does anybody here have a plan, or what?"

"Of a sort," Paige answered and crossed her arms. Her gaze shifted toward Maria, who had been standing silently at the back of the bridge with Ike, Brogan, and Miranda in such a way that it would have been easy to mistake the three for very eccentric-looking mannequins.

"Maria, sweetheart, if you wouldn't mind making a call for me, I'd appreciate it."

Maria gave Paige a smirk. "No need, Captain."

"I'm right here." A voice from behind them gave Rinkya and Rati a start. Artemis was standing there when she hadn't mere seconds ago. She stared passively at both of them.

"Excuse me, please," she said, and the pair slowly cleared her path, surprised at the softness of the pink-haired girl's voice as she stepped forward and studied the schematic before her.

"Now, I see why her sister was so good at ambushing us," Xerx muttered to Paige, whose grin was something between amusement and pride.

"I'm sure you heard the conversation, even though you weren't invited?" Paige said to the newly arrived Artemis. Her tone held an almost motherly sound of feigned reproach. Saying nothing, Artemis only grinned and nodded.

"As you can see, there's a few too many people between us and the dock," Paige explained, gesturing toward the image feeds on the holo display, showing the various Alliance patrols and police contingencies in the landing area. "Can you be a dear and solve this problem for us?"

"That's a lot of bodies," Artemis said and mirrored the captain's cross-armed stance. "How do you plan to dispose of them?"

"Woah, wait a minute!" Rati stepped forward. "No one said anything about killing anybody."

"But you consider them a threat." Artemis cocked her head to one side as a confused frown formed on her brow.

"Well, yeah but..." Rati started to stumble over his words as Artemis continued.

"I eliminate threats. Why would you keep them alive?"

Maria cleared her throat loudly, causing everyone to look her way.

"This is an exception to the rule, little one," she said to Artemis. "They present an obstacle more than a threat. Subduing them is preferable on this occasion."

After a moment, Artemis, her unblinking gaze fixed upon the massive tank, nodded slowly. "Is there any-thing else I should know?" she asked.

"Not unless anyone else has something to add," Paige said.

"Okay," Artemis said at last, once it was clear that no one else would be speaking up. In a sudden movement, she unsheathed her knives from their scabbards at her waist and flipped them around in her hand, making two silvery blurs as she headed for the exit. The doors slid open, and she was gone.

"Do we follow?" Xerx asked Paige. "Or do we let her do her business alone?"

"Oh, Zee honey, most people aren't fond of people watching them poop," Sarah remarked with a smirk; her quip earned her a gentle smack on the back of the head from her sister. Xerx snorted back a laugh.

"We'll need her to take care of the guards in the hangar," Paige said. "Then we can get started." She shifted her gaze back to Pip. "What's the ETA on the ship now?"

"She's in the glide path, best estimate thirty minutes," Pip said. Paige nodded and tapped the pistol at her thigh.

"Time to rock n' roll," The *Shadow Star* captain said as Brogan nodded and signaled to Maria, Miranda, and Ike. She then ordered Pip to dial up sickbay. "Kai, love, be sure to keep an eye on our vitals in case one of us needs the defib on our vests."

"Keeping two eyes," Kairen's voice sounded over the comm. "Good hunting."

"I'm pretty sure you'll want to let your wife know that you're about to go risk your life again," Alexa said to Xerx. At this reminder, he gave a start at the realization that he had never checked in on his comm after the kerfuffle had begun.

"Hey, see if *La Muerta* can deal with the guards by the *Reckless* too," Xerx said to Paige. He accepted a pair of pistols from Maria who passed beside him as the assembly began their trip to the hangar bay. They weren't the usual custom-made pair from his ship, but their magcels would turn anyone into a concrete outline with the same amount of efficiency. He buckled on the holsters, then checked his comm, and read the message notifications from Mobola before calling Neela, who he found was still at the hospital with Mobola and Pepper. The news that Salt had woken up and was practically good as new was at least a massive weight off his chest.

"We can go back to the ship," his wife said, "to give you support."

"I don't think the Alliance soldiers will take kindly to that." Xerx shook his head, as if she could see him. "Besides, Artemis is on the case, so that should free up Var."

"Artemis? Are we looking at a body count?"

Xerx put on his best reassuring tone. "She's under strict no-kill orders this time, I promise."

There was a significant pause before Neela spoke again, sounding defeated.

"I can't talk you out of this, can I?"

"We talked about this before, *Kipenzi*."

"I know." Xerx heard the tightness in her voice, a tone that twisted his heart. She wouldn't be happy, even if he did survive this, but she knew that there was little she could do about the situation either, and his vendetta would not be denied.

"Stay safe," she finally said.

"I will."

"Well, at least she won't kill you now," said Alexa, who appeared to have hung back to walk with him.

"She's not happy, though," Xerx said.

"Did you expect her to be?"

"Not really."

"Then she will understand."

The news of Salt's recovery had put him in far better spirits, as did Pepper's relay of the hospital staff's findings. He wasn't a doctor, but even he could have told them that the chemical they'd found him practically drenched in had been based on *riss*. He'd hung around Felyans enough to know their most common scents, after all. Nevertheless, he could now go into the fight without worrying about Salt's condition and armed with better knowledge of what the Doctor had done.

"Let's stop lagging behind," Xerx said, and he and Alexa doubled their pace to catch up with Paige, her crew, his cousins, and Sarah. He then switched his comm to the *Reckless*, knowing that Var would enjoy the reprieve from being confined to working on his significantly banged-up Gestalt.

"Var, you seen what's been going on?" Xerx said once the gruff-sounding Felyan answered on the comm.

"Been working on *Imani* most of the day," Var replied. "But I heard it broadcast on the emergency comms. Alliance military's got this place locked down and even has some guards around the ship."

"Well, Paige has Artemis coming over to rectify that," Xerx said.

"No wetworks, I hope?" Var said worriedly.

Xerx suppressed a laugh at how unnecessary death was the first reaction to the mention of Artemis' name. Not that it wasn't deserved, if half of Paige's stories about her were to be believed.

"Not this time," he replied. "Just keep on standby until I give the word. Then get ready to join the gang." He then threw Alexa a knowing look. "Bring fireworks."

"About time something exciting happened." There was a distinctive smile in the Hara'Kya Felyan's voice that made Xerx smile himself.

"See you soon, big guy. Keep your eyes open."

ELEVEN

Xerx watched the holo display from the emitter set in Paige's bionic arm, transfixed. Artemis worked quickly and efficiently at taking down her prey, and it was that efficacy that once again reminded him, much to his discomfort, about her blue-haired sister, Nemesis. He still had nightmares of that experience with her aboard his ship, even now. Artemis worked differently from her sister: quiet, deft, yet brutal. Even without killing, she treated each target with a seemingly cold indifference that left him wondering how he was ever going to fully win against the pink-haired death machine during Gestalt matches.

La Muerta indeed.

She made short work of the guards around the *Shadow Star*, sneaking behind them if she was able and taking them down with a fierce choke hold, silvery filaments of nanites emerging from her skin and blocking their mouths and nostrils in order to expedite their fall into unconsciousness, then just as quickly retreating once the deed was done. If a commanding officer called a check-in for a downed soldier, Pip did the work of making impressive voice filters to manufacture a fake response.

"That's a good way to give someone brain damage," Paige murmured after eyeing several of Artemis' takedown methods.

"She knows what she's doing, Captain," Maria said. "Artemis knows the limits of the human body; she wouldn't push beyond what suits her needs."

"You *would* know that," Ike said, speaking for the first time. Even a blow from Maria's elbow to the ribs couldn't stop his playful snicker, the spidersilk nanoweave of his tac vest softening the statuesque tank's prodigious strength.

"She makes it look like a bloody dance," Alexa remarked as she and her sister watched the holo with a disturbing level of fascination. Artemis moved like a ninja from an old Earth martial arts film as she meticulously finished her business, putting the soldiers out of commission one by one, freeing their way out of the *Shadow Star*. Next, she made equally short work of the guards around the *Reckless*.

"Done," Artemis whispered over the comm after she had finished off the last of their obstacles.

"Excellent," Paige said. "Standby." She then gave the signal for everyone to move out.

"Var, it's clear," Xerx said over the comm. "Time to lock and load."

"Way ahead of you, Captain," Var replied as the group descended the ramp from the cargo bay and into the cavernous hangar. Brogan took point with Maria while Ike and Miranda went to the rear with Alexa and Sarah. Paige and Xerx, along with his cousins, remained in the center. The two Felyans were thankfully dressed in civilian clothes and had donned hats to make them less conspicuous by their peers, though Pip had already embedded herself deep within the security system and set about erasing their images from the records.

A few yards out, Xerx caught the black and orange blur that was Var, catching up with them from the *Reckless* that sat over a hundred yards away. Running doglike on all fours across the tarmac like Hara'Kya Felyans were wont to do in a hurry, he arrived at his side, carrying two stun batons on his belt, with a pistol holstered at his back.

"Glad to finally be where the action is?" Xerx asked once Var had caught up.

"You have no idea." A toothy grin broke out on Var's long muzzle as he emitted a bark-like laugh. "I've been hunkered down in the ship's cargo bay all day doing prep work for the fight, then itemizing repair data after."

"Sorry about keeping you from the action," Xerx said. "I can just imagine you wanted to break stuff."

"Well, I did want to go with Neela and Pepper," Var said, then seemed to frown. A shudder passed across his shaggy striped fur. "Truth is, though, hospitals ... make me nervous."

"But you do much of the medical stuff on my ship," Xerx said flatly.

"Still makes me nervous," Var replied with a shrug.

"Indeed," Xerx said, an amused grin creasing the side of his face. "Well, you coulda fooled me."

"This is a break from the monotony, though," Var remarked, then rose to switch to bipedal motion. "Besides, I could do with a piece of the action."

Xerx grinned at the shaggy Felyan. "Got a point to prove, eh? I know how your kind got a bad rap after the Pup Kill incident. You know, to this day, it mystifies me why any Hara'Kya would've wanted to have anything to do with the Doctor. Even Izz couldn't figure that out."

Var snorted. "Xenophobia isn't unique to humans, Captain. There are a lot of voices among our kind that think mixing with non-Felyans is a worse crime than murder. The damned Doctor just knew how to manipulate that fear."

Along with Var's large, pawlike hand coming heavily down on his shoulder, Xerx felt an accompanying sense of satisfaction at his crewmate's solidarity, which needed no words.

"Don't worry," Var added. "I know how important this is. If I get to soften her up, I'll be sure to save the final blow for you."

With their new addition, Xerx, Paige, and their team made their way through the hangar, following the sound of falling bodies as Artemis took point and cleared a path of unconscious guards. The elevators to the landing area were still working but would be noisy.

As they discussed a strategy to infiltrate the landing bay, Pip called their attention to the security feed. Artemis was already making short work of the guards above as Paige observed the action on her holo emitter.

Dealing with the elite guards near the shuttle would prove more of a challenge. Everyone held their collective breath as one soldier that the pink-haired girl tried to sneak up on around a column caught sight of her a fraction too soon and drew his pistol with a speed that matched Xerx in full gunslinger mode. Fortunately,

Artemis was faster. She flicked the weapon out of his hands, then drew one of her own blades. For a moment, Xerx was worried that the pink-haired woman had been about to renege on her promise of no killing until he noticed how she traded blows with the soldier, landing her strikes in a manner so precise that no part of the blade touched him. That was until the soldier switched weapons, performing the action with a smoothness born of high-level military combat training. It was their saving grace that through it all, the surprise of the moment and the struggle to survive made him too busy to call for help. But the moment the guard opened his mouth to do just that, Artemis spat into it. There was no mistaking the black nanofluid. The soldier staggered back, grasping at his throat in combined shock and disgust before his eyes rolled back and he collapsed to the ground in a limp pile, as if all of his bones had been removed.

A collective sigh of relief cut the silence before Artemis moved on to the next couple of soldiers and took care of them with her usual swiftness but with much more care, keeping surprise on her side once again. Afterward, Paige gave the signal to move forward.

They took the freight elevator, which ended up being cramped, but the ride was brief. The door opened to the landing area, which was more sparsely populated with crates, leaving fewer hiding places, but Artemis had thankfully done her job clearing the way. Up ahead, their path seemed free of any complications.

"Am I the only one getting the feeling that this is too easy?" Rati said.

"You just don't know Artemis," Xerx replied. "She's damn good at her work."

"That may be, but I still feel like this is a setup," Rati said, far from placated by this.

"I'm not totally at ease either," Rinkya said. "Call it cop's intuition."

Pip's chirping voice on the comm interrupted their conversation as the team neared the maze of containers and stepped out onto the open tarmac.

"Ship's landed, Captain."

There it sat, the quarantine dry dock gantry lowering into place around it. Despite the mass of metal descending, the ship itself was unremarkable: a streamlined commercial transport, not suspicious-looking at all, contrary to the blues' misgivings. Still, even Artemis showed some caution about crossing over to the tarmac. Pip might have been controlling the cameras, but the tarmac would have left them wide open for someone on the ground to spot them.

"All right, now's our chance," Paige said. "Ike, Brogan, Maria, Miranda, you have the heaviest artillery; you're with me. Use stuns and tranqs, lethal force only when absolutely necessary. Pip can cover it up, but we don't want to overwork her. Xerx will deal with the Doctor."

"We'll need to get aboard, hopefully with you occupying her attention," Rati said. "We need to know what happened."

"Then keep close to me," Xerx said. "Var can keep you safe while you reach the ship."

"As will I," Alexa said. "Sarah, be a dear and help out Paige and her crew. Do what you're best at."

"The no-kill rule goes double for you, then," Paige said, fixing the black-haired woman with a stern look. Sarah rolled her eyes at this but assented.

"Pip, do your magic," Xerx heard Paige say over the comm. "No need to have more unwanted company drop in on us due to the camera feeds. Arty, we're going in. Back us up if we get jumped from behind."

Artemis had once again vanished, he noticed. There was little else except scattered palettes of equipment near the landing pad that she could have hidden behind, but there was no sight of her there. Nevertheless, Xerx knew she was waiting somewhere advantageous when she answered with a simple, "Yes."

The remaining guards were approaching the ship, aiming their rifles as the vessel's antigravs cycled down. It settled on the landing pad with a heavy thump that Xerx could feel through the ground. A near self-destructive thrill of anticipation bolted through him as he waited for his friend to lead the way.

The entrance hatch folded open, and at last, Paige gave the word.

"Now!"

"We run," Xerx said to his cousins, and the team made a mad dash across the tarmac for the cover of the equipment crates. "Stay close to me."

It was quite a lengthy sprint before either side would be in firing range, but the ship's engines were still cycling down, creating an ambient roar that would disguise their approach, giving them the same element of surprise that had served Artemis so well. Ten meters away, Xerx split his group off from Paige, heading toward a sizeable cluster of crates. He drew his pistols and set the accelerator to stun mode. It would slow their projectile speed, causing a hit that would feel like a strike from a two-by-four, but keep one's body intact.

"Miranda, high road," Paige barked, and the smaller of the two combat tanks broke formation. She ran like a cheetah and leaped upon a series of pipes, climbing to a natural stone overhang above an observation window one level higher. She settled in, brought her MAG sniper rifle to bear, and began adjusting the sights.

Now reaching the five-meter mark, Xerx lowered himself as he heard Paige over the comm shout "weapons free," and muffled shots rang from his left as he slid the remaining distance to the crates. Bouncing to his feet, he extended his arms above the crates, ready to join the fray if needed. Alexa slammed into the crate beside him on the left, holding a MAG pistol that looked more like a work of art than a weapon to those ignorant of her tastes in both form and function; Var arrived on the right with his cousins, all ducking below their respective cover. The Hara'Kya Felyan's clawed hands rested on the stun batons, ready for action.

Paige, however, had the situation well in hand. Their surprise tactic had worked, and most of the soldiers had been dropped before they could turn around. The others were still too slow on the draw, being hit by multiple stun-grade MAG rounds and turned into rag dolls.

Xerx glanced to his left and right, making sure the coast was clear before signaling over the comm to Paige.

"Clear on my end as well," she announced. "Pip, any more problems about?"

"Not as far as I can tell, Captain," the diminutive tank chimed in. "The golden goose is ripe for the taking."

"Stay down until I signal you," Xerx said, then turned to Alexa. "Stay with the blues. They'll need covering fire if things go tits up, and Var can help."

Alexa nodded, to Xerx's surprise. The Pirate Queen was never one to just sit around when there was action to be had. But he was thankful for her acquiescence, nonetheless. He dreaded hearing the end of it from Isibar if something happened to either of them.

"Be careful, Captain," Var said.

"Can't say I always am, but I sure as hell am gonna try this time," Xerx said before he stalked over to join Paige and her crew, still holding his pistols ready. He noticed Artemis slide down a nearby column from her hitherto unseen perch, and he could not help but be yet again impressed by that enigmatic woman's ability to improvise.

"You got eyes on things, Pip?" Paige said into her comm.

"Yeah, nothing yet," Pip said. Then a moment later, she spoke, her voice more tense than a moment ago. "Wait. We got movement in the entrance hatch."

Dr. Selene Hayashibara.

The real one this time.

Xerx had only seen her in the holos and pics that Isibar had provided, but there was no mistaking those thin, near-androgynous features. To his surprise, she hadn't changed one bit. And that surprise quickly festered into a throbbing sense of disgust. He knew that she was anything but stupid. And so it took a special kind of arrogant to have half the Colonies after your head and not bother to pop for any kind of cosmetic surgery. But then again, the clones they'd encountered here on Tophanavar had all looked like prettier, more feminine versions of her: voluptuous whereas the Doctor was basically a beanpole of near indeterminate gender. It gave him pause to wonder what the reason for them in the first place had been.

Not that it mattered now.

"You're up, Chook," Paige said, as she and her crew kept their weapons locked on her. Xerx stepped to the front, wondering if they had switched their weapons' accelerators to more lethal rounds; he hoped not. This kill was his.

The Doctor stepped out onto the first step of the ramp, her stance relaxed, her hands in the pockets of her long, white coat. She glanced over the company with a gimlet eye, but with a smirk that betrayed the rankling arrogance that Xerx had suspected.

"Well, if I knew I'd have an entourage, I would've put on makeup," the Doctor said. Even her voice, soft yet neutral, was of a sex that was impossible to determine. She set her pale blue eyes on Xerx. "Captain Xerxes Paraska, I presume? Did you arrange this little welcome party? What's the occasion?"

"Your funeral," Xerx said, taking aim. "You remember Isibar, Thane of House Paraska?"

"Oh, he's a thane now?" the Doctor said, amused in a way that suggested that she was either ignorant of her situation or gave zero fucks about it. "Things do change after a couple of decades, don't they? I still owe him for shooting me in the hand back on Icona."

"Izz wasn't aiming for your hand," Xerx said. And neither was he.

Pip's voice rang through the comm just as Xerx pulled the trigger.

"Captain, I'm getting some weird temperature readings from inside the craf—the fuck?"

Something blocked the shot. Something inhumanly fast. Something blacker than the stuff that Artemis spit out. It swatted the MAG round as if it were a fly, sending it into the cavern ceiling far above. Xerx stood, stunned to motionless silence. The Doctor hadn't moved, but her face had changed to a maniacal smile. It was a dark, disturbing thing that reminded him of pictures that he'd seen on social media boards on the StellarNet that altered pictures in slight ways, just enough to give one nightmares.

"My dear Captain," the Doctor said, as something moved behind her in the transport. It was vaguely human and easily two heads taller than her. And as if plastered on, a Cheshire cat grin spread almost literally from ear to ear on its as of yet unseen face. Nevertheless, those teeth were bright enough to stand out over its ghostly form.

"I never travel alone."

TWELVE

He wore a dark, half-cloaked suit that made him look like a dignitary from the Second Imperium, minus the ouroboros-like insignia upon the left breast. His eyes were hidden by sunglasses set upon his long nose that stood out from his ashen face, where his smile shone through with its unnerving, inhuman wideness. In fact, his form and smile were, ironically, the only "human" things about him, surpassing even the eight-limbed, enigmatic Vlissians, the encounters with which Xerx tried to severely limit. Their spiderlike way of walking, elongated heads, and mind-speech were disconcerting enough, but this … thing's … sheer alienness in spite of his human shape made even those mysterious aliens seem almost comforting by comparison.

"The hell is that?" Var said.

"Took the bloody words out of my mouth," Alexa remarked.

"Mine too," Rinkya added.

"Is he bleeding everywhere?" Xerx heard Pip say over the comm. "I can't get a clear image on any cameras."

"I call him Agent 10," the Doctor explained with unabashed pride as the man stepped around her and proceeded to march down the ramp with slow, deliberate steps. He paused only for the Doctor to plant a small kiss upon his ashen cheek, the act of which carried a sense of revulsion that seemed to reverberate among the entire team.

"I rescued him from the Imperium's ISID department," the Doctor continued, prattling on while Xerx watched, transfixed by the shadowy bleed from Agent 10's ebon body, which seemed to drag along its metal surface like a pool of slime. "You wouldn't believe the freakshow they keep in those ranks. But even they would have never allowed him to reach his full potential."

"But you have?" Xerx said.

"I have bigger and better plans," the Doctor replied with a disturbingly calm undertone. "Allow me to demonstrate."

The grinning menace began his threatening, purposeful approach, increasing his speed with every step. Paige and her crew raised their weapons. There was a bright flash followed by a deafening boom that echoed throughout the massive cavern that comprised the landing bay. Almost simultaneously, Agent 10's torso turned into black mist and a two-meter-wide crater appeared near the Doctor, covering her in tiny rocks and dust.

Xerx whipped his head about to see Miranda, perched on the upper walkway railing, high above the rest of the team. She was looking up from the sights of her MAG rifle as she retracted the bolt and chambered another of the huge sniper rounds.

"Too much chatter, not enough action," she stated over the comm, almost without emotion.

Paige and Xerx looked at each other and nodded. The woman had a point.

"Um... People, team, or whatever, that thing is rebuilding itself," Sarah said, snapping them out of their moment.

Black tendrils seemed to form from the air itself, forming veins of obsidian that ran like rivulets in reversed time, flowing into the man-shaped thing's body, coalescing into renewed body parts. The inhuman grin momentarily faded as Agent 10 closed his eyes and took in a deep breath; then he returned as nearly fully formed and resumed his approach.

Sarah and Artemis held back momentarily, Artemis seeming to assess the situation while Alexa's sister looked as if she was about to be sick. But the rest of the crew showed neither reticence nor illness, as Maria fired first. The *thump, thump* of her rifle's MAG rounds echoed in the vast cavern as they struck their target square in the chest. Magcel weapons could create a three-foot wide crater in solid concrete using only pebble-sized projectiles, but the hulking man-thing only staggered back from the successive impacts, apparently far less affected from such close-range fire than anything his size and mass ought to have been. A barely visible explosion of ink-black tendrils whipped away from his body at almost the same time as the weapons fired. Had they somehow taken the lion's share of the blow? Xerx supposed that Maria and Brogan were thinking the same thing he was, judging by their mutual slack-jawed stares.

All the while, the smile on Agent 10's face remained.

The *Shadow Star* crew's surprise only lasted a moment, and then the real fireworks began. The cavern erupted into a cacophony of sharp thunderclaps as Ike and Brogan came forward and added to Maria's firepower. They covered Maria, who switched out her MAG rifle for the plasma cannon strapped to her back.

Those shots fared marginally better. At least they caused patches of darker black to erupt on the monster's body. But even then, though his gait changed to a wincing limp, his pace did not slow down an inch, not even from the thunder-generating white-hot charges from the massive tank's BFG. Meanwhile, Paige, not one to have her crew do all the dirty work, stepped to the side, partially concealed by Ike's hefty form, taking aim with her own rifle with shots that were almost as precise as Maria's.

Another of Miranda's shots rang out. Seemingly too occupied with defending against the attacks from the others, the round struck 10 square in the head. What remained of him collapsed like a lead weight.

A cheer rose from Paige's group but was stifled quickly by the Doctor's resonant mocking laugh. They fixed her with a look of incredulous puzzlement.

"Please, continue," the Doctor said with a mocking sneer. "He learns from every engagement. You'll eventually find force ultimately futile. But I'm sure your efforts will provide him with valuable data."

As if on cue, Agent 10's body appeared to melt into a putrid black puddle as if he were dead and no more solid than ice cream left on a Pit Town rooftop at high noon. However, this puddle behaved very differently compared to a liquid. Even a shot from Maria's plasma rifle failed to cause a ripple.

Then, like someone who had a blanket suddenly thrown atop them, a shuddering form ascended from within the putrid-looking pool of black, coalescing into something that became more human-looking by the second. It ceased its groping, spastic movements as it rose to full height. The blackness then solidified into the creature's usual form and murky colors, down to his clothes, and with that disturbing smile still plastered onto his face. He then resumed his relentless ambling toward Paige and her crew as if he'd never stopped. Even Miranda's shots passed through it as though he were not there.

In fact, no ammo, conventional or otherwise, seemed to penetrate Agent 10's ironclad defense or offset its incredible regenerative power. The tendrils were a blur, swatting away the MAG rounds, and plasma bursts barely fazed him. He continued his unhurried pace, closing the gap between Paige's crew with death-like serenity and inexorability.

"Cover me!" Xerx heard Maria shout as she at last threw down the plasma gun. She unsheathed her machete-like blade and charged forward, bellowing out a war cry that resonated over even the gunfire. Ike stayed with Paige while Brogan broke ranks and followed Maria into the fray, his own Bowie knives in hand.

It was then that Sarah seemed to snap out of it.

"No! Don't!" she screamed and pushed past the *Shadow Star* crew, charging toward Maria.

"The bloody hell is she doing?" Alexa said. Xerx glanced the Pirate Queen's way and saw her taking aim with her pistols, trying to distract the monster. Over her own gunfire, he heard her say something about killing herself and going after her if her sister ended up dead. In the midst of it all, Xerx stole a quick glance back to the ship's entry port, where his heart instantly clogged in his throat.

The Doctor was making a run for it, in the opposite direction.

"The fuck you are!" he growled and immediately signaled to his cousins and Var. There was sufficient distance between his group and Paige, so he took his chance, leading the pack.

He leaped over the crates like a parkour runner on stims and, after one furtive glance behind him to make sure everyone was following, raced across the remainder of the tarmac to the shuttle. Var ran on all fours, close beside them on one side, while Alexa was on the other. Fortunately for them, it seemed as though the monster that the Doctor had unleashed was busy enough with Paige and her crew to not notice his half of the team, and he shepherded Rinkya and Rati in safely.

"I'll watch over them," Alexa said. "You go after your mark."

Xerx nodded and turned in the Doctor's direction—

—Only to nearly jump out of his skin as Maria slammed into the hull of the shuttle. She was nearly an inch from crushing him with the dent she made. Frozen with the shock of it all, Xerx could only watch as she groaned and slumped to the ground. There were black marks on her wrist as if something searing hot had tried to grab her. There was no blood, but he had never seen a wound that bled black.

A scream resounded in the cavern, and Xerx turned toward the fray just in time to see Agent 10 grab Brogan by the wrist and throat, holding his knife aloft, the same unnerving smile on his face. Smoke seemed to arise from the points of contact with the monster's hands. But a second later, he tossed the man, made of just as much metal and flesh, like he was no more substantial than an old moth-eaten blanket. Brogan was launched into the air, then carelessly left to fall full force into the ground.

"Xerxes Paraska, get off your arse and go!" Alexa's stentorian command shook Xerx from his moment of terror. The last thing he saw was Sarah as well as Artemis charging Agent 10 with the same amount of perhaps suicidal alacrity as Brogan and Maria had done. He couldn't imagine those two would fare any better, but there was nothing he could do to help them now, and so he ran full tilt in the Doctor's direction, going after the one factor he could eliminate.

There was only one way she could have gone, he surmised. The landing bay was large enough to accommodate military cruisers, but the human-sized exits that weren't massive elevators that brought parked ships to the docking area and back were few. The only other smaller exit was the one across from the bow of the shuttle, between two of the docking elevators in the distance. But he could see neither hide nor hair of her, and there were no crates that provided convenient hiding places as they did for his team.

He stalked away from the fray, taking only a moment to glance back once to find Artemis and Sarah now in the mix. Sarah was now in a full grappling match with the monster, attempting to push him back. Her contact with him seemed to be going over better than it had for Brogan and Maria. Despite her being half the combat tank's size, Agent 10 seemed to be unable to gain the leverage needed to throw her, and she appeared unharmed. But things in the struggle had nonetheless become ... weird. At their points of contact, where Sarah's hands were squeezing Agent 10's wrists, the air seemed to shimmer, as if it were under some kind of intense heat. Was he burning her hands? Sarah's face was a painful rictus as if this were true, but he saw nothing remotely like smoke.

The fight was cut off, however, when Artemis slid in from below and rounded Agent 10's back, slipping a knife into him. But that was the extent of what Xerx saw of it all as he turned around, shuddering only momentarily as ... Was it the monster? ... let out a scream just as inhuman as it seemed to be. Rather, it was like a chorus of screams running through a degraded StellarNet conference connection. It broke his concentration enough to forget his goal. But an outside force brought him quickly back into the present.

It was like he had been bitten by a very large bug, the shock of which crackled across his spine for one split second of pure agony. His body stiffened; his vision blurred, then cleared... and he saw the Doctor descend from the dorsal area of the shuttle, taking his momentary shock to make her escape, exactly where he thought she would. Xerx's confusion was replaced with fury and laser-focused pure willpower as he once again broke into a flat-out run, determined to overtake her. He slipped his knife from its scabbard, ready to make the killing blow the second he was within reach. The Doctor was nowhere near as fast as he was, nor did she seem to make a full effort to attempt evading him. She had a head start, but he was closing the gap.

Death is coming for her, Xerx thought. *Does she not even care?*

Is she laughing?

And what is that device she's holding up?

A shrill whine rattled his eardrums.

Then came an explosion that obliterated all sensation, and at the exact same time, bathed him in the most unbearably ecstatic bliss in human experience. Transcendent and incomprehensible, it slammed outward, firing like a rush of blood into his every limb.

Xerx heaved a shuddering gasp, nearly thrown outside of himself, barely aware of tripping over his own feet onto the tarmac. If there had been any pain, he was beyond oblivious to it, burned from within and without instead by raw, ungodly levels of scintillating pleasure. No words could describe what was happening to him; even his most sublime moments of intimate release with Neela could not compare to what surged through his every neuron, bringing him to levels of ecstasy that bordered on pain... and then crossed over.

He screamed.

And screamed.

And then it was over.

Alexa had smelled that chemical before the blues had gone inside with Var. She stood inside the hatch, out of line of sight of that aberration that the Doctor had set loose and was determined to stay there for as long as she could to protect the three Felyans inside the shuttle. For the first few moments, she had been content to wait where she was and save her ammo, but after Maria was slammed against the hull of the shuttle like a rag doll, she broke her position, leaping down from the ramp to her side. She noticed that she was still moving, though clearly in pain.

"Are you all right?" she asked the giant woman.

"I ... will be," she said, her voice a strained wheeze as she attempted to sit up.

"I have nanomeds," Alexa said.

"Already full of them, hon." Gritting her teeth, she gripped her shoulder and pulled. Alexa heard a sickening pop before Maria finally rose to her feet. Her weapon lay on the tarmac beside her, and she picked it up before running back into the fray. Ike was already helping Brogan to his feet, but she noticed that Sarah had joined in the fight and was actually holding her own against this Agent 10 better than Paige's biggest and battle-ready mercs. Relieved that she wouldn't have to give up her position just yet, she returned to the shuttle entrance, watching as her sister, who had shaken off whatever headache she'd been stricken with earlier, go after that ebony nightmare as if he were a pork chop. As much as she wanted to help her out, or at least provide a distraction, she felt that she'd be more of a liability right now.

"Whatever it is you're doing in there, make it quick," she shouted to the trio inside the shuttle. She didn't think it was a good idea to stick around where that thing on the tarmac could come back at any moment.

And then she heard Xerx scream.

THIRTEEN

Xerx remembered things, but only in a haze of agony and bliss encircling each other in an eternal dance, like the symbols of yin and yang. He was no Boy Scout; he'd tried various drugs that went in and out of style back in Pit Town in his wilder past, but he never suspected that there was a way to make torture out of pleasure.

The torment blessedly ended when he saw Alexa standing over him and felt the prick at his neck that finally turned the pleasure-pain into mere echoes: sparks of primrose bliss that fired intermittently in the back of his mind. His body was a lead weight and...

"Yeah, his pants are fucked. I'd burn them if I were you, honey."

The Pirate Queen's words bubbled up as if from beneath the ocean as he rose to consciousness.

"Agreed. There's no way I am letting him keep these. Even a molecular rinse wouldn't get the stains out."

That voice, the voice of his wife, was more surprising, but far from unwelcome. It jarred him more fully to consciousness, where he noticed the very prominent breeze upon the lower half of his body, ultimately explained by the significant lack of clothing there. His eyes fluttered open into subdued light, and blurry images coalesced into Neela, who was unsealing a vacuum storage pack containing a fresh pair of pants and shaking the creases out of them.

"At least this way, he won't have to go around getting revenge in his boxers."

He heard someone snicker in the background.

"They were my best fitting pair too," Xerx groaned in response, sitting up. As he expected, a white towel was wrapped around his waist, preserving his dignity, yet leaving his legs and feet bare in the unfamiliar bed.

"Oh, good. You're awake, then," Alexa said brightly, her voice much clearer now as images coalesced from indiscriminate blurs. "How do you feel?"

"You remember that time you brought me to that pleasure house on King's Knight and paid for an all-nighter?" he asked as Neela sat at the foot of the bed, opposite where Alexa stood, arms crossed. She wore a bemused expression while his wife tossed him the now clean and fresh-smelling pants and underwear, then gestured toward his boots and holstered weapons on the table to his left. He set to getting dressed, shifting his gaze from Alexa to his wife, then to Sarah, who was sitting in a chair in the corner, legs crossed. There was a visible level of tension in the air, suggesting that things were far from over. He was in an unfamiliar room that had the unnaturally clean smell and generic dressings of a hotel, though the long-diminished bite of riss could be detected very faintly in the background. Alexa was there with him, as was Sarah, looking anxious in a way that would probably have triggered his fight-or-flight instincts had he not known her better.

"I thought you said you didn't remember that night?" Alexa said.

"*You* don't remember that night." Xerx shook his head, making a humorless snort. "I just said I didn't to spare you any embarrassment. Those girls were ... well, good; You didn't notice how I couldn't walk straight for a couple of days after?"

"And when was this?" Neela asked. Her tone was curious but held a warning undertone of suspicion. Xerx smiled, letting his posture show her that there was no need to worry.

"Long before us, *Kidege*," he assured her.

"Just what did that bitch do to you anyway?" Neela said.

"Oh, that's right; things were in quite a bit of a rush up until now," Alexa said, digging into her pocket. She fished out and then held up a tiny device between the claws of her index finger and thumb. It was barely visible, the size of a ball bearing, and partly covered in blood.

"It looks like a chip of some kind," Alexa said to Xerx. "It shorted out the moment I plucked it from your skin."

Xerx couldn't help but smile in spite of himself.

"I didn't believe Izz when he told me about it," he said, receiving the tiny device and inspecting it himself. For something that had made hell out of heaven, it seemed almost insignificant. "He told me that the Doctor had implanted some kind of torture device in him back on Icona, but instead of using pain, it uses pleasure—" Absently, he shuddered, and his hand went to the back of his neck, rubbing at the patch of gauze he found there. Reflexively, his eyes watered at the memory of that ungodly bliss "—to the point where it overloads you. Something about her preferring pleasure over pain when getting answers from people." He frowned at the Doctor's damnable device. "So this means that I was out of the fight for ... how long? And where the hell are we, anyway? I'm guessing this isn't a hospital."

"At the Purring Princess," Alexa said, mentioning the bar/love hotel where they'd discovered Salt after his run-in with a Doctor clone. "Salt's new girlfriend let us use a couple of the rooms out back. I'll pay them generously for their hospitality, of course."

"I think I'm missing a piece here," Xerx said, now more than a little confused. "This was all after the fight at the spaceport? Did we win? And if not, how'd we get away?" He paused, then added, "Wait, Salt's got a girlfriend?"

"No to the first question," Alexa said. "As for the second, it was your crew's resident techie. It seems she did something that Pip said was—"

"Really stupid and ballsy at the same time," Pip's voice popped in on the comm at Alexa's wrist. A moment later, the holo console at the table at the room's far end sprang to life, revealing Mobola, a look of momentary uncertainty on her face.

"Are they ready?" Neela said, speaking to Mobola, who nodded.

"They're all waiting," the timid-looking girl said. She glanced anxiously at Xerx, who grinned her way, and a look of relief crossed her face.

"She took over the emergency service channels briefly and redirected the shuttle car systems, then procured us a couple rides out of there before we got our collective arses kicked," Alexa explained. "And as for Salt's girlfriend, he'll have to explain that to you."

"Hey, *I* was gonna explain how I helped you get away!" Pip snapped. Alexa shrugged, grinning cheekily.

"And what happened to Agent Freak?" Xerx said.

"Turned into black mush and poured himself down a drain," Pip said. "Captain's got me trying to track him down. Good thing your cousins made it out of the shuttle when they did."

"Why's that?" Xerx sat bolt upright, a sudden coldness going down his spine at the prospect of Rinkya or Rati getting hurt on his account. He then turned to Neela. "Are they okay? And what was all that about people waiting?"

"I didn't know they were still in the ship," Mobola admitted, her voice small.

"I keep telling her she couldn't have possibly known, but she keeps beating herself up about it," Alexa said, resting herself at the foot of the bed. "But so you don't get your knickers in a twist, they caught up with us just in time; all is well."

"Blues swarmed the spaceport after Squeak got out of the network," Sarah said, speaking up for the first time. "They shouldn't find anything, but we'll need to lay low for a bit." A sarcastic grin broke out on the side of her face. "Welcome to my world."

"Damn... I missed a lot," Xerx said, pushing back the burgeoning frustration that niggled at the back of his skull.

"Well, yes and no," Neela said. "Everyone's fine; Pepper and Mobola did a coffee shop crawl to stay out of anyone's way while she helped Pip with the spaceport systems, and we raised a little hell at the hospital and got Salt released a day early. He's in the room next door with Var waiting on news about you. And Paige and her crew are in the bar area making plans. Mobola's there now, with Pepper."

"And Rinkya and Rati?" Xerx asked.

"They went back to the precinct," Alexa replied in a placating tone, noticing the anxiousness in Xerx's question. "They slipped Mobola the info we needed from their standalone mainframe; now they're back with us."

"So, what's the next step? We got a plan to handle the dastardly duo?"

"That leads us to what Mobola said about everyone being ready," Neela remarked, standing up and pulling Xerx to his feet. "You and Paige now have a much better plan of attack, thanks to our cousins, the hows and whys of which you are about to find out." Alexa and Sarah followed as she led the way to the exit door. "Come on, *Kidege*. We'll get Salt and Var and then finish this bug hunt."

Salt was a sight for sore eyes to Xerx as they filed out of their separate room and passed through the back rooms into the bar. He greeted him with a bear hug that Var would have been proud of.

"Feeling ready to kick ass?" Xerx said, as Alexa and his wife led them along.

"I'm about ready to kill the bitch," Salt replied

Var grinned. "Well, now you have someone to take your anger out on."

"I'm still gonna need your help with this," Xerx said. "She already caught me with my pants down."

"How very apropos," Var said, with he and Salt sharing a very knowing snicker.

"I'm never going to live this down, am I?" Xerx asked once the double entendre sank in.

"Eventually, all things pass," Var said. "Though this will most likely pass like a kidney stone."

Xerx sighed. "If I give you one of my sidearms, would you just kill me now?" he said to Salt, who laughed all the more as Alexa and Neela brought them to the connected tables where Paige and her crew sat. A surprising addition to the retinue was the diminutive form of Pip leaning back a on chair with her feet on the table. Xerx noted what looked like a crown of aerials and a series of hexagonal processor units linked across her cranial ports like a mechanical web. Mobola, still looking as anxious as ever, sat nearby with Pepper.

"See? I told you he'd be okay," Kairen said. Xerx noticed the handsome man in the holo give Paige a smug grin. "You owe me now."

Xerx stepped up to the table and narrowed his eyes at the assembly, gesturing from Ike to Paige.

"Please don't tell me you guys were running a betting pool over whether I'd pull through," he said to the *Shadow Star* captain, who silently shrugged. Only a facetiously innocent grin remained on her face as everyone else cast her a series of unreadable expressions.

"Okay, I won't," she finally said and gestured to the empty seats in front of her. Xerx, rolling his eyes, took his seat. Neela seated herself at his right side and Salt at his left while Var remained standing, leaning upon a nearby column. Alexa dragged a nearby stool over and perched herself behind Sarah, whom Xerx noticed remained distant from the group but clearly within earshot.

A moment later, an orange-furred female Re'Kya Felyan approached, carrying a jug of beer and several glasses on a tray, setting it down on the table in front of everyone. She smiled sweetly at Salt, and he returned the expression, looking just a bit flustered as she took her leave.

Salt's erstwhile girlfriend? Xerx thought, suppressing a grin. It was too bad that there were more pressing matters than joking with Salt about the situation. But there would be plenty of time for that later.

"I guess she's the one we have to thank for the accommodations while I was in la-la land?" he asked instead.

"And the free drinks," Brogan added, lifting up his own bottle of lager before taking a hefty swallow. Paige, at the sight of this, fixed her crewmate with a frown.

"Go easy on the drink, Jay," she warned. "There's a fine line between accepting hospitality and taking the piss." Then seeing everyone assembled, she straightened up and began.

"Well, it's good to see we all came out of that shitstorm alive. But never start what you can't finish, it seems. Our target turned out to be better prepared than we thought, but by sheer fortune, we may have a solution." She then nodded toward Pip, who didn't respond for a moment until Brogan kicked her feet off the table and she toppled forward. Quickly, she straightened herself up and spoke.

"Okay, so while you were all dancing with the monster, it occurred to me that I had some serious hardware at my disposal, so I fired up the *Shadow Star* sensor suite and ran a scan of the quarantine zone, right?"

"Wait a minute," Var suddenly straightened and waved his hands. "You ran an active scan with ship sensors in the dock? Are you *nuts*? You could've fried any organic matter within a hundred meters!"

Pip stared up at Var, taken aback at the Felyan's reaction. Xerx felt like the tank's black eyes were going to laser a hole in his crewman.

"It's not like anyone was nearby, and, besides, the rock between levels would've absorbed the worst of it," she said, as if it were the most prosaically common knowledge in the universe.

Var opened his mouth to reply, but Xerx silenced him with a motion of his hand.

"Yeah, but I wouldn't rate my chances of having kids in the near future," he heard him mutter in spite of everything.

"As I was saying..." Pip began, then pointedly eyed the rest of the room. When no one else deigned to interrupt, she continued. "The scan threw me a curve. It picked up a match from the sensor log archives." She paused, giving a slight shrug. "Well, *almost* a match. Check this out."

A hologram of the most disturbingly unnatural-looking thing that Xerx had ever seen now hung in the midst of the attendant hologram members. It was something that he thought would be the result if a crab, a monster truck, and kudzu vines had produced offspring with construction equipment, and that offspring emphasized the "monster."

"These things infested a region of forests in the Knives of Blair some nineteen years ago," Pip explained. "They were a near-perfect blend of organic and mechanical. It took a whole bunch of processor power to break it down to molecular level and learn how to kill them permanently before they could multiply enough to overrun the whole planet's ecosystem."

Paige took over from Pip and continued the story. "As it was, we managed to synthesize a nano-compound that broke down the bonds between biomechanical interface nodes inside their circulatory systems."

"I get the feeling it's not that simple with the Doctor's pet monster?" Xerx said, leaning forward still studying the hologram.

"Bingo," Pip replied and brought up a hologram of Agent 10 in all his ebon glory. "This fella is a far more complex construct. Our compound might at best slow him down, but after seeing how we got our shit rocked, I'm pretty sure he's got adaptive systems, so it wouldn't be effective for very long."

Xerx sighed and leaned back in his chair. "So, we can't hurt him, and we can't slow him down in any effective way. Well, I guess we'll try harsh language, then? Maybe if we hurt his self-esteem, he'll just give up and let us take down Hayashibara and her clones?

"Oh, I didn't say it was *impossible*," Pip said with a knowing grin spreading across her face. "The scan revealed an ace-in-the-hole: someone else is also running this tech, but on our side!"

"What? Here, now in this room?" Xerx was incredulous. "Who would be running such advanced tech and keep it quiet, especially when it could benefit the team immensely?"

Pip opened her mouth to spout her big reveal when Sarah cleared her throat and raised her hand.

"Let me save you the trouble, tiny one," she said. "It's me."

"So, you're carrying a weapon or some sort of device?" Xerx asked, turning to Sarah. "Why hide it?"

Sarah rolled her eyes and sighed. "No, Xerxes, my dear dimwitted in-law. I *am* the weapon. My body's composed of the same tech. Damn fool of a father never truly knew what he was messing with when he created me."

Alexa shot Sarah a sour look, but Sarah just gave her a sarcastic smile.

"But to cut to the chase, what our diminutive friend over there was about to say is, *I* can hurt him."

Pip nodded, and Sarah now had everyone's undivided attention. They glanced at each other, exchanging looks of unfettered surprise, then fixed their respective gazes back onto her.

"Tore a chunk out of him with my teeth as I fought him," Sarah explained. "The wound remained for some time and didn't heal right away. In fact," she approached the table and placed her hands gently on the surface, "I believe I can kill him."

"So why didn't you finish him off while you had that advantage?" Xerx asked.

"Agent 10 doesn't lack for strength and has a significant weight advantage," Sarah explained with some chagrin. "Whilst it did minimal harm, I received an impromptu flying lesson from him—into a concrete wall." Her tone then lowered to something menacing as she cracked her knuckles and flexed her fingers. "I'd certainly be up for a rematch, though."

"Oh, you'll get your chance," Paige assured her, and Pip went on to finish her explanation, taking a thoughtful pose as her brow furrowed.

"So, now that we have a ballpark signature to work with, I've been able to tune the colony's security scanners to detect it, and minutes ago we got a ping." With a satisfied grin, she leaned back and placed her hands behind her head. "We found the bastard."

"*Think* we found him," Mobola corrected.

"Oh, no, he's there," Pip replied with conviction as Mobola fiddled with a hologram at her wrist. Her eyes suddenly widened.

"And ... he's moving."

"Moving?" Pip said.

Xerx suppressed a snicker, finding it amusing that his own wunderkind had surprised the eternally competent and cocky tech tank.

"You didn't check the most recent updates," Mobola said. "I've been tracking them." She made a gesture, and Pip's eyes widened.

"Hey, the clones are moving too!"

"The Doctor's clones?" Xerx asked.

"Ah, yeah," Pip said, sounding slightly awkward after Mobola caught her with her mental pants down.

She then spoke to Mobola. "Keep track of this for me for a sec."

Paige motioned to Rinkya and Rati. "This might be a good moment to discuss what you both found aboard the shuttle."

Rinkya seemed distracted while Rati spoke.

"I'll never forget what we saw aboard that damn thing," Xerx's cousin said. "It was like they'd all gone feral and then just dropped where they were. People looked like they'd been clawing at each other like animals; some had a frenzied look etched into their faces—for those who still had faces." He hissed in disgust and dismay. "Rinkya and I are gonna see that in our nightmares."

After taking a moment to compose himself, he continued. "We found a biochip left in a piece of luggage just as we had to bug out. We dropped by the precinct and had one of our own techies run it ... off the record."

He shook his head, rubbing at the bridge of his nose, a faint shake in his body.

"It was like a psychopath's grocery list. Creator only knows why she kept it, but I guess even psychos have to keep itineraries. It had schematics of the colony's water reclamation system with dissemination points marked off. I've seen these before; they're where the colony's planners marked off points for distributing waterborne antibiotics or recombinant nanotech in the case of a pandemic."

"Shit..." Xerx drawled. "She's going to contaminate the colony with that fucked-up *riss*."

"You know what this sounds like, *Kipenzi*?" Neela asked.

"Product demonstration," Xerx grimly replied. "But for whom?"

"That's the million-dollar question, isn't it?" Paige said. "We figured she'd be working for someone else. But good luck trying to figure that out."

"Based on what little we know about her, Hayashibara was never exactly the type to do something without an end goal at the heart of it, but to execute a plan on this scale, she's looking to hook a big underworld fish."

"Or maybe she's already hooked that fish," Paige added grimly.

"We'll have to stick a pin in that for now," Xerx said. "For now, let's focus on what we can fix." He then shifted his gaze back to Rati. "Got anything else for us?"

"Until now, she was testing individuals," Rati said, nodding. "It makes sense that her clones would've been keeping it on the low."

"And sending her data the entire time through their link," Sarah added.

"No chance you could figure out who it was going to?" Xerx said.

"If you're trying to figure out her client, then no," Sarah said. "They were all in communication with the real Doctor. So I'm guessing she was transmitting the data from her end using conventional means. The link was just to get it off-colony without it being traced."

"Sneaky bitch," Paige murmured.

Xerx slipped his pistol out of its holster, curling his lip with a grin of determination. "So we know what she's doing here; now all I need to know is where she is. She owed Izz; now she owes me."

"That's the easy part," Rati said as Pip made a broad gesticulation. Instantly, a highly detailed image appeared above the table, unfurling into a blueprint-style model of Tophanavar, resembling an upside-down pyramid. The colony's terraced levels were furrowed with a network of caverns running behind and beneath the habitat levels.

"Extensive work was done on this asteroid as the colony was being built, using Felyan and human engineering," Pip explained as the image zeroed in on an area beneath the reservoir at the bottom of the colony, "especially within the air and water circulation, utilizing artificial gravity wells. I've also pinpointed the dissemination points from the data we retrieved."

"So how do we get down there?" Xerx asked. "Those gates are most likely coded to maintenance workers."

"Not a problem," Mobola said and betrayed her own grin of pride. "I did a little backdoor work."

"With my help, of course," Pip added, not to be outdone. "We added your fingerprints and DNA profiles to the gate panels. As of today, you're part of the roster."

"We'll set about hunting the Doctor then," Xerx said and turned toward his cousins. "Here's hoping you can keep her pet occupied so that we can engage her swiftly."

"It's all a matter of when and where," Rati said

"Oh, hello there!" Pip immediately came to life and began to manipulate the hologram before her. Moments later, a blinking yellow icon showed a location only a few streets away on the same level. "Our boy is causing quite the ruckus in a nightclub a few blocks away."

"Distracting the blues," Rinkya said.

"And calling us out," Paige inferred as Neela shrugged.

"A trap is only a trap if you don't know it's there," she said.

"Well, then, I was hoping today would give us an opening before it ended," Xerx said, then holstered his gun. He was certain there was a predatory grin on his face, comparable to what had just now appeared on the faces of Paige and Sarah. "I was not disappointed."

FOURTEEN

Xerx, along with Neela, Salt, Pepper, Var, Alexa, and his cousins composed the group that would infiltrate the tunnels, while the *Shadow Star* crew would go with Sarah after Agent 10. With the plan in motion, they started off, leaving Mobola behind to work with Pip on the tech side of things. There was a hitch in the plans, however. Xerx should have expected it.

"What's up, Squeak?" Brogan said, being the first to pause when Pip called everyone to a halt.

"Something's wrong," the diminutive tank replied, rushing through an impossibly fast series of holos surrounding her. "I can't … I mean, there's no way to access the water system from the colony's network. I've tried everything that even resembles a backdoor subroutine, but I get nothing. All systems in the tunnels seem to be networked entirely separate from the colony, encrypted from real-world access points in the entrance hatch controls." She looked up at Xerx and his group, who, aside from Mobola, held blank stares.

"Now that's some seriously paranoid security," Brogan humorlessly remarked.

"It means that this is gonna take both of us to access it," Pip explained. "We're gonna have to be on-site in order to patch a micro-terminal to my rig and then either stop the dissemination of the chemical or flush the system if the Doctor succeeds." She shook her head. "It's the most bass-ackward thing I've ever seen."

Xerx held up a hand. "Wait a minute," he said. "You said 'both of us,' as in..."

All eyes immediately fell on Mobola, who, once the realization hit, suddenly looked as though she were on the edge of nausea, combined with a full-on panic attack.

"M-me?" she squeaked. "No ... please! I can't—"

"You're gonna have to," Pip said. "You're the only other one here who can access the systems the same way I can."

"But I'm ... I mean I'm not..." Mobola bit her lip, with shame mixing into her prior look of absolute terror. Pepper made a move to step forward, but Xerx was quicker.

"Don't frighten her more," Neela warned, seeing the swiftness with which Xerx rounded the table and stepped up to Mobola, while she pressed up harder against the column she stood against.

"We don't have fucking time for this," he muttered under his breath. But his expression softened as he came to stand before the shorter girl. She jumped as he put his hand on her shoulder, but overall, it didn't seem to make her any more or less afraid.

"Mobola, look at me," he said, his voice stern, but soft and not unkind.

"I know this is … less than optimal for us all. You're like Pip. You work in the background. But sometimes, in a scrape, you sometimes have to jump into the fire just like us. And do you think for a moment that any of us would leave you alone in a dangerous situation?"

"Captain Cockerel is right, you know," Pip's voice rang out, tangling the tension of the moment like a fly suddenly caught in a web. "You can do this. And you know why? 'Cause I goddamn need you as well. We're talking about bridging and controlling two separate networks in real time. I can do a lot of things, but that's a heavy data load, even for me!"

Xerx paused, staring at the tiny tank with as blank a stare as Mobola.

"Yeah, I said it," Pip said, her bravado not abating. "Pip Williams said it! I can't do this by myself." She then threw several MMA-style punches into the air in rapid succession, in spite of the grav sling she wore. "And who better than myself to keep those clones off your back, huh?"

"But … your arm…" Mobola said, pointing toward her friend's injured limb.

"Hey, don't ruin the moment, Mobo," Pip said flatly. Nevertheless, she rubbed at her arm, clearly regretting having thrown those punches moments before.

Another moment of staring passed… then Mobola snickered. A smile returned to her face, albeit faint. But for Xerx, that was enough. He stood back, removing his hand from his crewmate's shoulder. She seemed to tremble less, and her gaze shifted to the floor as she held herself. Tears, however, still flowed down her cheeks.

"So, can we count on you?" Xerx asked.

Mobola squeezed her eyes shut. Despite being somewhat more at ease, it seemed as though she was attempting to steady her trembling and stanch her tears by sheer force of will. Her answer, at last, came as a whisper, but with no lack of resignation.

"Yes, Captain."

Well, that's one crisis averted, Xerx thought, exhaling as a rare sense of relief flooded him. He then cast his gaze over his crew and stopped at Rinkya and Rati.

"Last chance to get out of this," he said. Both hybrids shook their heads, their unmoving tails broadcasting their determination as clear as the expression on their faces.

"We started investigating this, and we're gonna see it to the end, even if it's off the record," Rati said.

"Both of us," Rinkya added, curling her tail about her lifemate's.

So much for any hope that they would back out, he thought.

"Then we'd better rock and roll," he said. "These clones aren't going to kill themselves."

"We should be so lucky," Pip said with a laugh.

"Another nightclub, another shitshow," Paige said to the holo of Kairen. She slowed and brought her R8 to a halt. Not far behind, the rest of the team pulled up in their carcharadont-armored transport and disembarked.

It was still a full two blocks away from the incident, which was as far as the lines could go with the police blockade, and in the eternal twilight of the canopied district, they could see the flashing of lights from the blues' transports in the distance, reflected off the buildings.

"You say that as if it's unusual," Kairen answered dryly.

"Hey, quit clogging up the line!" Pip's voice broke into the conversation while her holo appeared beside Kairen's, distorting the former momentarily. Paige fought back the twinge of annoyance as she'd told her before to not intrude on private comms. "We've got work to do!"

"Just don't give me too many bumps and bruises to work with when you guys get back," Kairen replied, unperturbed by the interruption. In fact, he ignored the diminutive tank as if she were a gnat.

"I make no promises," was Paige's playful, but earnest, reply. "See you on the other side."

"I'll keep things warm for you," Kairen said in a voice full of promise before he ended the connection. As he brushed the fall of his blonde hair back, Paige grinned. She enjoyed their banter; Kairen had been a surprisingly good influence on her. She'd become a little reckless, giving little care if she lived or died. His presence had changed that, and she often looked forward to his touch after completing a mission—this time more than ever. Besides, she did owe him for being there for her during that funk on the way to the colony.

"Okay, now that he's gone, can we get to planning?" Pip asked, assuming an impatient posture.

"We talked about this before, you know," Paige warned.

"Yes, but this is important," Pip replied, undaunted.

"So, spill it then," Paige said as she routed their conversation to her team's comms. "What have you got?"

"First of all, this is the last bit of live data that I'll be able to give you until we're done on our end," Pip explained. "Good news is, though, we lucked out. Our boy is making such a big splash that the blues had to break ranks along sections of the blockade. Lots of property damage; stores gutted, vehicles thrown around, even a few deaths from those who were too stupid to bug out when it all went down."

A grid holo of the district spread out across the dashboard, with police bio-monitor signals indicated in glowing blue, and their target in a neon red, moving across several streets. Blues were attempting to engage, but the way some of the blue markers vanished made her suspect that they were having very poor luck. A yellow arrow wound through the streets that composed the most direct route to the objective through the areas where police were absent.

"You'll be able to slip through along that route," Pip said. "It'll be hard for Miranda to get eyes in the sky, though, as most buildings here are connected to the canopy and don't have rooftops."

Paige opened the door and stepped out of the car. "I'm sure she'll find a way, as usual."

Seeing Miranda looking her way, she nodded and charged on ahead. She watched as the mostly silent sister of her tank trio jumped between two buildings in the distance and landed atop a turret protruding from an old-Earth-style building, where she waited for them to catch up, pointing the way.

"Fucking ninja, that one," Brogan commented as he handed Paige her twin blades that he'd been sharpening and which she subsequently sheathed across her back. Ike threw her a MAG rifle, which she cocked and checked the sights of. The plan was set in motion as they closed in on the sounds of the commotion and flashing lights from the blues' personnel carriers. Maria, Ike, and Brogan took point while Sarah hung back. She would be using their suppression fire to distract the monster while she got a hold on it.

"Thanks for showing us the way," Paige said to Pip. "Hopefully, we'll have the situation in hand."

"No problem, boss," Pip said. "See you on the other side. Oh, one last thing. I think you've already noticed he's making a beeline for you."

As if on cue, the red marker broke away from the knot of blue marks on the holo map. Paige patched it through to her bionic eye, which projected it in a heads-up display to the upper right of her field of vision. Just as the diminutive tank had said, their quarry was coming their way, passing through buildings as if he were made of air.

"Well, that didn't take long," she said, squeezing her grip on her pistol and drawing her blade. She halted her approach and called the same for everyone. She glanced at Sarah, their canary in the coal mine/attack dog, whose jaw was set in a grimace of pain, the same as it had been at the kerfuffle in the spaceport. She'd torn a chunk out of him like he was a pork chop before; hopefully, she would take more than just a bite this time.

"Miranda," she said over the comm, "you have a bead on—?"

Before she could finish, the sharp energetic whine of her sniper rifle rang out.

"Guess that answers my question," Paige murmured aloud.

"He vanished," Miranda reported after several moments.

An ominous silence fell over her team, and suddenly, Paige found all eyes staring at her. She quickly realized that she'd gone quiet with the shock of it all.

"Eyes open, all of you," she said, recovering. Her voice cut through the tension of her team. "The second we have ground visual, keep it distracted. Leave the dirty work to Sarah."

"He'll ... be coming in through the walls or the floor," Sarah said, her voice heavy with the stress of whatever monster vs. monster mojo this creature had on her. "He thinks ... he thinks he has the element of surprise."

"Well, then," Sarah said, a grin as predatory as Sarah's nature erupted on her lips. "Let's prove him wrong."

That was when Miranda appeared, seemingly falling clean out of the air, to make a painful landing on the concrete in their midst. She then lay motionless.

An evil laugh trailed from below, muffled as if from some eldritch horror buried deep underground.

Xerx considered himself lucky to have Alexa there to have two of her personal shuttles bring him and his crew to the water reclamation access facility. Though open carry of weapons was not uncommon in the Alliance, or even Tophanavar, taxis were less amenable toward people who were obviously armed to the teeth, even if there were a pair of blues with them.

"Thank you for calming her down," Neela whispered to him during the ride, speaking about Mobola.

"I had to do something," he replied, giving a shrug. Mobola sat across from them near the door, leaning on Pepper's side as his wife leaned on his, watching the scenery pass by in light and shadow, saying nothing. "She still wants to be anywhere but here, though."

"As do we all, my love," Neela replied with a sad smile.

The driver pulled up to their destination, and everyone filed out, ready for action. Xerx watched Neela speak to Mobola, occasionally "assisted" by Pip. The conversation lasted for several minutes during their trip on the inclining road to the cliff face where the entrance to the water reclamation center lay.

"Seems your friends will be getting the lion's share of the action," Rinkya said in a jocular tone.

"Probably a good thing," Rati said.

"Yeah," Xerx said, his voice distant. "Nothing personal about killing that monster. This, on the other hand..."

The group fell into silence on the concrete path, with the exception of Neela and Mobola, still in conversation. That was when Xerx noticed Pepper coming to his side.

"What are they talking about?" he asked.

"Hopefully, Neela's giving a pep talk," Xerx said, removing his pistols from their holsters and giving them one last check. "None of us want her cracking up in the middle of this; we have work to do."

Pepper let out a guffaw as his father and Var caught up with them.

"Work indeed," he said as Xerx sped up to the front where Alexa had been keeping point. The incline ended with a massive steel door. It was time for action.

"Your time to shine, *dada*," Neela said, her use of the term of endearment disarming the shorter girl, who relaxed as Pip escorted her up to the front. She took tentative steps forward and kneeled down before the controls. She pressed her hand to the panel, and the lines of her *msaidizi* snaked outward from the furrow and slipped into the space between ID scanner and the frame.

"Let's hope she can do this," Alexa said, watching along with Xerx and the rest of his crew.

"She's got the talent," Xerx replied. "And Pip's doing the lion's share of the work. She just has to rig the connection. The hard part's inside." He then faced Neela, who stood at his opposite side from the Pirate Queen. "What was it you told her, by the way?"

"Just some things she needed to know," was Neela's vague reply. "I think she'll feel more useful now."

"How about less afraid?"

"Rome wasn't built in a day," Neela said. "But this will be a start."

Mobola's eyes went distant as she made the connection.

"Pip, are you there?" she asked, her voice now coming through everyone's comms, rather than her mouth.

"Sifting through a shit load of data, but hit me," came Pip's high-pitched, cheerful voice.

"Negotiating with host," Mobola said, her voice becoming near-monotone. "Gate controls accessed; ID protocols bypassed; systems access granted. Installing micro-terminal uplink."

"Aaaaaaaaaaand ... got it!" Pip said. "I'm in now; thanks a lot, little warrior! Uploading schematics and lifeform detection to the team."

No sooner than the diminutive tank had finished her sentence, the holoprojector on Xerx's wrist comm came alive with a network of tunnels, lit up by points of red and yellow. The tunnels he recognized from the water reclamation passages on the map of Tophanavar that Pip had displayed back at the bar; the lights were a new addition.

"What we've got here is the approximate location of all the Doc's clones and the distribution nodes for the chemical," Pip explained. "Fortunately, they're all connected to one central hub ... right here." One of the yellow points flashed orange.

"Which one of the red lights is the Doc?" Salt asked.

"Dunno," Pip said. "Bio-signs from these girls are too damn alike."

"So we just kill them until we get the right one," Var said. "Easy enough."

"They look somewhat different from the Doctor," Xerx said. "*I'll* recognize her, though. Remember, she's mine."

"We all know, dear," Alexa said. "The question is, are we ready?"

"Born ready," Xerx heard Rinkya and Rati say.

"You do the honors, then, Mobo," Pip said.

Mobola nodded. A moment later, there was the sound of a massive lock falling open, and the door slowly swung away from the frame. Alexa raised her ornate pistol and gestured for Xerx to join her on point.

"Hunting season is officially open," she said with a grin. "Shall we?"

With a nod, Xerx started forward into the dimly lit industrial complex, ominous laughter echoing around them.

FIFTEEN

During the prior shitshow of a mission, while Xerx had been unconscious, Paige instructed Pip to remotely launch their vehicles to their location, as there hadn't been time to get back to the ship and rearm. And so they took stock of all they had with them. There were plenty of previously useless MAG rounds and only a few other essentials that she hoped would be helpful. Now, even with Miranda having taken a pretty hefty lump after being tossed from her perch, it was time to use them.

"Wait until we have visual; then run our strategy," she said to her team after catching the phial of medical nanosalve that Maria had tossed her. Following Kairen's instructions over the comm, she plunged the needle into the tank's side and pressed the dispenser cap. Where others would have cried out, Miranda made little more than a grunt and stiffened. It would take time for the nanos to knit her bones and repair the internal bleeding, but she would recover.

"Charlie ... Mike," Miranda whispered. *Continue Mission.*

"Right," Paige said with a nod. She stood up... and all hell broke loose.

Black tendrils burst through the ground like massive snakes made of shadows, surrounding them.

"Weapons free!" she shouted as one emerged right beside her. She ducked the lightning-fast swipe of the ink-black appendage, then slashed at it. It flew in half, the stump becoming a pixelated shower of black that seemed to turn the surrounding ground into a void. She stepped away, stumbling once, swallowing back her rising fear. She scanned the controlled chaos about her, seeing her team surrounding Sarah, who stood at the center, waiting for her moment. At this particular moment, her crew was efficiently handling the situation, though it looked like a scene from some seafaring vid where the ship was attacked by some nautical horror. Still, Agent 10 had not yet made an appearance.

"Anyone have a target visual?" she called out over the comm.

"Only of a bunch of living ink blot tests," Ike replied.

"Same here," Brogan said.

"They keep coming, but no target," Maria said.

There was a pause; then Sarah spoke.

"He's right below us," she said as Paige bisected another tendril that erupted behind Miranda. She was sitting up, but swaying in a way that made clear the fact that she was still not combat ready.

"I hope you get to a hundred percent soon," she said as they were yet again surrounded. It was as if some giant squid lay underground, trying to tire them out.

"Charlie Mike," Miranda said yet again.

"Of course," Paige mumbled, then switched her attention to Sarah, who was the linchpin of their operation. "Hey, shark girl! Anything you can do to scare this bastard up to the surface for us?"

"How the—how in space would I know?" Sarah fired back. She was staying in the center as best as she could, surrounded by the bedlam, but Ike, Brogan, and Maria were moving about in such a way that it made it difficult. Their shots tore through the fuliginous tendrils, but they were repairing or replacing themselves with a speed that made their shots eventually useless—a fact that showed in the frustration on everyone's faces. Strangely, though, Sarah was the only one that the tentacles had not been aiming for.

From behind her, Miranda leaped to her feet. Catching this in the corner of her eye, Paige spun around to see the middle sister of her tank trio swipe her discarded sniper rifle from the ground. With machine-like precision, she began to circle the battlefield, taking out each tendril one by one and quickly spinning around to annihilate new ones that sprang up. It was like watching Hercules take down the hydra but with the recording sped up to three times normal. Miranda's accuracy never ceased to amaze her, and it somewhat eased the workload of her crewmates.

"Pip, are there any blues inbound?" Paige asked. "They were handling this thing, weren't they? Aren't they coming?"

"So ... you want them to die?" Pip asked dryly.

"Just answer the damn question."

Paige hacked away at yet another growing tendril before it had risen halfway from the ground, waiting for the diminutive tank to answer.

"Well...?" she asked, realizing that things were taking longer than expected.

"Pip Williams is currently occupied handling two major colony system networks," Pip replied tersely. "Please leave a message, and she'll get back to you."

"Fat lot of help you are," Paige growled.

"If only this were open air, we could just drone strike the area with TIP charges," Maria said. "Atomize the son of a bitch."

It was then that Paige looked up at the underside of the level above. Revelation hit her like a truck. A large number of overhead power cables fed into a lot of the buildings in this area.

"See the power relays overhead?" she said to her team. "We need a way to drop them." She gestured to the bundle of wires and nodes hanging from a connecting walkway between the buildings above.

"Captain, not meaning to piss on your campfire, but how're we supposed to get up there?" Brogan's voice dumped Paige back to painful, frustrating reality.

"Can just one fucking plan go right today?" she snarled.

"On it." The quiet voice cut through the comms. Paige and her crew looked up to see the figure of Artemis leaping from cable to cable with the grace of a soaring albatross, eventually closing in on the above power distribution node.

"Bless you, sweet angel of death," Paige muttered, her voice carrying a much-relieved tone. "Cut them down on my mark. Pip, we'll need a trajectory to mark the point of impact of the live power coupling. Miranda, what will the shock radius be?"

"Twenty meters from point of impact," Miranda said before the diminutive tank could answer. Instantly, a flashing purple icon appeared in her bionic eye's field of vision. She overlaid it on the terrain, showing it to be just ahead of where Sarah stood, then transmitted the image to everyone's holo displays as Artemis sprinted to the overhang, strafing away from the regenerating tendrils. She then crawled like a gecko toward the power node and drew her knives.

Artemis held her weapon ready. It was time.

"Everyone, scatter!" she barked over the comm. "Get as far away from this point as you can!"

Her crew obeyed and disengaged from the fight. It was a coordinated yet chaotic flurry of evasive movement as they ducked, swatted, and fired their way through the accosting black tendrils, moving in every direction. To her surprise, Sarah even managed to tear through one with her nails, stunning it as she subsequently hurried out of its range. She fired a succession of holes in the renewed appendage she was engaged with. Then, as it disintegrated into an ink-colored pool of dissolving viscera and corruption, she backed away from the flashing point in her HUD before giving the order.

"Arty ... now!"

Artemis cut the supports, and the couplings came crashing down, sparking with live energy. The lights in the surrounding buildings flickered off, bathing them in almost full darkness, with only the lights of distant high-rise buildings beneath the dim halogens at the base of the stone canopy above. A second later, a cacophony of light and sound burst from the ground. It flooded the tendrils with veins of rippling electrons and miniature cracks of thunder, vaporizing them and filling the air with an almost tar-like stench amidst the antiseptic bite of ozone.

Amidst the noise and light show, a human wail arose, echoing through the ground like the thrum of a speaker system adjusted for maximum bass at some hellish rave. It rose in pitch as the electrical fanfare continued. Almost near the point where the live coupling touched the ground, a black stain appeared, spreading like crude oil from a fissure in the earth. From it, Agent 10's humanlike shape appeared, twitching with the spasms of electrical currents that, while causing it obvious pain, did little else. The wail continued from his forming mouth, as shapes coalesced into the pale, black-clad figure that Paige and her crew recognized from the spaceport.

"Looks like we've flushed him out," Paige said, then slipped once again into her command mode. "All right, time to let him have it. Miranda, get some distance. Jay, Maria, switch to the big guns; Ike, you know what to do."

"Anything would have been better than nothing," Salt grumbled.

Everyone had given the opening a wide berth after the unexpected and creepy-as-hell giggling that had emanated from the maintenance tunnels' depths.

"The Doctor likes to play with her victims psychologically," Xerx said, reciting the warning his cousin had passed on to him. He allowed his own personal rage to swallow that brief shock of fear as he led the way into the tunnels. Pip had given him a HUD that displayed the tunnel schematics. They would expand at every entry point that Mobola accessed, giving Pip further info on the tunnel network to guide them. The team followed, Alexa by his side, followed by his cousins, then Salt and Pepper. Var and Neela took the rear, protecting Mobola and Pip. "You should've seen what she did to her victims on Halo Meridian."

"Do we want to know?" Salt asked.

"I ... really don't," Mobola hurriedly said, right at the end of the older Felyan's words.

"Don't worry," Xerx said. "I doubt she had the time to set up something as elaborate here as she did there."

"Yeah, she's probably in a big rush, considering how things turned out when she first showed up," Pip chimed in. A set of grids were in front of her field of vision, yet she could somehow keep track of them and follow the group at the same time. "She's probably trying to get everything set up and—look out!"

Xerx's vision focused from the HUD's tunnel map just in time to catch the glint of a knife thrown out of the contrasting harsh light and shadow of the SilicaPlas-laden junction ahead. Xerx dodged, but not quickly enough, feeling an icy pain cross his cheek and something wet and warm trickle down to his neck.

"Fuck!" he hissed as he aimed in the direction the projectile had come, flinging himself against the wall as his crew had once Pip had given her warning. "Can't see a thing!"

"On it," Pip said. In less than a second, the corridor came alive with human-shaped outlines just behind the walls. A set of girlish giggles echoed from the darkness as they ran in opposite directions down the junction and out of range.

"Please try to keep our captain from getting killed," he heard Var say to the diminutive tank. Xerx knew the tone of that growl in his voice. And so did Pip, he ventured to guess, due to the silence that followed. He grinned slightly, amused at how the little chatterbox could be so easily cowed by a perturbed Felyan. A bit more relaxed now, an idea came to him.

"Hey Lexy, you got anything in your bag of tricks for two knife-throwing assholes who like to play hide-and-seek?" he asked.

"I just might," she said. Xerx turned to the statuesque Pirate Queen and watched as she reached into her cleavage and removed a familiar-looking cylinder.

"You keep flash-bangs in your bra?" Neela and Rinkya said in unison, to which Alexa shrugged.

"Don't you?"

Alexa's face was utterly serious for a second before she broke into a wry grin.

"Relax," she said, just as the outlines came back into Xerx's field of vision. They were practically dancing, clearly in a gloating mood after giving him a bit too much off the top. "It's only for special occasions. Now let's see if they'll dance to *this* beat."

She pulled the pin and threw the grenade. It hit the wall between them just as she saw one of the outlines rear back with something in her hand.

"Fire in the hole!" Xerx announced. He squeezed his eyes shut and covered his ears, hoping his crew was doing the same thing.

The noise was more disorienting than the flash, sending a thumping sensation into his guts as a momentary flare of red-orange lit up behind his eyelids. He heard the telltale screams, then rushed in, pistol and knife drawn. He hit the door at the junction, spinning around to face the corridor which he'd run through. The MAG round made sure the one on the right was dead before she knew what was going on; the knife assured the one on the left a slower and more painful death for the other clone, hitting its mark in her chest. Both of them looked nearly alike: near-perfect clones of the Doctor. With the way clear, Xerx signaled for his team to follow.

"Your turn again," he said to Mobola, who stepped forward with Pip, shaking. Pip stood by her side, touching her elbow while Neela kept a steadying hand on her shoulder.

As Mobola set back to work, Pip stared at the two corpses, and Xerx saw her dark eyes narrow.

"Damn! I haven't seen replication that perfect since... and look at that subtle design alteration!"

"Something you recognize?" Neela asked.

"Yeah, I know this style!" Pip replied, her eyes widening. She gestured rapidly from the corpse on her right to the one on her left. "Alliance tech doesn't bother much with cloning, and what you have definitely can't make this kind of subtle variation. This is Jakartan tech! The same crèches that make tanks!"

"So she managed to find Jakartan crèches on the black market?" Rati asked.

"If there were any on the black market, maybe," Pip said. "But anyone who could swipe a crèche from Jakarta's Pride would be paid in planets by the highest bidder. Nah, she had to have been there. Pretty ballsy for someone who was supposed to be hiding from the Imperium. Hey, did you know that our crew was offered a job to swipe a crèche once?"

"You turned it down?" Rinkya said. A look of keen fascination was on her face, compared to her lifemate's passing interest.

Pip made a spitting sound. "Duh, of course we did! Even corporate couldn't force us to take on a job like that. Jarkartans are as fanatical about their gene tech as Alexa is about vinyl as a recording medium. Crèches are sacred items there, and their priesthood keeps tabs on those things tighter than a Beauvoir monk's—"

"Okay, time to focus," Xerx said. "We need to navigate this place, and time's—" He suddenly paused, then looked across at Alexa, lifting an eyebrow. "Wait. Seriously, Lex? Vinyl?"

"It's an ancient and underrated medium." Alexa turned her nose up, feigning disgust at his words. "And I won't hear a word against it."

Xerx rolled his eyes, and Mobola spoke.

"Access."

Pip stepped forward, setting down to business as if she had been nothing but business through the entire journey.

"Okay, we've got the map, and…" She blinked, then gestured through the holos that surrounded her. A look of frustration quickly shrouded her face.

"What's wrong?" Xerx asked.

"Where the hell did they go?" Pip said, more to herself than anyone.

"Where did *who* go?" Salt asked, joining the crowd along with his son.

"The bio-signatures of the clones." Pip looked up, an expression plastered upon her face that was one part disbelief, and the other, utter indignation. "They just … vanished."

The door opened with the same ponderous pace as the main entrance. And the chorus of giggles came from the inside. The lights in that corridor had not yet come on, and Xerx frowned. He glanced back toward Pip, then saw an explosion of red points come across her field of vision.

"What's going on?" he asked, returning his gaze back toward the doorway. The same red now blanketed his vision.

"Hard cover!" Pip shouted, running along the wall and pressing herself against it. Neela grabbed Mobola while Xerx, along with Alexa, his remaining crewmates, and his cousins followed suit along either side of the door as a familiar whining noise crescendoed and the stone of the floor erupted into particles and dust.

"Lance rifles!" Var shouted as Xerx sheathed his knife and drew his second pistol. He risked a glance into the doorway as the rain of weapons fire ceased. The lights had switched on, lining a much higher stone ceiling. The corridor looked like the walls of a maze, atop which three of the clones sat, aiming their rifles, priming for another shot. Those things were miniaturized particle beam weapons, usually mounted to ships. To shrink that tech to portable size was expensive, and each one had to be crafted by hand. Such a weapon was a statement of just how important this objective clearly was to their opponent.

Luckily, for all their deadly power, Lances took a long time to recharge between barrages.

"Priming," Xerx said. He looked across the doorway, where Neela stood.

"Go fishing," he said to his wife, inclining his head toward the opening. Neela nodded and extended her arm in a gesture that was almost like tossing a baseball. The glint of her *msaidizi* shot outward from the organism on the back of her hand, into the kill zone the clones had created. The action would most likely have slowed them down with just how curious it would have seemed, Xerx figured, and rightly so, as a choked gasp broke the ensuing silence. Neela yanked back, although a force attempted to jerk her into the doorway by whatever her tool had caught hold of. Gritting her teeth, she quickly pressed herself against the wall just in time to avoid another barrage and the explosion of debris it caused.

The clone was dead on arrival, the barbed end of her *msaidizi* having pierced her throat. The rest was wrapped around her neck. A look of horror and pain was plastered on her lifeless face.

"Remind me not to piss off your wife, Captain," Var said and released a wheezing laugh.

"Good advice," Alexa said, raising an eyebrow. "Dibs on her gun, by the way."

"If you can retrieve it without dying, it's yours," Xerx said and reached into the doorway to return fire.

But before he could pull the trigger, he realized the clones had vanished.

"Dammit! Where'd they go?" Xerx darted his eyes over every corner of the hallway that he could see. Like here, there was a junction farther away, but without Pip's readouts working for these particular clones, there was no way to know if they were just playing the same game that the previous two had tried.

"Any more tech issues?" he asked Pip—or had been about to, if she hadn't interrupted his sentence with an excited noise.

"Hey, I got life signs again!"

"Again?" Neela said, beating Xerx to the question. "What happened the first time?"

"I think it's a bio-cloaking genome," Pip said. "I've heard of the Imperium testing it out, but it wasn't ready for field use."

"So the Doctor's using her clones as guinea pigs for more than just this super-*riss*?" Rati asked.

"Seems that way," Pip replied with a smug grin. "I just had to calibrate my scans. They can't hide from me now!"

"Let's hope you're right," Xerx said. He stepped into the doorway cautiously, keeping his guns ready, but as far as he could tell, no human-shaped highlights appeared in the HUD.

Confident as he dared to be that the area was clear, he signaled his crew once more. Alexa came to his side, having taken up the fallen clone's rifle, and everyone took their positions yet again.

The hunt was far from over.

SIXTEEN

Paige came to realize that Artemis' appearance had been a godsend.

They were nailed down before she arrived, like that time they'd been caught in a war zone on Tantagel IX that had turned hot. But the electrical shock had flushed Agent 10 out good and proper from his subterranean hideaway. Artemis leaped from her perch high above, allowing her implanted grav chutes to slow her descent at the last moment, landing behind the monster. She plunged her knives into the back of his knees, and he released a sound that made Paige want to take refuge in a room awash with microphone feedback. In addition to being a distraction, Artemis' attack gave her team the opening they needed for Sarah to break through.

"Sarah!" shouted Paige. "You're up, honey. Go give that monster hell!"

"Monster, you say?" Sarah flashed her a wild-eyed look and grinned, her mouth filled with needlelike teeth set in oily black gums. "I'll show you a fucking monster!"

She launched herself toward her waiting opponent. Her clothes flowed over her skin like viscous fluid as she moved, forming black chitinous plates over her body.

Her hair stiffened and took on the appearance of porcupine spines, and her fingers extended into long black talons. Her jaw opened unnaturally wide, and she bellowed a guttural challenge at Agent 10 as she charged toward him.

Paige was taken aback, less so by the transformation and more by the fact that Sarah had cursed. It was something that the artificial woman—or at least what had formerly appeared to be a woman—never did.

Sarah barreled into Agent 10 like some obsidian guillotine and appeared to slice him clean in half. She stumbled but quickly regained her footing as the creature reformed itself into a single humanoid shape once more. The pair then set about one another like feral beasts challenging for dominance. Now, with Sarah on the far side of the enemy, Paige gave the order to open fire.

With unerring accuracy, Miranda blew chunks out of Agent 10's head, though it reformed quickly. In the meantime, Maria had brought her own personal heavy weapon to bear. Named "Tiny," it was originally an aircraft-mounted MAG cannon, modified to allow her to carry and fire from the hip. The weapon boomed with every shot, and Paige marveled as the huge tank's arms just seemed to absorb the full force of the weapon's horrible recoil, which certainly would shatter her own prosthetics had she been the one attempting to fire it.

The rounds ripped through Agent 10 and Sarah alike, though neither seemed particularly disturbed by them. Paige added her own fire to that of the others. Minimal as it was in damaging it, the distraction was enough to allow Sarah to start causing some serious-looking wounds to her opponent. Agent 10 snarled, cringing at the hail of bullets that preceded Sarah's next pass. Sarah slid like a baseball player, deftly ducking the barrage as if she were made of rubber.

The monster's hand suddenly expanded to a size that could fit easily over her waist and grasped her with a force that might have killed even Maria. Sarah roared, though Paige was unsure if the sound was pain or frustration. The creature then lifted her off her feet and began to constrict his grip. Artemis jumped in with her twin daggers but was just as quickly swatted away by an extra limb that, along with a nightmarish set of eyeballs, grew out of the abomination's back. She made a shallow dent as she impacted the side of a wrecked taxi nearby with a resounding thud, then let out a wet-sounding sigh as she fell to the ground. Paige and Brogan both winced as Ike shook his head. They knew the sound of pulped organs when they heard it.

"Artemis!" Maria screamed. Paige knew this was serious, as the Amazonian woman rarely used her partner's actual name. She gestured for Maria to hold station, but she was already marching forward, firing round after round into the creature, a look of absolute fury in her blue eyes. She tucked and rolled under the swiping motion of the extra arm, but it bent in an unnatural way, catching her when she was halfway to her pink-haired partner. Like Sarah, she became trapped as she was hefted into the air, and, with one swift motion, pummeled into the ground, where she lay motionless in a puddle of the corroded slag that formed out of the monster's old emergence point. Paige felt sick at the sight of what had just happened. And all the while, she was helpless to do anything more than watch while firing useless ammo.

"Kai...?" she whispered over the comm.

"She's okay," Kairen said reassuringly. "Life signs are stable. It takes more than that to take someone like Maria out."

"And Artemis?"

"Erratic ... wait. No. They're stabilizing."

"That's both a relief... and not surprising, come to think of it," Paige said, remembering how effective the enigmatic pink-haired girl's nanos could be. Hadn't she heard that she'd once rebuilt her entire left arm from organic waste in a septic processing tank?

The monster suddenly let out another ungodly screech. Brogan and Ike reeled, and Paige stood transfixed in combined pain and awe as Agent 10 violently shook his occupied arm, upon which Sarah was attached, her lower half flopping about. Spikes radiated from about her waist and pierced the creature's limb where it gripped her. It was a sight not unlike an enraged cat that had chosen to bite the object of its ire with every shred of its furor. She slashed down with her claws and severed the limb that gripped her. Separated from its host, the limb melted into black fluid and splashed to the ground, leaving smoking puddles on the road. Sarah then lunged at Agent 10 and sank her unnaturally large maw into his shoulder.

In spite of the creature's desperate attempts to be rid of her, she managed to gain an even more secure purchase with her arms and legs, sinking her elongated talons into his body. Black ichor flew into the air and rained down as noxious raindrops as Sarah methodically began to consume chunks out of its body in a sight both fascinating and loathsome. She'd heard the Pirate Queen make discreet remarks to this, but she never would have believed it without seeing it for herself. Outside of her darkly sarcastic attitude, for someone who otherwise tried to behave as prim and proper as Sarah, normally never even cursing, this most likely was a side of herself that she supposed the woman made sure that no one ever saw.

"Captain," Brogan's voice broke over the comm. "Something's happening."

Paige snapped out of her trance to focus more fully on the situation to see what Brogan was talking about. Thankfully, Artemis had recovered enough to rise to her haunches, parts of her body setting back into shape with dull but disturbingly audible pops. She made several loud hacking coughs and vomited up silvery black fluid, then rose unsteadily to her feet, and staggered toward Maria. Both looked the worse for wear. As for Agent 10...

"Yeah, I see it too," Ike said.

"What do you—?"

Paige stopped before she could truly begin as she realized what was going on.

"He's retreating," Maria said. She sounded almost punch-drunk, but coherent. The monster was sinking back into the roadway, dematerializing bit by bit as Sarah was still in full ravenous beast mode, imbibing his flesh with mindless gusto, having eaten deep into his torso, leaving absolutely nothing behind.

"Sarah?" When she showed absolutely no sign of even recognizing her voice, Paige practically screamed over the comm. "Sarah! Snap out of it! Get off of him! He's taking you with him! Do you even fucking hear me?"

But the ebon form of Agent 10 sank deeper and more quickly into the decaying sludge upon which he stood, carrying the oblivious Sarah with him, pulling her into the substrata of the colony.

Paige and her crew watched, painfully aware of the uselessness of their weapons as the agent sank into the tunnel of his own making, pressing the structure of the colony down along with him and creating an ersatz tunnel that he carried the rampaging monster that Sarah had become, with him.

And then, a wild card appeared in the form of a pink streak, leaping from where only a moment ago she been lying motionless. She sailed into the air over the wreckage of the combat zone, landing in a precision squat beside the tunnel, looking intensely downward into its depths. Only too late did Paige notice the intent in her large, green eyes, but Maria cried out before she could.

"Don't!" she screamed. But it was as if the pink-haired girl was driven by something beyond their ken as she stepped back, blades at the ready, and then strode purposefully forward, dropping forward into the tunnel's depths and disappearing below its lip. This was the last of Artemis that Paige saw, as she disbelievingly watched the pink-haired angel of death tumble into the sinkhole like one afflicted with a suicidal determination.

In a moment, the reality of what had happened fully sank in.

"Shit, shit, *shit!*" Paige ran to where Agent 10 once stood, Maria limping to her side, then falling to her knees at the chasm's edge. The rest of her team joined her as she gazed despairingly at the ruined ground, her black hair that whipped in the breeze obscuring the tears in her eyes.

"We'll get them back," Paige assured her crewmate, seeing her state of grief, unusual as to be disturbing. She had no idea how they were going to do it, but it was all she could do to give the massive tank some consolation.

"Alexa's not going to like this," she said, quiet and overflowing with a new feeling of self-hatred. She'd approved the plan. Had she sent Sarah to her death? And why did Artemis have to be such a wild card?

"Hey, Captain."

Paige straightened up at Pip's voice, swallowing back any unsteadiness in her own as she spoke. "What have you got?"

"Did you tell that thing that I said something bad about his mother?" Despite the quip, Pip's voice was ominous without her usual playfulness.

"Well, Sarah might have," Paige said, half-mired in a morose humor of her own. "I couldn't really tell amongst the growling. They both ... vanished. Why?"

"Funny." Somehow Pip managed to communicate an eye roll over the audio with her response. "Anyway, my scans show him making a beeline for us."

It was a long way down, and on more than one occasion, Artemis wondered if she would survive the journey.

The tunnel was nearly a sheer ninety-degree fall, hurling her down a steep incline that she'd only seen before at a water park in one of the orbital habitats around Halo Meridian, using the weirdness of centrifugal force to slow down one's fall farther away from the station's axis to keep things relatively safe. But there were no such safety measures in Tophanavar's artificial gravity field, which pulled her down into its infrastructure, the residue of the Agent 10 creature lubricating her descent over uneven ground, and nearly hurling her into hazards of rebar, nanocrete, and exposed pipes. She deftly avoided collisions with superhuman reflexes, rolling and weaving out of the way, trying to slow her descent by gaining some kind of foothold, but the lack of friction, combined with the speed of her fall and the tenacity with which she gripped her knives, making certain that any attempts to put their use toward the task of breaking her descent were done with minimal danger of injury or their loss. Because of this, the resulting attempts at breaking her fall, whether by foot or blade, made for a series of tumbling follies that might have been hilarious to an outside observer, had they not been nigh lethal.

And even in her fall, there was no sign of the creature, causing her to wonder how fast had it plummeted into the ground, with the Pirate Queen's sister in tow.

Her nanos allowed her to see in the scant light of this cavern, keeping watch for any sign of the creature. And at long last, she managed to spot it ahead, pushing and dissolving its way through the solid matter of the asteroid's bedrock as if it were shoving aside a granitic pudding. Buoyed by this, Artemis gritted her teeth and brought her knees to her chest, squeezing herself into a compact position like a spring. Gone were the foundations of the colony, and she was sliding through slime-ridden rock. And thanks to another turn of fortune, the creature had changed the trajectory of its angle, slowing her down as the incline settled out into something more parallel to the colony's gravity field.

"He's coming this way?"

Xerx was in pain ... both physically—from a couple of rounds that had grazed him in the last few run-ins with the Doctor clones—and of course, mentally. And apparently, this was a shared exhaustion that he could read on the faces of his entire team. Only Pepper had taken lumps of his own when diving in to defend Neela against one of the clones, who was surprisingly adept at hand-to-hand and had been wearing knuckle dusters. That bruise was now swelling pretty badly, and although the sound of water was close, there was none nearby except in the massive pipes that lined the walls and ceiling.

"Yeah," the diminutive tank replied. "Paige and her crew are on the way, but it's gonna be a bit. Luckily, you cleared the way." Suddenly, she brightened as script flew across the holos about her head. "Oh, hey, good news! Know how Mobo and I identified that the creature leaves a unique signature on the matter it passes through?"

"Not really," Xerx said, looking confused.

Pip fixed him with a disdainful look. "It does help if you pay attention."

"It does help if you just get to the fucking point, quickly," Xerx fired back. He fixed Pip with an irritated look of his own.

The pair stared at each other for what seemed like an age until Pip broke the silence, her expression once again becoming neutral.

"Touché. Well, Agent 10's bio signs are really weird. He's not quite organic and not quite mechanical, so it makes him hard to track."

"So how long before he gets here?" Xerx asked.

Pip shrugged. "He's basically carving his own entrance here," she explained. "He doesn't seem to be moving fast, so it'll be about ... I dunno, ten, maybe twenty minutes?"

"I thought you had schematics of the city's tunnel-ways?" Rati said, cutting into the conversation and sounding more than a little annoyed.

"Oh, excuse me," Pip snapped. "I didn't realize the colony updated newly bored tunnels in its infra-structure by biological aberrations into its archives in real time!"

Rati opened his mouth, but having no retort, quickly stopped. Rinkya put her hand on his shoulder, shaking her head.

"You two done?" Xerx said, testily eyeing both his cousin and Paige's loaner techie.

"Just one thing," Pip said, still without her usual san-guinity. She shifted her gaze to Alexa. "Your sister's with Agent 10. Artemis too."

Alexa's eyes widened, then narrowed. "Define 'with.'"

"Apparently, she started literally eating him and wouldn't stop," Pip said. "And she disappeared into the ground with him when he escaped … still eating him. And neon hair dove in after them. So, when they show up, just be careful where you shoot."

Alexa stood silent for a moment, processing the news. It, in fact, turned out to be one of the rare times that Xerx had seen the Pirate Queen out of tongue. A moment later, she frowned and sighed.

"Damn girl gets herself into more trouble every day," Alexa said at last. "We'll have to deal with it accordingly, I guess."

"All we can do," Xerx said. "So let's finish this. I can hear water, so we shouldn't be too far, right?"

"Schematics show the dissemination point in the cavern beyond," Pip said, gesturing to the final door ahead. "Just don't fall into the reservoir. God only knows where those currents will pull you, and I don't think it'll really matter at the other end, if you know what I mean."

"Don't worry," Xerx said, checking his ammo. He'd been as sparing as he dared, but MAG pistols had more limited shots than a rifle. Still, he was trained by the best, and he knew that all he needed was to see the science bitch to end her. "The only one going into the drink today will be the Doctor's corpse. How many are beyond the door?"

"Four," Pip said. "I think."

"You *think*?"

"Hard to say," Pip said. "Some materials in the cavern block readouts. We'll both get a good reading once Mobo does her thing."

"Then it might be more," Xerx concluded grimly.

"God, I hope not," Salt said, chiming in.

"Well, given how many we've killed, she can't have many more to put in our way," Xerx said.

"Famous last words," Neela said. Her response made Xerx frown. Such pessimism was uncharacteristic of his wife.

"Got a bad feeling?"

"Not really," Neela said. "Just promise me that you won't do anything stupid when we go in there."

"Do you see ending a terrorist and murderer as doing anything stupid?" Xerx asked.

"Only if you're outgunned."

"Then I'll try not to be outgunned," Xerx said and signaled to Mobola, who stepped forward to do her usual magic.

"Last one," he said to her with confidence. "You did great!"

She didn't respond until she had finished the process with Pip, and the door began to open. As usual, she ran back to the rear of the group beside Var's protective frame, but she took the time to give him a small, but not quite sheepish grin, which made Xerx smile in return.

That smile quickly vanished when he faced the slowly opening door again, and Pip shouted, just as the images lit up in his HUD.

"They're right behind the—!"

Alexa shoved him aside, fully facing the two clones that stood in the way as he toppled to the floor. Their rifles were aimed, and one fell to her shot, but the other fired. Xerx turned over from his prone position to see a splatter of blood fly from where the Pirate Queen's not-quite-bronze skin ended and her green shoulder scales began. She staggered back, and immediately, he realized that what she was hit by had not been a MAG round. Even low-caliber rifle fire would have come out the other end, but he could clearly see what looked like a black pellet lodged in her skin.

Alexa abruptly contorted. Her fist balled up, and her sharklike teeth set in a rictus of what Xerx thought was pain... until he realized what it really was.

When her scream lilted into something that sounded about as far from pain as possible, he knew exactly what happened. Heart sinking with the realization, he scrambled to his feet as Alexa dropped to her knees, her scream warbling to an almost orgasmic sound, her legs crossing as she bent over, one hand moving to between her legs, the other grasping her right breast. He shifted his gaze to the clone who stupidly stood in the doorway, gloating at her work—just as the crack of several weapons sounded, and five MAG rounds sank into her body. He turned back toward his crew to see everyone aiming their now-hot pistols and rifles into the doorway.

"Guess the Doctor didn't make these assholes too bright," Xerx said before hurriedly attending to Alexa. His team watched helplessly, not really having seen everything that had happened in those few moments. Fortunately, he had, and he reached for Alexa's shoulder blade. The Pirate Queen herself seemed to now be caught in some sort of blissed-out seizure, but far from helpless, it appeared, as her limbs went suddenly rigid, except for her right arm, which flailed out and grabbed his hand. With slow, almost deliberate movements, she then removed her opposite hand from her crotch, and dug her claw into her shoulder blade, grunting momentarily at the pain, then relaxing somewhat, her gaze focusing, her jaw clenched. She fished out the device—the same one as what had sent him into agonizing ecstasy back at the spaceport—and shattered it between her prodigious claws. Instantly, her shuddering settled down. She gasped and then began breathing, first in pants, then slowing to normal, as if she'd been holding her breath after a long dive.

"I'm... I'll be okay," she said, her voice a quavering whisper. "At least I now know ... why you soiled your knickers the way you did."

Xerx helped Alexa to her feet, and she steadied herself on his shoulder on wobbly knees.

"Are you sure you'll be all right?" Neela asked, stepping forward.

"Just peachy in a tick," Alexa said, bracing herself against the wall. "I admit I was rather curious as to how those things made you feel." She grinned in a particularly hungry way that made Xerx want to step as far away from her as possible. "Now I'm afraid my poor boy toy is going to have an exhausting night."

"You fished out Tyger again, didn't you?" Xerx said flatly.

"You're going to have to pour one out for him tonight, I'm afraid," Alexa said, not wasting any more time. As soon as she took her first steady step, Xerx signaled his crew to move forward into the now fully open steel doorway.

The chamber was massive, nearly half a mile in diameter, with a ceiling some fifty to sixty feet above the underground lake. Multiple waterfalls from pipes high above, each of which seemed to measure twenty feet across, fed the reservoir from thirty-foot intervals along the sheer rock wall. The path that lay before them was barricaded with stone guardrails along the edge beside the water and with massive columns that appeared to have been carved out of what had once been the solid rock that composed the asteroid's interior. The path, rails, and columns curved along the circumference of the cavern, toward another entrance on its opposite end, into which many of the pipes fed.

But what drew Xerx's immediate attention was the fact that there were no signs of the remaining clones. Upon realizing this, he slowed down.

"Talk to me, Pip," he said. The waterfalls were not deafening, but he spoke over the comm to cut through the noise. "The others have sensor blocking?"

"Not likely," Pip replied. "I sussed out their bio-signs; you should be able to see them now. If you can't, then they're not here." A red icon appeared, overlaid upon something behind a second massive stone column about a hundred feet up ahead.

"Is that—?"

"The dispersal unit?" Pip said. "Should be."

"I'm going for it."

Neela grabbed his shoulder before he could take another step. He turned around, and before he could ask, he felt her lips on him. It was all too brief, but the meaning was plainly obvious.

"Be careful, *Kipenzi*," she said.

"I will."

Xerx signaled for his team to move forward slowly and keep an eye out. Then he strode forward, guns drawn, adrenaline making him feel giddy at first, then increasingly more suspicious as he approached his goal, even though he was aware of his team following farther back. The entire way, his eyes darted around the cavernous reservoir area, and, finding nothing but the steady echoing din of flowing water, his thoughts began to race.

This is a trap. It has to be. There's no way in hell that bitch would just leave this unguarded. Where the hell is everyone? Where is the Doctor? This is a trap. I'm putting my crew and my cousins in danger, including Iriid's wife, who happens to be the fucking Pirate Queen! This is a trap. What the hell am I doing? When I find that murderous psycho, she's gonna be super dead for this alone. This is a trap. This is a trap. This is a trap...

MAG fire nearly frightened Xerx's internal organs out of his mouth and the contents of his slowly filling bladder into his pants. He spun around, guns drawn... and saw the broken corpse of a clone lying on the floor in a growing pool of her own blood. His team seemed to be coming down from an adrenaline high on their own while Pip had a crescent-moon grin across her small monochrome face.

"Nailed it!" she said over the comm.

"What happened?" Xerx asked.

"Remember, the rock here interferes with sensor readouts," Pip explained, "so I figured, if I was a homicidal clone, where would I hide?"

Xerx nodded, feeling his blood thrumming in his ears from that fright before he turned around, keen to ferret out another one of the annoying clones.

Instead, they decided to save him the trouble.

From behind the column, another one emerged, leaping toward the opposite cavern wall quick as a flash, her movements swift and nimble. There was a familiarity in these movements that spiked a sense of alarm that Xerx had hoped that he would never feel again. An image of glowing blue hair shot across his subconscious as he raised his guns and fired.

She was fast.

Obnoxiously fast.

Frighteningly fast.

His shots trailing behind her, the clone charged his way, running down the wall as if Tophanavar's augmented gravity held no sway over her. His training kicked in, and Xerx dodged at the perfect moment, avoiding the MAG fire from her own pistols as he tucked and rolled dangerously close to the edge of the reservoir's churning waters, then sprang back to his feet. He glanced over the momentary cover, giving his opponent no time to make a precise shot, making a mental map of the area. It was then, when he refocused on his target, he saw that she'd vanished once again. He snarled in frustration, but then Pip's voice broke into the comm, strangely whispering.

"She ran up the wall, hopping along the stalactites. Don't look up yet; she doesn't know that I'm tracking her. Any moment now, she'll be coming your way."

"Just tell me when," Xerx whispered back to the diminutive tank. Now feigning confusion, he looked every which way but up, gripping his pistols tighter.

"Almost there..." Pip said, "And ... Route 1, now!"

Xerx obeyed, swinging his arms blindly in the direction Pip had indicated, letting instinct guide him as he opened fire. He squinted against the rocks and dust that rained down, then ran toward the other side of the column, catching a glimpse of the clone in his field of vision as she fell and hit the ground painfully. He'd only caught a glimpse of his objective, which now lay in view: a hexagonal container attached to the barricade at the water's edge by a set of wires. But first, he would have to deal with the clone.

He heard his team open fire and then heard scrambling sounds alongside him, moving directly above. Without looking, Xerx fired in the same direction. A feminine-sounding cry of pain made him realize he'd nailed her.

She fell in an arc over him and landed about ten feet away, near the machine, writhing in what appeared to be a considerable amount of pain. Another near-perfect copy of the Doctor, dressed in a catsuit of spidersilk and Kevlar with gun holsters sewn into the fabric. She was also more muscular than the others.

"Guess you're what passes for the elites," Xerx said, approaching her as her writhing settled into a limp, gasping slow attempt at crawling. He heard a faint grunt of approval from Pip at his tenuous video game reference. Upon closer inspection, he noticed that there was no blood, meaning that he'd hit a protected spot, but as he was well aware, even body armor didn't cut the stunning pain of being shot.

"Kinda cute that you thought you were a gunslinger," Xerx said, pausing, once he was certain he was in a range where he could not possibly miss. He took aim for her head. "Trust a trained pirate blood. It takes more than a gun."

"You talk too much," she sneered.

"Yeah, I've been told that."

He fired—and missed.

Well, I didn't see that one coming, Xerx thought as, appearing to recover instantly, she leaped his way. Where there had been a pair of pistols like his own in her hands, there was now a set of very sharp knives. Still keyed up on adrenaline, Xerx dodged the first and second swipes, which missed his face by inches. She was determined and horrifyingly fast, but throughout the fight, Xerx had come to realize that as quick as she was, and equally good at acting hurt, she was no Nemesis. Flailing with hidden weapons at too close range, she had made a gamble. And she'd just lost.

Xerx kicked her in the midsection, full force, and sent her flying across the ground.

"Light her up!" he commed to Pip, who relayed the order. The clone did her last dance as his team's MAG rounds tore through her, the majority aimed at her unprotected head. She lay still, and all was silent.

Breathing heavily, Xerx took a moment to come down from the adrenaline high, suppressing his rage at the Doctor's apparent disappearing act. Then he set his sights on the container.

"Let's get this over with," he said.

Artemis tucked in and sprang to her feet, chasing after the creature that seemed to sense her approach and picked up its pace. But it could not outpace her enhanced muscular attenuation as she put forth a burst of speed that could have kept up with a maglev nearing its cruising velocity. Her target in sight, she leaped forward, her knives aloft.

She sank her knives into the creature's impossibly roiling flesh. But the moment she did, she was hit with a pain that jolted up her forearm, akin to being electrocuted with a low-level charge, while at the same time, having her arms submerged in acid. She gritted against the pain... and that was when the voices began anew.

They had begun before her fall, carried on the colony's recycled air, starting as a whisper, then grew into sneers that taunted her ... then goaded her into the fight, even when it appeared that Paige and the others had had things under control. But a piece of the creature rose like a thin tendril from the ground behind her while she watched the mission unfolding, content with observing unless they truly needed her. She managed to free herself the first time it had grasped her by the wrist, but the voices called to her—the voices of her handlers.

The ones who she had obeyed perfectly, only to be locked away in that cell on Hemlock IV.

"Imperfect."

"Prototype."

"You'll never be what we needed."

Artemis was at first caught unaware. And this was when the creature seemed to sense her moment of distraction. It threw her off, sending her flying weightless, away from the creature while Sara slowly, absently consumed it.

Artemis, her body reacting by instinct, righted herself into a protective crouch as she made her eventual impact with the tunnel wall, breaking her fall with the augmented strength in her legs. She slid down to the floor, residue of the creature lining the cavern, inert, but with a smell that was borderline nauseating.

Her hands now free, as well as her legs, Artemis shook the residue from her knives, just in time to hear the voices again.

"Useless."

It came from behind her. Artemis spun around, taking a defensive stance against a towering sight that she assumed was impossible.

She then realized it was only a facsimile of a ghost from her past. The man, or rather, the solid, muscular shape of the man was that of Agent 6, one of her trainers, who had visited a thousand cruelties upon her.

As he had during countless torture sessions that he called "training," the doppelganger assumed a martial stance and swiped at her with a flurry of blows, which

Artemis deftly avoided. Once she tried to block, but the force of it cracked the bone in her arm, sending a jolt of pain throughout that limb, which her nanos took a moment to heal.

"Imperfect thing ... must be contained."

A woman's voice. Exactly like her own, but the words spoken with far more disdain and disgust than she'd ever been able to muster. The form matched the voice—which was a form exactly like her own. It was Agent 3, her genetic donor. She appeared to her right, lithe and fast, striking at her with even greater speed than the Agent 6 copy. This time, Artemis was ready and sliced through her arm, the severed appendage falling to the ground, not in a solid form, but liquid, instantaneously splattering to the cavern floor as a puddle of malodorous, black sludge.

Nightmares of her past began to surround her now: several other forms appeared from the residue in the cavern, all of whom Artemis recognized: facsimiles of Agent 5, wiry, yet relentless in his fighting prowess. Then came Agents 7, 8, and 9.

This thing was trying to overwhelm her.

No. She realized it as her nanos brought clarity in the midst of battle. It was trying to distract her. As connected to it as she had been, she had been connected to the creature as well, and a cacophony of thoughts and memories came to her mental access. And above all these thoughts was the understanding that it could not outpace her.

The simulacra rushed her, and she leaped back before springing into the fray, transforming into the angel of death with her knives, avoiding the blows of her former masters, and carving into them like the food processors that she'd seen Maria use in the mess hall while watching her cook. They'd trained her well, and she'd surpassed their expectations, but still, she was thrown in that constricting cell on the prison world. And she would let Maria kill her during sex before she'd ever go back there.

Having mowed through the crowd of facsimiles, she continued her pursuit, but even as she turned in the direction of the creature and ran full tilt, the voices still taunted her. Each word drilled more deeply into her mind.

"Failure."

"Imperfect."

"Should have stayed on Hemlock."

"Shut up," she hissed as more simulacra peeled off of the walls and rose from the floor, to impede her way... and to give her more targets. These could try to goad her into a fight, but their fighting prowess left much to be desired. They were fodder for her knives as she continued her pursuit.

With the Doctor nowhere to be found, but their otherwise primary objective within arm's length, Xerx was forced into the agonizing choice to abandon his pursuit. Prioritizing this objective over the other, letting a known terrorist walk versus sacrificing the sanity of the entire colony through yet another one of her twisted experiments made him want to howl in impotent frustration. The clone was dead, and he was coming off of the adrenaline rush, but he was far from calm. He knew his team could see him standing there, shaking, fists gripped upon his pistols in a way that would have asphyxiated them had they been small living things. And worst of all, he was just this close to not caring.

"Where is she, Pip?" he said through gritted teeth. "Where is the goddamn Doctor?"

Pip spoke in a surprisingly petulant tone, nearly matching the aggression with which he'd addressed her, her reaction shaking him from his haze of near-rage.

"I don't know. There's too much interference in this cavern, remember? She could be hiding in here still or…" she gestured toward the cavern's opposite door across the lake and sighed in frustration, "she might have already escaped."

Xerx sighed, a dullness coming over his body.

"*Kidege*, her monster is still coming," Neela said. "We can't get to the Doctor, but we can stop this."

At last able to move again, Xerx holstered his pistols, then approached the container.

It was tied to the railing of the path's edge with what looked like zip ties. On its surface was a device that cycled through some kind of sequence but with no letters or numbers that he was familiar with. From his point of view, it appeared to be lattices of vanishing and reappearing lines and shapes, like dancing stick figures.

"A device is attached," Xerx said, calling his team to his side. "I can't read it."

Mobola, Salt, Pepper, Rati, and Pip came the closest, but while the first three shook their heads in equal confusion, Pip's eyes widened.

"It's Cistercian cipher," Pip said. "What they use for numerals on Jakarta's Pride."

"You can read it?" Xerx asked.

"Well, duh! Where do you think I was born, Xiao?" Pip replied with an exaggerated eye roll. "It's part of the basic teaching set they download into us before decanting."

"So if they're numerals... then they're counting down?" Rati asked. His tone was flat with dread. Pip nodded.

"So it's a bomb?" he asked as everyone, save Xerx and Pip, now gave the container a wide berth.

"Don't be stupid," Pip snapped. "She's not going to use an explosive device." Her tone shifted to a mocking affectation of stupidity. "'Gee, let's just destroy my whole reason for installing this thing, huh?'"

Xerx was taken aback by the diminutive woman's acerbic demeanor and regretted his behavior toward her just a few moments ago. But he now at least began to understand why Paige and crew sometimes called her "Little Tiger." Silently, he watched as she continued to study the device, then pointed to the seams atop the container.

"It's a sublimation dispersal unit." She then gestured to its base. "There'll be valves at the rear. It's used to disperse decontaminants, drugs, even pesticides over a wide area, through both air and liquid. And yes, the timer's counting down to its release."

"You sound pretty calm," Xerx said, his own calm slowly receding as he was reminded of the tight schedule on which he, Salt, and Pepper had been working to repair the *Reckless*' tesseract drive during the pulsar incident. "How much time do we have left?"

Pip stretched out her arms and cracked her fingers. "It would only scare you. But I've got time enough to stop it." She then felt at the bottom of the timer and popped open a formerly unseen panel, removing a wire from it. She then reached into the satchel that she had strapped at her waist and removed a silver needlelike object, which she screwed onto the end of the wire's copper plug.

"What are you doing?" Xerx asked.

"What I do best," Pip said with a smile, before shoving the needle into her forearm, much to Xerx's dismay. He'd seen her do this before, and it never stopped being nauseating. But it was the only thing she could do without the far less traumatic *msaidizi* implants his wife and crewmate possessed.

With the connection securely made, Pip's eyes went fully black as she leaned forward and rested her hand on the surface of the device.

"Well, the good Doctor didn't want us to have an easy time of it," Pip muttered. "This system is rigged to the gills with barrier subroutines. Gonna take a bit longer than I thought."

"Will you still have enough time?" Xerx asked. A spike of fear caused his voice to falter somewhat.

"Oh, yeah, no worries."

"Pip's confident ease set Xerx more at ease—that was, until a familiar voice, mocking and androgynous, broke in over the comm.

"No, she won't."

The spike of rage to which he'd become accustomed subsumed his fears completely.

"Stay on the task," he whispered to Pip; then he stepped back from the canister, casting his gaze around the chamber.

"So, Doc, you think you're slick just 'cause you can break through the comms?" he said, drawing one pistol. "Show yourself; I'll train you to be smart without your brain meats."

"I love the chutzpah of your family," the invisible Doctor sneered. "But in a moment, it's not going to matter."

"What do you—?"

The crack of the sudden explosion and succeeding loud splash shook him to his knees. The accompanying shriek brought him back to his feet, where he was greeted by the sound of his entire team crying out at once.

"*Kipenzi!*" Neela screamed, gesturing toward the container—where it no longer was ... and neither was Pip.

"*Shit!*" he yelled, running toward the masticated section of the walkway. The slipperiness of the water that covered the floor nearly sent him careening into the churning water himself, but he broke his momentum on the remaining undamaged section of the railing. Still, it was too late.

"*Pip!*"

This time, the one to scream was Mobola. There was a sound of shuffling and struggling bodies coming from his team, but Xerx was too distracted with steadying himself to see what was going on.

"Seems your arrogant little friend didn't think explosives were in my skill set," the Doctor said. "Well, I've been working on that, as you can see."

"I'll fucking kill you!" Xerx screamed into the comm.

"I rather doubt that." The Doctor's smug voice was like something slimy and unwelcome on his ears. "You've got yourself a problem bigger than myself, I think. In fact, I'd start calculating where the little tech tank's body will wash up if I were—oh! I see someone else is taking the initiative!"

Xerx froze in place. "What do you—?"

"Stop her!"

The voice was Neela's. He spun around to see what had just happened, but it was too late. Before he knew what was going on, Mobola shoved past him at a speed that he had never seen come from her, taking her swiftly out of reach. He could only watch on helplessly as the normally painfully timid girl leaped over the ruined side of the walkway and dove into the tumultuous water. Stunned with the uncharacteristic audacity of her actions, he scrambled back to the edge, where Neela joined him, and soon the rest of his team, whom he had to wave away. There was no telling how much damage those explosives had fully done.

"We tried to stop her," Neela said, her voice hollow, her hand over her mouth in utter disbelief. Tears spilled over onto her cheeks. "Var grabbed her; she kicked him in the gut; she ducked Salt and Pepper and dodged Alexa and me. I'd never seen her show such an attachment to anyone. And I'd never seen her move so fast."

The Doctor's voice cut into Xerx's momentary shock and hopeless terror, predicated by a sharp whistle that rang out over the cavern's constant running water, coming from the tunnel at the end of the path on the cavern's opposite end.

Xerx looked up through vision that had just begun to blur with tears.

She was right there.

The Doctor had been there the entire time!

"Believe me, I didn't feel like staying here, but I had to pick up my pet," the Doctor said as a black form emerged beside her, barely human-looking, but with a disturbing grin that was unmistakable. There was, however, an extra addition to his form: a writhing, equally black mass attached to him. Was that Sarah? Black ichor began to spill into the reservoir, but proving more viscous than the rest of the water, as it did not spread out. Despite her being far out of range, he took a shot, but he only ended up hitting one of the solid metal pipes above the cavern and ricocheting into bare stone far above. He fired again, and then Neela stopped him, pushing his arm down.

"Your next shot might hit us," she said.

"Yes, listen to your wife." Xerx could feel the sneer in the Doctor's voice like acid on an open wound. "Ricochets can be quite hazardous to your health."

"Mine won't," Alexa piped in as a shot from her lance rifle tore through the Agent's head. The aim was perfect with the aid of its auto-targeting, but the Agent's head re-formed as it always had. At least she didn't have the temerity to aim for the Doctor and take his rightful kill. Immediately, the Doctor reached into her pocket, and a shimmer enveloped her and her pet monster. Without thinking, she took another shot at the monster, but it seemed to vanish into the shimmer. There was a tiny splash in the water directly below. Alexa sighed.

"It's an entropy bleed shield," she said. "We could walk through it, but that's the only way any shot will land on them now."

"You people have been quite the pain to deal with," the Doctor said, laughing softly. "Well, it doesn't matter. Last I checked, even tanks needed oxygen, and your little crewmate does as well. Not that that matters either with those currents. It looks like my experiment is on. Anyway, I just wanted to drop off something that belongs to you."

The writhing black form fell from the monster and landed wetly on the ground at the Doctor's feet.

"She's proven to be a real issue for my dear Agent," the Doctor continued. "It will take time for him to recover, but fortunately, he doesn't need as much of ... himself ... as any normal human. And I do believe this poor dear has found some parts of him to be quite indigestible." She sighed, and Xerx could make out her shaking her head. "Well, anyway, I have work to do. My experiments won't conduct themselves, after all."

The next voice was impossible. Tiny and bright, with a smug edge of its own.

"Probably should go back to the drawing board, Doc."

"Pip?"

"Just a minute," she said. "Mobo's still bringing me up."

A moment later, both Mobola and the diminutive tank broke the surface of the water, gasping and coughing. Relief fell on Xerx like a blanket as he and Neela kneeled carefully at the walkway's damaged edge and reached out for them. It was clear that they were fighting the current, but once Mobola had gripped his hand, he could see what had kept her from being swept away as she withdrew a single thread of her *msaidizi* from the opening in the back of her hand. It unwrapped itself from the piece of the guardrail still moored to the path and retracted into her hand. Neela had Pip, whom she pulled to safety. In her hand was the device that had been attached to the container. Its display was off.

"Looks like you lose," Pip shouted to the Doctor, then broke into a fit of sputtering and coughing. But her words received only silence. Xerx glanced back toward the now-empty opening, but he was too relieved to be angry for the moment, as he and Mobola stood up, and the rest of the crew approached them, each hugging the two heroes in turn.

"I can't believe you survived down there," Xerx said to Pip.

"Huh? Oh, yeah, I didn't actually realize I was underwater until I was a few feet down," Pip said, waving it off, as if no one had thought only moments ago that she was certainly dead, and they would have to face Paige's undying wrath for it. She looked down at her forearm and wiggled the now ragged-looking cable still plugged into her arm. A nasty-looking bruise was forming where the rushing water had forced the needle to move around inside her flesh. She pulled it out and discarded it, with not so much as a flinch. Her other arm hung limply where the grav sling had been smashed. She frowned, flailing the injured arm pathetically. "Guess I'm missing the Dorado MMA finals next week."

"You talk as if this was no big deal," Neela said, keeping Pip's cockiness in check. "You could have died, you know."

"Maybe," Pip said and went to hug Mobola's waist. "And thanks, you. I can't imagine what kind of courage you had to muster up to do something that crazy."

Mobola said nothing, only gave a tired smile, and then slowly hugged Pip back. If she hadn't been soaking wet, Xerx would have sworn that tears were falling from her cheek.

Once Var had assured him that both women were otherwise okay to move, Xerx, though touched at the display before him, ordered his team to follow the pathway to the second tunnel to search for any signs of where the Doctor might have gone. Though relieved at not having lost two people on his watch, Xerx could not help but feel that steady background frustration. Still, through it all, he was reminded of all that Isibar had told him about the Doctor's caginess. Everything to her would be a chess game; that was how she rolled. And it was why it had taken so long for him to track her down. She would always try to be three to four moves ahead of her opponent.

"You think we could follow her through whatever mess that her toy made in the tunnels?" Xerx asked Pip.

"Maybe, but I don't think that's wise," Pip said. "My crew's taking a big risk to do that themselves."

"I think we should tend to Sarah first," Neela said.

"I'll tend to her," Alexa said, catching up and following at Xerx's opposite side. "If you think she's bad normally, in that state, she'll eviscerate whatever comes too close. I don't want any of you getting hurt."

Xerx nodded and then gestured down the path. "Be my guest," he said as Alexa took point and double-timed her way down the path. The rest of the team kept their own pace. Xerx looked back and saw Mobola, still soaking wet and with a haunted look in her eyes. She looked at him, then looked away. He gestured for her to come to his side. He didn't look back afterward, knowing that she would second guess herself but ultimately not want to disobey him.

"I didn't get to tell you that that was one of the most reckless things I've ever seen any member of my crew do," he said, looking ahead. He waited a moment and then betrayed a smile. "Good thing that's what I named my ship."

"You're ... not angry, then?" Mobola asked, her voice almost a whisper.

"You saved someone's life," Xerx said. "And you showed ingenuity by anchoring yourself while going down." He tapped the top of her hand, near the holes in her gloves. "Just how long do those things stretch?"

Mobola shrugged, shaking her head. "Honestly, I don't know. I never asked."

"You never tested them?" Xerx asked. "You're not curious to know what else they can do?'

"The story behind them isn't..." He saw Mobola bite her lip and look away, holding her arms.

"Hey, don't worry about it," Xerx said. "I won't pry. What matters is that you showed that you can do good in a scrape, just like we can. You're getting a big bonus in your pay, to say the least."

Mobola smiled. She tried to make it look shy, but its genuineness shone plainly through.

They arrived at the opposite entrance, where two holes of crumbling infrastructure sat in both the right and left walls of the tunnel. Alexa was kneeling beside Sarah, who writhed on the ground as if in agonizing pain, her skin as black as Agent 10's but without the constant oily sheen. Still, her teeth were bared. It was the mouth of a beast, with fangs longer and sharper than Xerx had ever seen before.

She screamed, and the sound caused Var to nearly retch.

"Is she ... okay?" Rati asked, still reeling from the noise.

"Is she even human?" Rinkya said.

"She's not technically human in the first place," Alexa said, shoving her back down as she raked clawed hands that looked more like demonic talons her way. "She's an artificial lifeform created during our father's experiments, part of the Alliance attempts at a super soldier program."

Sarah lunged at Alexa a second time, barely missing her forearm with her teeth.

"Bloody try and bite me, you fucker!" Alexa said. She shoved Sarah back to the floor once again before explaining to the team. "Alliance desperately wants something that can go toe to toe with Imperial tanks."

"So how do we stop this?" Var asked, wrinkling his muzzle at the sight.

"*We* don't," Xerx said, gently blocking the massive Felyan's approach with his arm. "She does. Lex knows what she's doing."

"Wake up, you rabid bitch!" Alexa screamed; then she swiped her hand full force across her sister's face. The blow echoed into the tunnel. Xerx could practically feel the appalled expressions on the faces of his team members who were not in the know. And for the first time since this mission began, he found himself having to suppress a laugh—especially when it appeared to work. Instantly, Sarah stopped writhing, instead, lying deathlike in the pool of black ichor, her breathing slowing down to a regular rate, and her skin color shifting from midnight black back to her pale almost-white complexion. Even her teeth and claws seemed to retract into something that could pass for human.

She rolled over onto her side and promptly vomited up a second puddle of foul-smelling black fluid. Everyone, Alexa included, stepped away.

"I need a bath," Sarah groaned, rising on all fours but looking as ungainly in this position as a newborn deer.

"You could jump into that water if you'd like," Alexa said, standing at the ready for a fall as her sister placed a hand on the cavern wall and painfully rose to her feet. "But I don't recommend it."

"Remember when your dad forced us to eat our vegetables, and I threw the plate into the wall?" Sarah said.

"Then he fixed you a second plate of nothing but vegetables and made you eat them?" Alexa said, a grin cracking the side of her face.

"This was worse than that," Sarah said, leaning on the wall.

"I imagine it was," Xerx said. "So you did try to eat him?"

"You might need to fill in some blanks, in all honesty," Sarah replied. "I barely remember after I tore his arm to shreds. How much of him did I eat?"

"It was hard to tell," Alexa said. "When we saw him, there wasn't much left. He looked like some kind of fucking creepy grinning dwarf. He sloughed you off like some aberrant tumor. I don't think they knew how to kill you, so you're lucky to be alive."

"So you reckon I'm a living being, after all?" Sarah said. She shook her head, and the spines that covered her scalp melted back into her familiar-looking long black locks. "How sweet of you." She then placed a hand on her jaw and adjusted it with a loud click. "Shame she got away."

Xerx frowned at the conversation. The disappointment in Sarah's voice was deeper than he expected, but she had done a lot for them just now.

"Not for lack of trying," he said with confidence. "But the story's too long to tell right now. We need to get the hell out of here."

"He got away," a voice said, coming from the tunnel. Before Xerx could ask any kind of question, he saw the pink hair first, soiled with the black ichor from the Doctor's pet monster. From the shadows, Artemis stepped, walking slowly, hunched over in obvious exhaustion, yet grasping her dual knives in trembling fists, as if they were appendages, as moored to her body as bones to muscle.

Following her was a chorus of voices.

"Useless..."

"Killing machine..."

"Deathbringer..."

"Good for only killing..."

"Failed experi-"

The chilling litany that followed her from the bowels of the cavern was, by increments, silenced once Artemis spun around and stabbed into the darkness from which she emerged. A form that resembled a hand reached out and grasped itself about her neck, holding her in what looked like a half-Nelson, attempting to drag her back into the enshrouding darkness. Seconds later, several other appendages sprouted from the blackness beyond, attempting to anchor her. The pink-haired girl's movements were methodical in dispatching the as-of-yet unseen entities that tried to reach for her, her face emotionless except for the intensity of her almost-glowing green eyes from which the black rivulets seemed to pour down her face with the intensity of tiny waterfalls. Nevertheless, there was an exhaustion there, as if she'd been fighting to reach this place for hours.

Not understanding the situation, but recognizing Artemis' need for help, Xerx forced down the initial fear before drawing his pistol. He aimed at what appeared to be nothing, save the appendage. He could only imagine the body beyond it in size and scope, and he hoped it would be enough.

"Don't shoot," Artemis said, even as the fuliginous arms pulled her back into their dark embrace. She reached up and slashed the appendages where the wrists met the hands, and Xerx watched as they did not so much melt off of her as splash to the ground, no more solid than the water that flowed from any faucet. She pulled free from the severed embrace, even as several other arms reached out to hinder her, then were dispatched with equal efficiency and ferocity, splattering to the ground like ink from a broken pen, splatters of black partially coating her clothing.

"Useless ..." He heard the voices whisper, the sound fading, stuttering, as if from a dying man as one hand loosened its grip after the pink-haired angel of death took a final stab into what appeared to be an empty void.

"I am *not* useless," she said, staggering into the opening. Xerx saw that Artemis' face was dispassionate, but her eyes betrayed a flaming resolution as she stepped into their midst, then leaned against the far wall, sinking to the ground. She drew her knees up to her stomach, sheathing her knives.

"Arty?" Xerx said, tentatively stepping up to her. "Did you just follow that ... thing here?"

Artemis, her head against her knees, made the faintest approximation of a nod.

"I'm late," she said.

"Ah... why did you even try to follow it through the tunnel?" Xerx asked, not sure if he wanted to know the answer. Maria had once told him that with her, it was often best not to ask "why" to anything she did. But curiosity this time had won out.

"They called me."

He had been about to ask who, but realized that it would have been a foolish question. He'd heard the voices, taunting and sneering, as she sliced through whatever had been in the tunnel, trying to drag her back into its darkness.

"Is Sarah okay?" Artemis asked.

Xerx gave a quick glance to the Pirate Queen's sister, who seemed none the worse for wear, if just filthy, and nodded. "Seems that way," he said.

"Good."

"Are *you* okay?" Xerx asked.

"No."

"Are you ... hurt?"

"No."

Xerx paused in momentary consternation.

"Then what's wrong?"

"I'm waiting."

"For who?"

"I'm not useless." This came out as a whisper as a slight tremble went across her body.

Again, a reference to the voices. And for some reason, Xerx felt that this was something more personal than he felt prepared to delve into. Nevertheless, he could not help but wonder what the hell could have been happening to her back in that tunnel.

"Freeze!" An authoritarian voice abruptly echoed from the depths of the original tunnel through which the Doctor had appeared. "Drop your weapons!"

The order was followed by a series of flashlights, each resting atop several pistols in the hands of a police squad. Another glimmer of motion caught his peripheral vision, and he turned to see a second unit of blues on the cavern's opposite end emerging from the door to the walkway and training their weapons in the direction of his crew. Xerx lifted his hands, and the crew followed suit.

It was then that Paige suddenly emerged from the adjacent tunnel that Agent 10 had bored into the situation, followed by her crew, each aiming their weapons in both directions of both squads of blues. Maria, upon the sight of Artemis and ignoring the blues' threatening postures, ran to her, still keeping her rifle's sights on the blues before dropping to her knees and embracing the pink-haired girl with obvious relief. At least now, Xerx understood who his enigmatic friend had been waiting for. He figured, with some bemusement in spite of the situation, that he was going to have to hear the story from both of them later on, provided they wouldn't all be spending an inordinately long time holed up in a jail cell.

"Oh dear, this is awkward," Paige said with icy calm. And the hair on the back of Xerx's neck stood on end. The blues didn't know what had happened, and this situation seemed about ready to go very badly on several levels.

"Everybody!" Rati said, suddenly asserting himself. "Just cool it for a moment." Xerx breathed easier at this, yet inwardly kicked himself for having momentarily forgotten his cousins' positions on this colony. The young hybrid stepped forward into the middle of the fray and flashed an ID holo in the direction of the blues in the tunnels while his mate stepped out of the tunnel and did the same to the ones on the path. "I don't think you have the right grasp of the situation here."

"Detective?" One of the blues stepped forward, a plain-looking man with a thick mustache. He lowered his gun, then emphatically signaled to his squad, who all lowered their respective weapons. He then placed his finger to his temple, speaking into his comm subvocally. The squad of blues on the cavern's opposite end immediately stood down. Brogan and Paige, in turn, nodded to their respective team members, who lowered their weapons.

"The hell are you doing down here?" Mustache Man said now that the situation had been relatively defused.

"Solving the real problem, Officer Calais," Rati said. He spoke in a reproachful tone that emanated rank. "Rinkya and I were there with these guys, deep cover op, couldn't say a word; sorry, my friend. What you need to know right now is that all these guys just saved the colony. And I can prove it."

EIGHTEEN

Tophanavar's market level was busier than ever with the exhibition tournament, but Xerx didn't mind. Now that Rinkya and Rati had been given some much-deserved time off by the force, he was able to spend some of it with his cousin like he'd wanted. They had even been able to watch *Imani*'s next fight, which was, once again, against *Tiberius*. As expected, Artemis had knocked him out of the list of finalists with a shank in the spinal conduits when he'd turned around too soon. It was an embarrassing defeat, but at least he'd given it a good run. And after all that they'd been through, he wasn't even upset. After everything, it was good for the crew to finally have time for themselves. Repairs to *Imani* could wait until they hit hyperspace. Neela and Rinkya were spending the day shopping, as were Mobola and Pepper, the latter having been even more impressed by the former's act of bravery and was probably showering her with an embarrassing amount of compliments. Salt was most likely with that bartender girl he'd seemed to have gotten sweet with, and Var was either aboard the *Reckless*, enjoying a rare quiet day, or getting drunk somewhere. Everyone, even Alexa and Paige's crew, had received commendations from the colonial government, and all spaceport fees for both the *Reckless* and *Shadow Star* had been waived. Conversely, the Alliance authorities had made a swift and wordless departure the moment this kerfuffle had blown over.

"So you're saying the Doctor took off in an escape pod?" Xerx said, finishing off his final Takoyaki. He smiled with satisfaction, surprised that space gypsies were not only so adept at making it, but actually harvested supplies of squid farmed on their ships.

"Broke into the government protocols and shot past the temporary traffic ban," Rati explained before taking a bite out of his beef stick.

"And what about the ... constructs that Arty said that she had to fight through to get to us?"

"There wasn't anything when we went down there with Paige, except for a lot of black good puddles," Rati said. "But at least it explains why they seemed splattered along the wall in some places like someone had been fighting."

"Seems *La Muerta* did you guys a community service," Xerx observed.

"I'm thinking we owe her one, then," Rati said.

"Probably, but she doesn't like conventional rewards," Xerx warned his cousin.

"What do you mean?"

"She deals in favors."

"Meaning..."

"She may do something one day that she'll expect you to look the other way for."

"I was afraid of that," Rati grimaced, then sighed. "But I guess that's the price I pay for helping out mercs and pirates."

"You say that like it's a bad thing," Xerx said with a chuckle. "Don't worry about it; on any good day, Arty's usually a peach."

"I'll take your word for that," Rati said. "But getting back to the Doctor, you'll need to know that the ship docked with a frigate, and it jumped almost immediately."

"Did you get its registry?" Xerx said.

"That's the creepy part."

His cousin then pressed a thin piece of paper into his hand. The digits for the ship's registry were written prominently on it, along with a name: Donnie Newman.

"Should I know the name?" Xerx said with a confused look.

"The registry belonged to Rinkya's dad."

Hearing the tone with which he mentioned his life-mate's father, he suspected the worst. "So, is he...?"

"We don't know," Rati said grimly. "He left on a job one day when she was a kid, and ... vanished."

"Not to sound like a dick," Xerx said, "but you ever thought that he might've skipped out on her and her mom?"

"Not according to people who knew them," Rati said, sounding not the least bit offended. "They were crazy in love. And besides, divorce between humans and Felyans is almost unheard of. Something has to have happened to him. Also, ship registries have records in both corporate and government databases, making them too much trouble to fake, even by pros. So, if the registry really is to Rinkya's father, then this is too big a lead to pass up."

Xerx nodded understandingly. He and his crew tended to hop around the colonies quite a bit, so they could do their own searches to find out where the ship had come from and, even more importantly, where it was headed. And Rati knew he had connections that neither of his cousins possessed.

"But it's out of your jurisdiction," Xerx said understandingly. "I'll see what I can find. But it's probably gonna take time. And I mean lots of time."

"She's been looking for years," Rati said, a sad smile resting on his face. "She can wait a little longer."

"Like me and this vendetta, it seems," Xerx said, the memory of his failure souring his thoughts. He'd gotten in touch with Isibar, who was understanding about the whole thing, as expected, but he could not help but keep wondering if there could have been anything done differently that would have had a different result.

Coulda, woulda, shoulda, he thought, and once again he brushed away that depressing trail of musing.

"By the way, I never got a chance to thank you. You know, for everything. You and Rinkya didn't have to stick your necks out for us."

"You're family," Rati said, slapping Xerx on the back. "Rinkya and I may not be pirate bloods, but we're here for you."

"Thanks," Xerx said. "I don't get around to seeing you guys often enough. Gestalt season's over for a bit, so that's why our next stop is An'Re'Hara."

"Hey, great!" Rati's tail shifted rapidly as he grinned. "I'll let Dad know you're coming!"

Xerx laughed. "Oh, I told him already. One does not arrive on the doorstep of a family of fifteen unannounced."

"Well, just be careful," Rati said. "I think some of them haven't gotten out of their biting phase." Then, seeming to catch himself, his eyes brightened. "Oh! There's one thing I forgot to tell you."

"About the ship?"

"No. Well, it's about *a* ship, but not the ship we just spoke about," Rati said, clarifying. "This is about something else that Rinkya and I found in that ship the Doctor arrived in. We hope it might give you a clue as to where she might go next."

He opened his holo emitter and switched on an image of something that Xerx both hadn't seen in a long time and hoped to have never seen again. He narrowed his eyes at the sight of it: a swallowtail-style banner, deep red, with what appeared to be a black, curved "X" sewn crudely onto it.

"You've seen this before?" Rati's question sounded more like a statement.

"Unfortunately," Xerx grimly replied. "And it doesn't surprise me that she would have connections with them."

Maria found her again, in the same place, watching the *Shadow Star* crew finishing their final checks on loading *Tiberius* onto the ship. Artemis loved looking down on the world, especially from high vantage points, even if others had to endure chronic pain in order to reach her precarious perches. Maria had no issue with heights, but her compounded battle injuries often made joining her petite pink-haired companion difficult. She did often wonder what Artemis thought of this, as her emotions were often difficult to gauge. But she never showed any sign of reticence when she wanted to join her, being the more extroverted of the two. Besides, with her tendency to hide in the ship's ventilation ducts and service passages, she was good at making herself scarce if she truly wanted to be alone. She'd lost count of the number of times she'd done a series of acrobatics, squeezing herself out of an air vent in order to join her in bed.

Artemis fixed her with her large green eyes, her knees propped up to her chin the same way she'd found her after their adventure inside the tunnels that Agent 10 had dug into Tophanavar. Paige had them follow, rappelling down into the bowels of the colony and then following the trail of black slime until they'd run into Xerx and his crew, face-to-face, with Artemis huddled against the wall. She'd said little as she embraced her; that was expected as well, but she knew that something was bothering her, the same as now.

She walked over to where Artemis sat, near the exit hatch, tucking herself in beside her, though with some difficulty, due to her extreme size difference.

"You want to talk to me now, little one?" Maria asked, cajolingly.

Artemis' gaze shifted her way, then back to the sight far below as the final stabilizer arms locked about the massive mechanized gladiator.

"You seemed to not be ready before," Maria added, slightly less confident now.

"I am more, aren't I?"

"More than what?" Maria asked. "I'll need a bit more than that."

"More than a merchant of death."

"Who said that you were?" Maria replied.

"Lots of people," Artemis said. "I was called that ... before."

Maria knew exactly what she meant by "before." She knew her past, her use as an assassin for the Second Imperium. She might not have been a tank, but she was just as much a pawn of their machinations.

"Of course you are, silly," Maria said, playfully flicking at Artemis' left pigtail, held aloft by a double skull barrette. "We're together because of it."

"It's just..." Artemis began, then sat silent once again for over a minute. Nevertheless, Maria sat patiently, allowing her to continue. She was both distraught and yet relieved to see this much emotion being displayed by the usually stoic girl. "It's just that the things that they said ... that *he* said—the Agent." For the first time since she'd joined her up here, she turned to face Maria, frowning. "He *knew* me. And he created things that looked like him—Agent 6. I killed him, Maria. The *real* him. Permanently." She turned away and bit her lower lip. "Then he made other copies of other agents. All the ones who trained me, tortured me."

So that was why some of the splatters of black in the cavern looked like a murder scene.

"Maybe they gave that thing his memories?"

Artemis could only shrug, then fall silent again before speaking.

"I don't like it."

"Well, if that isn't the understatement of the year?" Maria said, brushing the back of her fingers against the pink-haired girl's cheek. "You're never the most forthcoming person ... and you've been even less so about what happened before we caught up with you. Perhaps a few more details would help?"

"It taunted me," Artemis said, though at first, she turned away before giving a faint nod. "I was too fast for it. Though it taunted me. It sent copies of the Agents to slow me down. It kept taunting me. Said I was a failure. That I was only a killing machine, and that I bring death everywhere I go." She shuddered visibly before speaking again, this time her voice lowering to a whisper, as if she were afraid the words would bring forth some kind of curse.

"He said that I would cause the deaths of those I care about... and that I couldn't be anything more than that."

Again, her eyes settled upon Maria, a streak of a tear moving down her face beside the permanent black tear-like marks on her face. "What if it's right?"

Maria, saying nothing, leaned in closer, slipping an arm around the petite woman, smiling a reassuring smile. It was a smile that Paige had once said could warm an entire room. She hoped it had the same effect on Artemis' mood. She leaned in and placed a soft kiss on her strangely cool forehead. Her body always felt cooler than any other human, in fact, warming up only when they made love.

"If that were true, then do you really think I'd be here now, given our history?" Maria said. "Think about it. You pilot a competitive fighting machine and have thousands, if not millions of fans; you have friends who care about you, and I'd like to believe you care about them. Even ones that are hard to like, like Sarah."

Again, Artemis went silent, leaning into the embrace, before again talking.

"I don't want to be *La Muerta* anymore."

Despite how somberly Artemis had said it, Maria couldn't help but let out a small laugh. Thankfully, Artemis was rarely offended and showed no signs of it affecting her emotionally.

"Then tell Xerx to stop calling you that," she suggested.

"It doesn't really bother me," Artemis said. "But I feel that I need to prove it before I ask him to stop." Again, she slipped into that brief, almost pensive silence. "I just don't want that to be all that I am."

"Artemis."

Again, she looked Maria in the eyes, this time with true surprise. She so rarely used her actual name, after all.

"You might have been born for the sole purpose of killing ISID enemies. It might have been all you ever knew for thirteen years, and ... well ... changing your reason for existing takes a long time. Few people know it better than I do, and even I never fully achieved it. I'm ham-fisted at domestic tasks," she pointed to her boots, "and I don't think I'll ever break the habit of wearing these. But I'm a bloody good soldier, at least working for Paige. And I get to do it on my own terms."

"So you're saying I should embrace my nature?" Artemis said.

"Yes and no," Maria said with another soft chuckle. "What I mean is that you don't have to kill someone if you don't want to."

Artemis cocked her head in the way she normally did when processing something new and interesting that someone had just told her. Then she held out her hands, making a weighing motion.

"I guess perhaps I *am* an angel of death after all," she said, before Maria smiled at her. It was a sweet, kind expression and signaled what was to come.

"Perhaps," the statuesque tank replied, brushing her finger upon the pink-haired girl's very full lips. "But you're *my* angel of death, little one.

She then pulled Artemis closer. The smaller woman didn't resist as Maria leaned forward and kissed her deeply.

If she couldn't clarify Artemis' confusion, she could at least make her forget it for a time.

EPILOGUE 1

A Felyan male's lack of a refractory period could be as much of a curse as it was a blessing, Alexa had heard. And she supposed, in her half-sleeping state, that it was something of a curse for Tyger—especially after her having been nailed with that pleasure-pain chip earlier. But she'd gotten the best out of him compared to any time before.

She stroked the brown fur with black stripes on the sleeping hybrid's chest and then frowned at the shallow cuts her claws had made, especially after she'd intended to be careful. But so soon after such a ridiculous high the chip had given her, normal sex was merely chasing the dragon. And poor Tyger had paid for that chase. He wouldn't like that. She imagined that he would also be quite sore tomorrow after all the exercise she'd put him through. It was at least a good thing that her retinue had given him a good meal and plenty of rest beforehand. She made a mental note to leave him with a few of his debts paid out and with the best painkillers money could buy before he left in the morning.

Still, though he was probably the best of her "boy toys," he wasn't her Iriid. There was nothing emotionally involved between them. She merely needed someone to scratch the "itch" that her frequent periods of heat produced, and he was damn good at it. Had her father known what kind of monster he was creating with this biological demand when he made her? Still, she supposed it was better than what her poor sister had been burdened with. And today had probably been the worst for her. Still, they made it through, and Sarah had seemed none the worse for wear ... she hoped. Despite all the trouble that followed her sister, Alexa was happy that she'd bounced back. She was probably in her suite now, either sleeping or zoning out on StellarNet shows; it was perhaps the only reason she'd been blissfully unaware of the noise that she and Tyger had been making these past couple of hours.

But out here in the Colonies, away from home with her beloved, she knew that more trouble was soon on the horizon.

Her comm signaled for her. She turned toward the holo it emitted into the room's dimness. It was Xerx.

Speak of the devil...

EPILOGUE 2

Kairen didn't look like much, most people would say. His slender build and nebbish appearance, however, belied his knowledge, skill, integrity ... and best of all, his bedroom prowess. And in that regard, Paige felt like she'd won the lottery.

"Going for a record now, are we?" he whispered into her ear before returning his lips to her neck. "Maybe I'm tired."

"Like hell you are," Paige said, on the edge of a chuckle, which turned into a giggle as Kairen caressed a particularly ticklish spot on her stomach. "Because I'm certainly not."

"Are you sure about that?" Kairen teased as his hands traced their way to her breasts, the feel of his body against hers revealing sharply differing textures that belied his true state of arousal. Paige bit her lip at these sensations and smiled.

"I know how you get when we go off on a mission," she said as Kairen brushed his tongue across her earlobe.

"Can you honestly blame me?"

"I guess not. But I'm here now, aren't I?"

"Yes. You are." Kairen spoke softly, shifting his attention to her cheek as he purred against her. "And I'm glad you're yourself again."

"Things worked out better than I'd hoped," she said, her thoughts skipping momentarily to the corpse that they'd recovered from Xerx's adventure in the water reclamation passages. Her crew had placed it in the cold section of the ship's storage. In lieu of the true prize, the company would deem it acceptable for research value.

"The company has something of the Doctor either way," Kairen said as Paige turned his way. Their lips met, but all too briefly, as a moment later, her paramour gave a brief pause.

"Hey, did Ike double-check this time?"

"He'd better have," Paige said and then fixed him with a half-amused grin. Not that she blamed him. Despite the fact that Pip had been rescued from certain death today, and by the most unlikely of people, it didn't mean that she wouldn't stop her usual attempts to spy on her intimate moments with Kairen. God only knew how she kept scrounging resources to design those damn micro-cameras.

"I'm surprised you're asking now and not before the last two times. If he hadn't, then we've most likely been giving our resident pervert a right show and are about to give her yet another."

"I guess I worry too much," Kairen said.

"Sometimes, love. Sometimes."

Kairen said no more as Paige, for the third time, thanked him for his support.

Her comm signaled her later that night. To her dismay, it had fallen off the nightstand and back into the bed, right beneath Kairen, who slept as soundly as if he were on the best drugs in the universe. He barely stirred as she fished it out from under him and glanced at the holo.

It was Xerx—with another request. She should have figured.

"It can wait until tomorrow, Zee," she mumbled as she placed the comm back on the nightstand and happily snuggled next to Kairen, joining him in sleep.

EPILOGUE

Dr. Hayashibara knew that she would have to ditch this ship. There was too much danger of the Alliance recognizing its status as a ghost ship; too many questions would be asked. And she would need to disguise herself again.

She'd finished placing her warrior into the crèche. He would survive, even though that Xerxes Paraska and his friends had certainly surprised her with their own monster. Who knew it would have decimated her dear Agent 10 in such a way? But it was no matter. He would recover, and she would deal with this situation soon enough. For now, it was time to make sure that more important matters were underway.

She cleared her mind and then opened it to her plethora of replicant "sisters," hard at work in the far reaches of the Alliance and Imperium, her beautiful colony at its business. And now, it was business that she needed to attend to.

Sitting in the pilot's chair, she let her mind drift, following the velvet cords that linked her to each of her family. She was both loosely yet unbreakably connected to each one. And when that pirate blood and his crew killed them, she felt each and every one of their deaths: a drowning into darkness that they would never return from. It was like limbs being repeatedly amputated. The need of a presence was there, but the actual presence was forever gone.

But this one was still alive, still active, and still about very important things.

The Doctor looked into the important business; she was a passive observer known only to herself and the replicant, who shared her personality and desires, but whose will could be bent away from too much autonomy.

The room was dimly lit, save for the lights that shone on the black, throne-like seat upon the dais at its center. Behind it, equally lit, was the banner of the Helix: the shape of the DNA of mankind. And the man who sat upon the throne in a priestly frock and collar gazed down upon the replicant. His narrow face was worn with the emotions of life, digging trenches of crow's feet and brow ridges into his graying flesh. A still-thick crown of gray-brown hair was slicked back from its receding hairline in an almost obsessively neat coiffe. His pale eyes were gray and narrow.

"It is a pity that a full demonstration of the product could not be given," he said. "Nevertheless, we will still purchase it. But we demand a discount."

"Fair enough," the replicant said. "Then we will recalculate the amount at 20% less than the original fee. I trust this is acceptable?"

"It is," the man said. "The payment will be sent to your accounts within the hour." He then smiled wanly.

"In spite of the setbacks, things are still running in a timely fashion."

"If death is coming, we will bring it to them first," the replicant said.

"Humanity will thrive," the man said. "Humanity first."

"Yes, Father," the replicant said. "Humanity first."

EPILOGUE 4

Xerx had had his fill at the Purring Princess. He thought he'd have learned his lesson when he'd played along with Var at that drinking match back in Pit Town on Siberna. Hadn't he been part of the reason for the bartender posting that sign that read "DO NOT CHALLENGE VAR TO A DRINKING CONTEST?"

Still, here he was, somewhere between buzzed and full-on drunk, trying to hail a cab back to the space-port. Neela probably would have been pissed at such a situation, but she had been with him and was still in there, enjoying herself with Var, who was into his fifth cup of that disgusting *asak* drink. And Salt, who seemed joined at the hip with that Felyan bartender girl, had absconded with her to parts unknown over an hour prior, leaving Pepper and Mobola there, still celebrating. He'd had a full day, however. Aside from saving the entire colony, he'd spent quality time with his cousins and his crew and got the ball rolling on his investigation. Hopefully, Alexa and Paige might be able to eventually dig up something on that missing ship. Now, he just wanted to go to bed.

As he transmitted the cab request on the kiosk outside the bar, he squinted against a brilliant light that appeared in the bar's darkly tinted window. At first, he thought it was the headlights of a passing vehicle until he looked up and realized that the light was coming from above rather than ahead.

He shielded his eyes against the growing disc of brilliance. It cast his surroundings into stark contrasting shadow and light. All the while, a deep, pulsing hum began to reverberate in his ears and throughout his body. Then, from the center of the near-blinding brightness, a dark shape coalesced from which a form descended, angel-like. The disk of light then began to fade the closer she came to the ground.

"Kumiko?" Xerx rubbed his eyes and squinted against the black blur the light had left on his retina, regarding the girl before him. He had not seen her in years, not since their last run-in on Siberna, and her hair was longer than he recalled. Aside from that, her skin was still nearly as pale as a tank's—not surprising as her mother was one. She still kept her habit for old Earth goth apparel, rocking a crushed velvet pinafore with steel buckles.

She made no response as she continued to descend toward him. In his slightly impaired state, it took him a moment to realize that Kumiko was accelerating as she approached.

"Uhm, Kumi," he slurred, "you planning on slowing down?"

She didn't respond. Instead, she leaned into a full-on dive. Xerx, sobering up significantly from fear, braced for impact immediately before she zipped straight overhead. He turned in time to see Kumiko intercept a bedraggled-looking clone of the Doctor raising a gun toward him. There was an expression of combined surprise and outrage plastered on the clone's face as Kumiko, using her momentum, threw the clone over her shoulder and into a nearby wall, the plasterwork spiderwebbing with the force. The clone dropped to the floor and burst into white-hot flames, disintegrating at the snap of Kumiko's fingers, as if she'd fallen into a blast furnace.

"Ugh. You're drunk," she said, turning to face him. She fixed him with a look that bordered between amusement and annoyance.

"Just buzzed," Xerx said on the edge of an involuntary belch. "And what are you so pissed about? It's not like I'm that way all the time."

"True," Kumiko shrugged. "But you picked a bad time for it."

"Why?"

As if to answer his question, he felt the cold steel of a knife suddenly at his throat.

Xerx sighed, more annoyed at this sudden turn of events than afraid.

"And today started out so nice."

He glanced into the nearby store window to see the heretofore unseen second clone sporting an insane grin: the look of someone with nothing to lose.

"I didn't think it'd be that easy," she said.

"Only because I didn't think there were two more of the Doctor's little copies running around," Xerx said nonchalantly.

"I'm surprised you think at all," the clone replied. She was panting as if this moment were giving her some sort of sexual satisfaction. "Well, not that it matters." She then spoke to Kumiko. "As for you, you snowflake-looking bitch, you had better stay out of this if you know what's—"

Her words devolved into a scream as Kumiko made a simple gesture. The knife fell to the ground, followed by a pile of what appeared to be black sand. There was a sound similar to concrete being poured out of a bag, and Xerx turned around to see the lower half of what was left of the clone's body disintegrate into the accumulating pile of black dust.

"Took you long enough," Xerx said, rubbing his neck. "You thought her having a knife at my throat was funny?"

Kumiko shrugged and made the "little bit" gesture with her index finger and thumb. Xerx made a gesture with a different finger, and both of them shared a moment of laughter.

"Remind me to never piss you off," Xerx said. "So why'd you come down to the interstellar boonies? You missed all the fun."

"Not really," Kumiko said, then pointed at him as the blinding light re-emerged from behind her.

"I'll explain on the way," she said. "But I need you to come with me. Right now."

THE END

COME FOLLOW THE NORTHWEST
PASSAGE WITH US!

SUPPORT US ON PATREON!
www.patreon.com/WildSpaceSaga

WILD SPACE SAGA CONCEPT AND COMIC ART
BY TERENCE PEGASUS AND BRANDON HILL:
wildspacesaga.deviantart.com

ART BY BRANDON HILL:
brandonhill.deviantart.com

FOLLOW BRANDON HILL'S FACEBOOK PAGE
AT "AuthorBrandonHill"

Follow us on Twitter!
@DecKrash
@WildSpaceSaga

Be sure to check out Brandon Hill's other e-books, paperbacks, and hardcovers, available on Amazon Kindle and Nook:

Wild Space Saga:
Wild Space Saga, Book 1: "Between the Devil and the Dark"
Tales of Wild Space, Book 1: "Lifemates"
Tales of Wild Space, Book 2: "Rites of Passage"

The War of Millennium Night:
"From Slate to Crimson"
"Double-Cross My Heart"

The World of Five Nations:
"The Hidden Meanings"
"Elven Roses"

Virtual Law:
"Reunions"

COMING SOON

Wild Space Saga, Book 3: "Twisted Faith"

The fortuitous arrival of Kumiko, a powerful tertiary who has taken a liking to the newborn daughter of the Felyan Empress and Seth Ramirez, the human envoy to An'Re'Hara, leads Xerx away from what was intended to be a relaxing visit to his cousin and his sizeable family to ferreting out a dark plot that may destabilize race relations between the normally peaceful Felyans and humanity, many of whom have taken Felyans as husbands and wives. This leads Xerx, Alexa, and the *Reckless* crew to Zynj, the former capital of the ancient First Imperium, now an irradiated, polluted rock, inhabited by insular people who sell the scraps of their once-great cities to survive in their underground warrens: the perfect hideout for the human supremacists of the Helix society. Will the courageous captain and his crew be able to stop Helix and foil the will of their charismatic leader, or will the already beleaguered Alliance soon have two powerful enemies to contend with?

BOOK CLUB QUESTIONS

1. Looking from the beginning to the end, do you feel that Sarah needed more fleshing out as a character? If yes, why? If not, how do you think her character developed?

2. Was there a good emotional impact regarding the situation with Paige and Pip? If so, in what ways? If not, what do you wish would have occurred?

3. How was Kairen a help to Paige?

4. Do you feel that Kairen is a character who is worth seeing more of? Why or why not?

5. How do you feel about Xerx not wanting to involve his cousins in this vendetta?

6. In what way was Neela right to be worried about Xerx's involvement in this vendetta against Dr. Hayashibara? If you don't think she was, why not?

7. Do you believe that the reasons for Xerx to pursue his vendetta were enough to make the reader(s) emotionally involved? Why or why not?

8. Did the Gestalt battles seem enjoyable and interesting to you? Why or why not?

9. Would you like to see more Gestalt battles added to the story? How would you make them more interesting?

10. Is there anything that you would like to add to the Gestalt battles?

11. How does the location of Tophanavar appear?

12. Did Tophanavar seem like a real, living place? Why or why not?

13. Detail the Felyans and hybrids as a species. Are they well-defined?

14. What else would you like to explore with Felyans as a species?

15. Which member of the *Shadow Star* crew did you think was the most interesting and why?

16. Which member(s) of the *Shadow Star* crew would you like to see explored in further books and why?

17. Did the interactions between Pepper and Mobola appear important to the story? Do they convey strong romantic tension between the two? Is there any more that you would like to see that would flesh it out better?

18. Does Dr. Hayashibara feel like a compelling villain that
    you would like to see come around time and time again
    in the series? Why or why not?

19. How do the chapters of the story seem to form a uni-
    form tale?

20. In what way is Xerx's cause in pursuing the Doctor a
    worthy one or not?

AUTHOR BIO

Brandon Hill is a native of Louisiana and an avid reader of science fiction and fantasy, who began writing in the eleventh grade. Of himself, he says, "I am a 'classic nerd' and prolific writer who has had dreams of authorship since childhood. I sketch perhaps even more prolifically than I write, and have drawings of just about every character my warped imagination has come up with. I hope to continue sharing these ideas, characters, and stories with others for years to come."

Terence Pegasus is a native of Northampton, Northamptonshire in the United Kingdom. Sharing the same love of science fiction and fantasy, he enjoys making kitbashes of various Warhammer 40K parts. Sharing the same love of sci-fi and fantasy and having forged a friendship with Brandon that began in the mid-90s with a mutual interest in 80s cartoons and sci-fi series, he and Brandon began their work on Wild Space Saga, eventually sharing his unique characters and integrating them into the story and providing his concept and technical work to its ever-expanding universe.

Discover more at
4HorsemenPublications.com

10% off using HORSEMEN10